CARGO

D.V. BERKOM

CARGO

A Leine Basso Thriller
Copyright © 2015 by D.V. Berkom
Published by

First print edition August 2015
All rights reserved.
ISBN-13: 978-0692487686
Cover by Deranged Doctor Design

1

THIS WASN'T RIGHT.

Kylie leaned over the side of the *tuk tuk* and gasped for air but only succeeded in choking on the thick exhaust of heavy evening traffic. The neon signs of Bangkok's Soi Cowboy District streaked past at dizzying speed, shifting her unsettled stomach into epic nausea.

I didn't have that much to drink.

She'd been at the bar for less than an hour, waiting with her friends from the hostel for the legendary lady boys to appear. The thought that the bartender had spiked her beer skated across her mind, but she rejected the idea. Why drug a customer who was obviously part of the backpacking crowd and wouldn't have much money?

The motorized rickshaw turned down an unfamiliar street, heading in the opposite direction from the hostel.

"Wait—where are we going?" she asked, her breathing shallow. The words echoed in her brain, like she was standing in a hole. Slowly, she swiveled her head. Alak, the guy she'd been talking to who worked at the hostel, sat across the seat studying her closely, as though she were an insect pinned to a bug board.

Frowning, she glanced in the rearview mirror. The driver was watching her, too. Dread crawled deep in her stomach, clawing at the thought that the two men knew each other, knew what was wrong with her, expected it, in fact.

I have to get out...get back to the hostel. She curled her fingers around the metal rail that surrounded the backseat and leaned toward the open doorway. *I need to call Mom and Dad, tell them I'm ready to come home...*

Alak grasped her arm and pulled her back. Unable to keep her grip, her fingers slid from the railing.

A dream-like fog descended over her. Why did she come to Thailand? There was a reason. *What was it again*? A picture of her little brother, Brandon, flashed through her mind—of him lying in the middle of the street in downtown Phoenix, a pool of blood surrounding his head like a dark red halo.

Such a sweet angel.

She tried to move her arms, but nothing worked. The first flush of alarm faded into the background, and she floated in a viscous sea, no longer afraid of where Alak and the driver were taking her. Her brain screamed at her to be more concerned but she couldn't drum up the energy to care.

A montage of images obliterated Brandon: Angie and Beatrice, the twins she'd met from New Zealand, laughing and throwing back shots in the open-air bar with their tour guide, Charlie; Alak buying her beer and asking her questions about home; the little boy, Jaidee, sitting next to her at the bar until Alak shooed him away.

The *tuk tuk* lurched to a stop, and Kylie slipped off the backseat and onto the floor, mute, numb, and so weak she couldn't move. As though belonging to someone else, her arm flopped to the side and her hand touched air, now free from the vehicle's confines. Someone seized her under the arms and dragged her from the *tuk tuk* and onto the street, her shirt bunching beneath their hands. Jagged gravel scraped her exposed back. She opened her mouth. To what? Cry out? An instant later the pain floated off, and she fought to remember what she was going to say.

Poor Brandon. He's with the angels now. She struggled to keep her eyes open, but then gave up. *What's the point?* Her eyelids fluttered, sensations dissipating like mist in the desert, leaving only a pinpoint of herself.

A moment later, even that was gone.

L EINE BASSO SAT inside her car across from the café
where the two women were meeting. The former
assassin adjusted the volume on the receiver so she
could hear everything her daughter and the Modeling Magic rep
said. The women had just set their drinks on the table and taken
a seat under the café's awning.

It was another cloudless, Southern California day: blue
skies, low-seventies, comfortable. Leine was getting damned sick
of comfortable. She could use a little stormy weather. Maybe
some rain, or a blizzard. Hell, even the dusty Santa Ana winds
would have been better than this seventy-degrees-and-sunny-
every-day monotony. Normal people didn't live like this.

At this point she'd welcome an earthquake.

Leine focused on the two women's conversation, half-enjoying
her daughter's debut as an operative for SHEN, the anti-trafficking organization Leine worked with. The mother half of her
was not happy April slid into the role without talking to her first.

Not that she was overprotective.

Leine could have kicked herself for using photographs of

April when she contacted the cover agency, but it sounded like a good idea at the time. She'd been trying to obtain a physical address for Modeling Magic so she could slip inside their offices and rifle through their paperwork and computers for information regarding a recent case. Presumably, four women had been offered modeling contracts and given an assignment overseas, an offer to which all four had eagerly agreed. Their last known location in the States was the greater Los Angeles area purportedly at a property owned by Modeling Magic, Inc.

So, she'd called her daughter and asked if she could use her photos to lure the woman into giving up the address for a meeting.

"What? Why would you do that?" April had asked. She wasn't the kind of person who would want to make her living as a model. Not because she couldn't. It was more because she hated the idea of the impossible-to-replicate airbrushed perfection most of the models projected. And because she'd rather write. At the moment she was deep into the first draft of a literary novel. She insisted she was going to be the next Margaret Atwood, although Leine was happy to see her continue to work a day job.

"Down, girl. I'm only going to use them to arrange for a meeting with a company we suspect is a front for trafficking."

"Oh. Well, then, of course you can. Do you need me to go undercover?" April had tried repeatedly to get Leine to include her in assignments from SHEN, but Leine refused. Leine did, however, encourage ongoing self-defense training and was teaching her how to handle various weapons.

"We'll see. It depends on what happens after I send the pictures."

"You know, Mom, I'm getting pretty good with a gun, and it would be fun to work with you. Lou even mentioned he might be able to use me sometime in the future. Just think what that kind of experience would do for my writing."

"You write literary fiction. There's not much call for gunplay and Krav Maga," Leine said. "If you end up writing thrillers or murder mysteries, let me know. I'll hook you up with Santa, and he can send you on a ride-along with somebody from the LAPD." Santiago Jensen, or Santa, as he was more affectionately known, was a detective for RHD, the Robbery Homicide Division of the LAPD, and Leine's new roommate. She still wasn't sure how to refer to him. Boyfriend seemed too tame and a bit juvenile, and partner sounded like a business arrangement. She avoided the political correctness of "significant other," which she hated more than monotonous, sunny weather.

Leine figured a ride-along with a member of the LAPD would have a fifty-fifty chance of coming back to bite her in the ass. It would either scare the hell out of her daughter or add fuel to the fire. She wasn't entirely sure which way April would go, and didn't want to find out.

April sighed. "You need to let me grow up sometime."

"Yeah. I know. Let me live in my fantasy world a little longer, okay?"

Her daughter had laughed. "Okay. Go ahead and use the photos. You've got them on your phone, right?"

But it hadn't worked. The rep suggested meeting at a popular coffee house in Beverly Hills.

April was ecstatic when Lou gave her the green light to work undercover at the initial meet. Leine would have put the kibosh on the whole affair, except Lou and April did an end run behind her back and planned everything. The idea of being left out of her daughter's undercover activities gave her a bad case of heartburn, and she volunteered to monitor the meeting.

Leine returned her attention to the conversation. There wasn't much ambient noise other than a bit of traffic, so the sound quality was excellent. The mic April wore as a button on her blouse had a wide range, so would easily pick up the rep's words. The tiny receiver in her ear allowed Leine to coach her if the need arose.

"Thank you for meeting with me," April said. "I'm really excited about this amazing opportunity."

"My pleasure, April," Melissa, the rep, said. "I always like to schedule a preliminary meeting with potential applicants in order to get a better feel for whether our agency will be a good fit. So far, I like what I'm seeing." Somewhere in her early thirties, Melissa was dressed for the part in a designer jacket and skirt with expensive shoes, topped off by a trendy hair style and a shitload of jewelry.

"So what are my next steps? My girlfriends are all, like, over the moon that I'm finally going to pursue modeling."

Melissa chuckled. "Well, first of all, do you have a passport? It's possible we may be able to get you in on a shoot overseas. One of our models has the flu and we've already scheduled the venue and all the equipment and personnel, so postponing isn't an option."

"I have a passport, but don't you have other girls who are trained? I've never modeled before. The idea makes me kind of nervous."

"Oh, don't worry. Our photographers are the best at making our models look good. I like the idea of having a fresh face with little experience. Vulnerability translates well in the photos." Melissa paused. "Besides, our client is quite particular about body type and coloring. You'd be perfect."

"Awesome. Where would I be going? Paris? Milan?"

Leine smiled. April could definitely play the part.

"This assignment is actually in Dubai."

"Wow. That would be amazing."

"It's a pretty cool job, I'll say that." Melissa opened her briefcase and pulled out an envelope. "Here's the contract. Go ahead and look it over, and if you see anything that you don't understand, let me know. I'll be happy to explain it to you."

April took the papers from her and paged through them.

"I'm going to run to the ladies' room, so take your time. Do you want anything else?" Melissa gestured toward April's drink.

April shook her head. "No, thanks. I'm fine."

Melissa picked up her purse and disappeared into the café. April watched her go and then slid the empty manila envelope closer.

"How am I doing?" she asked, her voice low.

"You're a natural, honey." Leine hated to admit it, but April had a knack for subterfuge.

"I'm still nervous that she'll see the wires."

"She doesn't seem suspicious, does she?"

"No."

"Then I wouldn't worry." Leine knew how she felt. She'd hated wearing a transmitter, always worrying she'd be compromised.

"Did you put the tracking thing on her car?" April asked.

"Yep," Leine replied. The signal from the GPS device she'd slapped on the rep's Lexus was strong.

"You sure I don't seem nervous?"

"Not at all. It's natural to think the target knows something. Don't worry."

"The paperwork is asking for my birthdate and my social."

"Just put down the driver's license number and birthdate Lou gave you this morning. If she asks, tell her you forgot your social, and you'll call her with it this afternoon."

April fell silent while she filled out the forms. Melissa returned a few minutes later.

"Well? What do you think?" the rep asked.

"Do I sign here?" April turned the contract toward her.

"Yes. And initial there, and there."

When April was finished, Melissa tucked the contract back into the envelope and put it into her briefcase. She held out her hand.

"Congratulations. You've just signed with Modeling Magic. May this be the beginning of a long and happy relationship."

April smiled and shook her hand. "Thank you. When do I leave?"

Melissa glanced at her watch. "I'll have to clear it with the home office, but remember I told you we're in a bind? If everything checks out, your flight leaves at eleven tomorrow night."

"Wow. That is soon. What should I bring?"

Melissa slipped her sunglasses back on and smiled. "Just yourself and your passport. Everything else will be taken care of."

I'll bet, Leine thought.

LEINE FOLLOWED MELISSA OUT OF THE PARKING LOT, STAYING several car lengths behind her. Twenty minutes later, she drove into the lot next to a high-rise and parked. Leine continued past her and pulled to the curb a few cars down. The rep exited her car and walked into the building. Noting the absence of security cameras outside the door, Leine settled in to wait.

At five o'clock, several people emerged from the building and headed for their vehicles, including Melissa and a younger woman. After a brief conversation next to Melissa's Lexus, both got into their cars and left.

Leine waited until each of the cars in the parking area had gone before she exited her vehicle and moved to the doorway. She paused a beat to gauge her surroundings and then slipped inside.

The cool, elegant interior matched the modern architecture of the building. Spotlights transformed lush plants and contemporary artwork, giving the lobby a sophisticated ambience.

There were no obvious security cameras in the lobby, either. She checked the building registry next to the elevators for Modelling Magic, Inc. They weren't listed. Two suites had no designation, one on the first floor and one on the fifth. The office on the first floor turned out to be vacant. She located the stairwell and climbed to the fifth floor.

Leine eased the door open to make sure no one was visible before she stepped into the hallway. The carpeting muffled her footsteps as she made her way past various offices. At the end of the hall was a door with the logo for *Modeling Magic, Inc.* written in gold and black lettering along with the suite number and hours of operation.

She observed the empty reception area and scanned the office hallway through the side window, searching for light indicating someone working late. The office appeared deserted. She listened for several minutes to make sure her assessment was correct before she took out a small envelope the size of a credit card. Inside was a set of picks and several turning tools. She selected what she needed and raked the lock. Easing the door open, she slipped inside.

Skirting the reception desk, she proceeded down the hall toward the back. She passed a conference room and two offices before coming to one that had Melissa's name plate on the wall next to the door. Leine peered through the glass. A large desk with a computer flanked by filing cabinets, two chairs, and a loveseat filled most of the space. Leine picked the lock on the office door and went inside.

Glamorous photographs of male and female models covered one wall. Bookshelves lined another, with a third taken up by floor-to-ceiling windows.

Leine started with the files. She didn't expect to find a paper trail, but she wanted to be thorough. Once she was satisfied that Melissa hadn't left sensitive information in the filing cabinets, Leine moved to the computer. In her experience, most people mistakenly thought a password-protected computer was enough to keep prying eyes from the files stored there. She took out a small black device, which she connected via the USB port, and turned it on. The compact piece of hardware was compliments of her days working as an assassin. Before she left her former employer, she had a friend reverse-engineer it for her. She'd found it useful on several occasions.

The lights on the device blinked amber while it tried first one and then another password combination, accepting and rejecting them at high speed. She brought out a magnifying glass and checked the keyboard, noting the keys that appeared the most worn. She entered them into the device and initialized another program that ran simultaneously to the main one, searching those specific strings of letters, numbers, and symbols at the same rate.

Several minutes passed before she got a hit on the secondary program. The device entered the string of characters and the screen changed from a password prompt to a screensaver depicting a white, sandy beach with a palm tree and turquoise ocean beyond. Icons populated the desktop. Leine clicked on an email program at the bottom of the screen, which opened to reveal Melissa's correspondence. She skimmed the dates and subject headings, pausing at a recent notice from a commercial airline.

She opened the message and scanned the details. It was for the flight to Dubai leaving the next evening—the one Melissa told April to be on. Her daughter's name had already been added to a list of other young women and men taking the same flight, all of them unaware of their true destination. Relieved her daughter was only being used as bait and wouldn't be on the flight, Leine closed the message and checked for flight statuses closer to the time of the disappearance of the four women from Iowa.

In a subfolder, she found an earlier email noting several passengers headed to the same destination. The four women were listed.

Leine copied the flight information onto the device's SD card and then searched through the rest of the emails for correspondence pertaining to them and the other names on the list. For good measure, she copied Melissa's document folder and the rest of her emails.

Finished, she removed the hacking device, shut down the computer, and slipped from the office, locking the door behind her. Once back inside her car, she transmitted the information to Lou over a secured network. From there, he would book two operatives on the flight to Dubai. In a perfect world, the information would lead them to where the women from Iowa were being held. If everything went as planned—and, when operating in a foreign country, that was a big if—both groups of victims would be on their way home by the end of the week.

Score one for the good guys, Leine thought, and pulled away from the curb.

3

A DOG'S BARK dragged Kylie out of a deep slumber, and she fought the dense fog that had settled in her brain. A woman's voice echoed somewhere far away and brought her to the surface. Scrunching her eyes against the pile driver banging inside her head, she tried to swallow but only succeeded in running a thick, cottony tongue over her desiccated bottom lip.

Where am I? The smell of cooked rice, seared meat, and human excrement rolled her like a tsunami and she doubled over, retching.

When the nausea passed, Kylie pushed up to a sitting position and opened her eyes. Metal bars surrounded her on three sides of a small enclosure, with a pitted, mildew-stained block wall at the back. A dozen young women of varying races and ages either crouched on the rough concrete floor or leaned against the block. Most wore blank expressions. One woman, a hijab covering her head, squatted in the corner crying softly.

Outside the cell, a combination of crumbling concrete and mortar told of years of neglect. Paint still dotted the surface, but age, wear, and humidity had faded and chipped the walls so only small sections of blue remained. Above her, a rusty metal roof, more rust than roof, covered the space.

Kylie pulled at the sodden material of her shirt, attempting to peel it away from her body. It didn't do any good. She stood up, swaying slightly at the rush of blood from her head. The thick humidity was like breathing through water. Lifting the hair off her neck, she headed toward the bars at the front of the cage, her bare feet cool on the rough concrete floor.

Think, Kylie. How did you wind up here?

Images floated through her mind of sitting at the bar with Angie, Beatrice, and Charlie. She closed her eyes and concentrated, trying to tease a strand of memory from the gaping hole in her consciousness.

Alak.

A small, dark-haired woman wearing a colorful skirt stood next to her, staring through the bars. Kylie touched her arm to get her attention. The woman looked at her hand, and her gaze skated to Kylie's.

"Where are we? I—" Kylie fumbled for the words to make sense of what was happening, grasping at something solid to tether herself to. "I can't remember how I got here."

The woman shook her head. She said something in Thai, but Kylie hadn't learned enough of the language to understand her. She glanced at the other women sharing the cell with her.

"Does anyone here speak English?" she asked the group, feeling foolish for traveling through a foreign country and not learning the language. A few of the women shrugged or shook their heads. The rest ignored her.

In the distance, a door banged open and voices filtered through the dark hallway. Heart in her throat, Kylie backed away from the bars and took a spot next to the wall between two of the women, hoping she blended.

Wishful thinking.

A slight man with a face marred by an old case of acne stopped in front of the cell. In his hand was a large key ring. Behind him, a man with a face like a ferret and carrying a rifle dragged a young boy by the arm.

"Jaidee!" Kylie's initial caution was forgotten at seeing the kid she'd met at the bar the night before. Her shock was matched only by her dismay at his filthy face and split, bleeding lip. The boy's eyes lit in recognition, but any happiness at seeing someone he knew was short-lived. The man with the keys opened the cell door, while the other one shoved Jaidee inside. The door slammed shut behind him.

Kylie waited until the men left before she knelt in front of Jaidee and brushed his hair back from his face. By the looks of his trembling bottom lip he was trying to be brave, but his eyes were brimming with tears.

"Shh, you're going to be fine, Jaidee." Kylie gently rubbed the dirt from his cheek with her thumb and used part of her sleeve to wipe away the blood on his lip and chin. That small gesture of kindness was all he needed—the dam broke and Jaidee collapsed into Kylie's arms, sobbing his fear and frustration into her neck. Kylie let him cry and watched as a few of the other women drew closer, murmuring soothing sounds, concern evident on their faces. Soon, Jaidee was surrounded by all but one of the women in the cell as they took turns comforting the young boy.

Curious, Kylie left the group and walked over to the holdout —a Thai woman about Kylie's age wearing an expression that said she'd been through worse than being locked up in a dark, putrid cell. The micro-mini-skirt, stiletto sandals, and tight, midriff-baring top gave the impression she earned her living in the sex trade. An angry scowl on her face, she stood with her back to the wall, arms crossed, glaring at Kylie with obvious suspicion.

"What you want?" she asked.

"You speak English?"

"No," she sneered, looking away.

"I don't know what your problem is. We're all in the same boat here." Kylie's voice trailed off as she gazed at the other women fawning over Jaidee. Part of her wanted to curl up in a corner and cry, hoping the other women would comfort her, too. But the pragmatic part, the part she'd been relying on while traveling alone through Southeast Asia, told her whatever came next wouldn't be good and that she'd better suck it up sooner rather than later.

Unwilling to be on the receiving end of more bitchiness, Kylie gave up trying to talk to the woman next to her and moved to the other side of the cell. She sat on the grungy floor and closed her eyes, trying to think positive thoughts, but dark images crowded her mind. She didn't remember doing anything illegal, and doubted she was in an official jail, although she wasn't sure. Maybe she'd gotten uncharacteristically shit-faced the night before and did something stupid that she couldn't remember. But a far more terrifying reason began to wiggle its way into her mind.

They didn't call Bangkok the sex capital of the world for nothing.

Did Alak use Jaidee to distract her so he could put drugs in her beer? A shiver tracked up her spine at the thought of what would come next. *But why is Jaidee here?* Was he a plant to get information from somebody in the cell? Or was he going to the same place she and the others were headed? She drew her legs up and wrapped her arms around them, resting her head against her knees, pushing away the image of someone so young being used for sex.

How stupid was I not to keep an eye on my drink at a bar in Bangkok? She'd heard stories about girls being drugged, raped, and left somewhere. It happened lots of places, even back home, but she'd thought she was with friends.

Stupid, stupid, stupid.

And why weren't Angie and Beatrice here? The New Zealand twins had been at the bar and were much drunker than Kylie remembered being. Were they working with the tour guide, Charlie? Maybe they were all working together with Alak. Try as she might, she couldn't believe the two sisters had any part in what happened.

Her parents were right. They didn't want her to go by herself, said it was too dangerous, especially in Kylie's delicate emotional state. Kylie had argued each point her parents had made as though her life depended on it, and in a way it had. Sure, she was over eighteen, barely, and could do what she wanted, but Kylie grew up wanting to please her parents. Still did. Even so, she *had* to go on this journey alone.

Back home, she was going through the motions, not happy, not sad, just numb. Afraid to allow herself to feel anything, she refused to listen when her mother and father spoke about Brandon. Talking was their way of grieving, of releasing the pain and anger they both felt at his death, but that wasn't the way Kylie was built. Her friends had noticed and tried to shake her out of the funk she was in, but nothing worked. The claustrophobia had increased as the months wore on, to the point where she was going to suffocate if she didn't get out of Phoenix.

And now, a month and a half into her solo journey, here she was, a prisoner in a shitty cell in Bangkok, staring at a bleak future.

Jaidee had calmed down and was playing a game of tic-tac-toe on the dirty floor with one of the other women while the rest looked on, enclosing the two in a protective circle. Kylie glanced at the bitchy girl, who was watching Jaidee and the women.

When she caught Kylie studying her, she rolled her eyes and looked away.

Kylie stood up and walked over next to her. The woman stayed put but didn't acknowledge her. Kylie leaned against the sweaty cinder block wall and watched Jaidee and the women.

"Looks like he's having fun," Kylie offered. Her voice shook as she spoke. The other woman didn't respond.

Kylie really wanted to ask her what was going to happen to them, but didn't dare, didn't want to screw up the chance to connect with someone. She took a deep breath and clamped down on the fear rising in her chest. *Chill, Kylie. You're going to get out of here.*

"What do you think they want with him?" she asked, nodding at the group gathered around Jaidee. Again, she received no response. "He's so young. I don't understand why he's locked in here with us."

The woman scoffed and yanked out a pack of clove cigarettes and a lighter. Her hand trembled as she lit up. She sucked in a lungful and propelled the smoke into the air, turning it temporarily blue. "That because you stupid cow from America."

"Whoa. What did I ever do to you?"

The woman frowned, blinking back tears. Kylie softened and leaned closer so the other women couldn't hear their conversation.

"Are you all right?" she asked, regretting the question as soon as it came out of her mouth. She expected the woman to shut her down with an icy look. When she didn't, she added, "I don't mean to pry. I'm just really scared."

The other woman sighed, and turned to Kylie. The depth of emotion gazing back at her radiated anguish so deep Kylie was certain it would never heal.

"Oh." Kylie exhaled and looked away, embarrassed to have

witnessed such a private response in a stranger that she'd thought was just a cold bitch.

"My name Sapphire," she said, offering her cigarette to Kylie.

"Kylie," she replied. "Thanks, but I don't smoke."

Sapphire shrugged and took another drag, streaming the smoke through her nose. She smoked it down to the filter, dropped the butt on the floor, and stubbed it out with the toe of her stiletto.

"The last I remember, I was at a bar in the Cowboy district," Kylie said, hoping to draw her out. "I woke up here."

Sapphire studied her for a moment, paying particular attention to her eyes. She nodded. "You were drugged."

"I thought so. Is that how you got here?"

Sapphire smiled ruefully and shook her head. Her glossy black hair cascaded forward, giving her a sultry look. "I made boyfriend angry. He say I too much trouble." Her lips twisted like she was going to cry, but she didn't. "He sell me."

"He *sold* you?" Kylie stared at her in disbelief. "Your boyfriend can't just *sell* you. That's illegal."

Sapphire cocked her head. "You understand what I mean boyfriend?" She paused for a moment, thinking. "Okay, okay. Not boyfriend. Wrong word. He *Maeng Daa*...how you say...pemp?"

"You mean pimp?"

"Yes. Yes, pimp."

Even though Kylie had assumed she was a prostitute, she'd never met one before. Anger sparked inside of her at the thought of anyone believing they could own another person.

"It okay, you know." Sapphire nudged Kylie with her elbow. "Not lot of jobs in Bangkok, but I make good money." She shrugged. "Maybe I do again."

"What's going to happen to us?"

Sapphire exhaled another blue cloud and gazed at the far

wall. Then she looked Kylie up and down and shook her head. "You no want to know."

Kylie's breath caught and the blood drained from her face. Sapphire's words reverberated in her mind. Her heart fluttered and she had to force herself to breathe, like she was being squeezed from all sides. Leaning forward, she gripped her knees.

What if they were going to use them in snuff films? Kylie had heard of movies where people were tortured and murdered in real time, the live action streamed over the Internet to online customers. Or, maybe they wanted to cut out her organs and sell them.

A moment later the door at the end of the hall crashed open. Everyone inside the cell turned as a squat Asian woman dressed in a shimmery silk suit strode down the corridor toward them, followed by the man with the acne scars and two rough-looking men carrying guns. The woman, who appeared to be middle-aged, stopped in front of the cell and barked something at the guards. It didn't sound like Thai to Kylie—the words had a harder edge. The man with the scars produced a key and opened the door. One of the armed men walked into the cell and growled something to Jaidee. He grabbed him by the arm and yanked him away from the other women.

"No!" Kylie shouted. Her stomach twisted at Jaidee's cries as the man dragged him away. She fought the urge to follow him. The boy's eyes went wide, and he stretched out his arms, terror plain on his face.

Heart in her throat, Kylie spun around. "What did that guy say?" she whispered to Sapphire.

"He say he must be man and stop crying to women," she replied.

The woman in the silk suit scanned the remaining prisoners in the cell with a calculating eye, lingering on Kylie longer than the others. Her hair had been heavily shellacked, resembling a black helmet. Kylie was surprised the woman's heavy makeup hadn't melted from the thick humidity.

The woman said something to the gunman who pointed his weapon at Kylie and her cellmates and shouted orders in Thai. Not sure what he'd said, Kylie didn't move as the women began filing out of the cell. Sapphire turned back and nodded her head toward the others.

"*Mama-san* say we go."

"Go where?" Kylie asked, nausea rising in her throat. She didn't like the *mama-san* or whoever this woman was and didn't want to go anywhere near her.

"Wherever she want." Sapphire shrugged and joined the rest of the women.

Kylie hung back, her natural obstinacy rearing its head. Terror fueled her anger, and she decided she wasn't going anywhere, with anyone, ever.

After the last woman had exited the cell, the remaining gunman, obviously upset that she didn't follow orders, waved the barrel of his gun at Kylie and yelled. Kylie crossed her arms and flattened her back against the wall. Her knees shook, but she stood her ground. The words "fuck off" caught in her throat.

The *mama-san* laid her hand on the gunman's arm and he backed off. She walked back into the cell, stopping just short of where Kylie stood. Kylie was at least a head taller, but the woman's bulk and gravitas told her she had all the power in the situation. A cloud of sickly sweet perfume engulfed Kylie and her eyes watered.

"You go now," the woman said in English, her eyes narrowing. "He kill you if you no do what I say," she said, nodding toward the man with the gun. "You my property, now." With that, the *mama-san* stepped away from Kylie and motioned to the gunman.

Kylie darted to the side as he approached, intending to run past him, but he stopped her short, blocking her escape with his gun.

In panic mode, Kylie turned away, but he seized her around the waist and wrestled her to the floor. The *mama-san* grabbed her legs, surprising Kylie with her strength when she secured her ankles with a plastic zip tie. Kylie screamed at them to stop and kicked with both feet. The *mama-san* drew her hand back and struck her hard across the face. Stunned by the pain, Kylie went mute as hot tears skidded down her cheeks. The gunman flipped her over and the woman lassoed her hands behind her back.

Her wrists and ankles burning from the forced restraints, Kylie bit her tongue until she tasted blood, now afraid to anger either one of them. The *mama-san* said something to the gunman, and he dragged Kylie from the cell, taking her down the hall and into a rabbit warren of alleys.

They continued along a passage to where another gunman stood near an open doorway. The man had a fierce expression with a deep scar running from the corner of his mouth to his ear, reminding Kylie of the bad guys in the late-night kung fu movies she'd watched with her brother before he died.

As they drew near, she realized he was culling the women —the man with the scar would nod at specific girls as they passed and another man would pull them out of line and hand them off to someone else. When she and the gunman dragging her made it to the front of the line, the man with the scar directed them through an open doorway toward an idling van.

Blaring horns and countless cars and scooters filled the crowded, narrow street with dozens of people racing by on their way to somewhere. No one paid any attention to them. Exhaust saturated the air, and Kylie held her breath so she wouldn't choke. Advertising signs written in Thai cluttered the street, assuring her she was still in Thailand.

The man carrying her shoved her head first into the open cargo area of the van. Kylie tucked her head and rolled to keep her face from skidding across the floor. She rocked to a sitting position, scuttling out of the way when another woman was pushed in after her.

Kylie scooted back against the bare metal side of the cargo van and pulled her knees up. The door slammed closed. She raised her head and found herself staring into Sapphire's almond-shaped eyes.

"You should not fight," Sapphire said, nodding at Kylie's bound hands and feet. Sapphire's hands and legs were free.

Another captive, a woman in her early twenties with light brown hair, sat across from them, her back to the rear doors. Her face was bruised and swollen. Kylie wondered what she'd done to deserve the beating. She caught Kylie looking at her and turned her head.

The cargo area smelled of diesel fuel and rotting fish and was cut off from the front of the van by metal bars. There were no windows, and no interior handles visible for either the back doors or the side. The man with the scar climbed into the driver's seat and slammed his door closed. He maneuvered into traffic, horns blaring from every direction.

Soon the driver broke free of the gridlock and the van began to move at a more determined clip. Kylie was grateful for the slight breeze coming through the driver's open window, but the air was still thick.

"What's your name?" Kylie whispered to the battered woman. She needed a diversion or she'd scream.

The woman shook her head and began to cry. The driver yelled what must have been a command to be quiet, for she immediately fell silent. Kylie did the same, not knowing how to speak to her in her own language. Sapphire settled in, stretching her legs in front of her, and lit a cigarette. The driver glanced in the rearview mirror, but didn't stop her.

Kylie sighed as her own tears pricked at her eyelids. A group of missionaries visiting her church who'd been held at gunpoint in the Sudan had said that when in a dangerous situation in another country you shouldn't react—no crying, or anger, and especially no demands. The more docile you are the better chance you have of survival.

She hadn't passed the first test. It was hard *not* to fight back. She'd just screwed herself.

Kylie stared down at the welts and bruises on the sobbing woman's face and neck and, although it went against everything Kylie believed in, steeled herself to be as accommodating to her captors as possible.

But would it be enough?

4

"Y OU BOUGHT HIM a what?" Leine asked as she dabbed perfume on her wrist. She and Santa were in the bedroom, getting ready to go to his former partner's birthday dinner.

"You know, like a punching bag, only better." Santa shadow-boxed in front of Leine, a grin on his face. "This one comes with a masked cartoon bandit, complete with a revolver."

"And just where is he going to put it? Did you talk to Dana?" Dana was Don Putnam's wife of over thirty years and ruled the part-time pugilist with an iron hand. He bitched about it incessantly, but Santa had confided that Don secretly loved how ballsy his wife was. She was the reason Putz was still out on a medical after an earlier cardiac event, and was trying to get him to retire permanently from the LAPD.

"She said I can install it in the garage provided I don't stoke his dreams of coming back."

"But you want him to come back. How's that going to go over?"

Santa shrugged and gave her a sly grin. "She doesn't have to know."

Leine rolled her eyes and grabbed a sexy black dress from the closet. Santa whistled as he came up behind her and wrapped his arms around her waist.

"I love that dress. You know I won't be able to keep my hands off you if you wear it."

Leine turned in his arms and smiled. "I'm counting on it."

Santa returned the smile and took a step back, wagging his finger. "Oh, I get it. You're wearing that so we don't end up staying too long. Is that your nefarious plan?"

Leine brushed past him, headed for the bathroom. "You think you know me, don't you, pretty boy?"

"Damned right I do. And your plan would work if it was anybody else's party." Santa grabbed a crisp white shirt and dark slacks from the closet and laid them on the bed.

"That isn't why I'm wearing this dress. If you must know, it's because Bodacious Brodie's going to be there, and even though I'm totally secure in my wily feminine ways, she's a knockout and I'd rather you looked at me." After Putnam was sidelined on the medical, Heather Brodie had been assigned as Santa's new partner. Leine made her peace with the change, but damned if she was going to let an opportunity slip by to remind Santa what he had at home. "Besides, you two are together every day."

Santa raised his eyebrows. "The great Leine Basso is *jealous*?" He grinned and shook his head. "That's something I never, ever thought I'd see."

Leine gave him a look. "Be serious. I'm not jealous. I'm—" She paused for a moment, searching for the right word. "Competitive. Completely different animal, darling."

"Yeah. Whatever you say, Leine." Santa chuckled to himself as he got dressed. "I just can't believe you'd think a California surfer girl could hold a candle to your indescribable charms. Been there, done that."

"That's sweet of you, but I'm not worried. Really."

Traffic was light, and half an hour later they arrived at the Putnam's bungalow. The grounds were immaculate, benefitting from the birthday boy's forced retirement. By the sound of it, the party was in full swing with most of the guests congregating in the backyard.

"You go in," Santa said as he opened the trunk, revealing the punching bag. I'm going to snag a couple of the guys to help me set this bad boy up in the garage."

Leine rang the doorbell and walked into the house. Several people greeted her on her way to the backyard. As she suspected, Heather Brodie was surrounded by a gang of off-duty, single cops, a couple of whom Leine recognized from RHD. She had that thrown-together, California-casual look with a body that made men salivate and put women on edge. Her natural blond hair had a just-got-out-of-bed look, and the woman never seemed to need makeup. Not that Leine wore much, actually hated the stuff, but still. She was tempted to hand out bibs to the men surrounding her.

Most of the women had grouped up and were enjoying cocktails at one of the tables so Leine headed toward them, grabbing a beer from a cooler on the way.

"Hey, Leine. Glad you could make it," Dana called out. Don's wife looked as though she'd already had a couple and was in her happy place. Leine took the empty seat next to her and they touched beers.

"Where's Santa? Don't tell me you guys drove two cars?"

Leine shook her head. "No, he's installing that punching bag he bought Don."

Dana nodded. "Oh, yeah. That's right. I told him he could put it in the garage if he promised not to aid and abet Don in his never-ending quest for reinstatement."

"Yeah, I don't know how well that's going to work."

Dana chuckled. "I know. But I had to have him promise

something." She gazed lovingly at Don Putnam, who was at that moment manning the grill and holding forth with a group of guys Leine didn't recognize. Apparently, these men were realists and didn't think they had a chance with Bodacious. That, or they were happily married.

"The job's going to kill him, one way or another." Dana sighed and turned her attention back to Leine. "So I hear you picked up intel on a modeling agency front who's shipping unsuspecting women to Dubai." She shook her head and took a swig of her beer. "I hope your people find them. They're not what I'd call progressive about women over there."

"So what do you think of Don's replacement?" Leine asked, ignoring her invitation to a feminist discussion. Dana was quite vocal about her views, and adding alcohol to the mix could set her off on a tangent. Not that Leine disagreed, but it was a birthday party, and she preferred to keep things on a less contentious footing.

Dana cocked her head and studied Heather. "She's cute, I'll give her that." She took a drink of her beer. "More importantly, what do you think?"

Leine shrugged. "Santa says she's got good instincts and she's teachable, so it's all good."

Dana laughed and shook her head. "That's not what I meant, and you know it." She gave Leine a sidelong glance. "I think the dress says it all. You could definitely give Barbie over there a run for her money."

Leine smiled and the two women touched beers again. "It's all in the presentation, Dana."

"That's what I love about you, Leine. You never have to guess where you stand. It's so rare these days."

"Don't I know it."

Santa appeared a short time later along with two other guys

from the LAPD and went to visit with Don at the grill. Leine's phone buzzed and she excused herself.

"Leine, it's Mindy Nelson."

"It's great to hear your voice, Mindy. Long time. How are you?" Mindy Nelson had worked as the executive assistant to her old boss, Eric, the same time that Leine was at the agency. A couple of years before Eric died, Mindy decided to quit the workforce to raise her family. One year ago, she and her husband, Paul, lost their six-year-old son in a gang-related shooting in downtown Phoenix.

"Not too good, Leine." Mindy cleared her throat. "Kylie took off on a backpacking trip across Southeast Asia, alone."

"Is she okay?" Leine asked. Brandon's death had been rough on the family, but it was especially hard on their daughter, Kylie.

"That's why I'm calling. Lou told me to get in touch with you. I—I don't know where to turn..." Mindy's voice cracked and she sucked in a ragged breath. "Leine, Kylie hasn't been in contact for over a week, and she promised to either phone or video call us every few days. She hasn't missed more than two days in a row."

"Don't worry, Mindy. You know how kids are. They find something exciting to do and forget all about their families." Leine could empathize. A couple of years back, April had been in Europe for months without contacting Leine. Of course, their situation had been different. April blamed Leine for the death of the man she thought of as her father, and refused to contact her.

"No, I don't think that's what happened. When we didn't hear from her, Paul contacted the hostel where she was staying in Bangkok. They hadn't heard from her for several days and her things were still there."

"Would you like me to check things out for you?" Mindy had been the voice of reason in Leine's otherwise chaotic career as an assassin. She credited her for talking Leine down after she realized that she'd killed her lover in a case of mistaken identity carefully orchestrated by her douche bag boss, Eric. Leine showed up at the Nelson's house the day after Brandon was senselessly murdered in downtown Phoenix. The ability to share the grief of losing someone so close helped keep the monsters at bay.

At least for a while.

"Would you? Oh, Leine, Paul will be ecstatic when I tell him." The relief in her voice was palpable.

"Of course, Mindy. You don't ever need to ask. I'll always be there for you and your family."

"Thank you, Leine." She read off the address for the hostel where Kylie had been staying, and gave her Kylie's phone number and itinerary.

"I'll leave tonight."

"Please find our baby, Leine. I don't think either of us could handle losing another child."

"I'll do everything I can."

5

L EINE ZIPPED HER carry-on bag closed and slid her phone into her jacket pocket. Santa leaned against the doorjamb, watching her with his arms crossed. She lifted the suitcase off the bed and set it on the floor. They'd both stayed at the party until Leine had to leave to pack for the red eye to Bangkok.

"The girl's been out of touch how long?" Santa asked.

"A week, maybe longer."

"She could be anywhere."

"I know. But I have to try." Leine extended the handle of her case, scanning the room to see if she forgot anything.

"I know I don't have to tell you to be careful. Bangkok's not LA."

Leine gave him a look and said, "Are you forgetting what I used to do for a living?"

"Of course not, but it's well within my rights to remind you to be careful." He shrugged. "What the hell else am I going to say? Try not to shoot anyone while you're overseas? Don't end up in a Thai prison?"

Leine grinned. "Good to see you haven't lost your sense of

humor." She walked over to him and touched his face. "I love you. And I love that you're worried about me."

"I love you, too." Santa kissed her and leaned back. "What about April?"

Santa and April had developed a bond similar to the one she'd had with her former lover, Carlos. Leine's daughter had held out for months, wary of anyone romantically connected to her mother, but finally succumbed to Santa's superior charms and cooking ability. Leine didn't blame her for taking her time trusting him. It wasn't like Leine's track record with men had been what anyone would call good, or even normal. In the beginning, even Leine half expected her relationship with Santa to fail. To both women's surprise, it didn't. Santa showed himself to be a persistent suitor, able to look past Leine's former profession as an assassin as well as her reticence to commit.

Santiago Jensen was in love. Slowly, he'd been able to convince Leine to give him a chance, and later, to move into his apartment, which Leine had resisted like a cat resists a visit to the vet. She didn't want to mess with the trajectory of their fledgling relationship and figured moving in would do just that. Especially when the daily monotony started.

But it hadn't. In fact, to Leine's immense relief, cohabitating had actually strengthened their bond, taking her completely by surprise.

"The role she played in the Modeling Magic case is over," Leine said, answering his question. "Lou was just using her as bait. It's up to someone else to follow the four missing women. Besides," she added, "Mindy's a good friend. I'd do anything for her and Paul."

Santa nodded, conceding her point. He shifted his stance, a thoughtful look on his face.

"What?"

He shrugged. "Nothing."

"It's not nothing," Leine said, checking her watch. She rolled her suitcase to the side and sat on the bed. "I know that look. You want to talk." She patted the spot next to her. "Let's talk."

Santa studied her but didn't join her on the bed. He appeared to be wrestling with something, so Leine waited, knowing he was a deliberate man, one who needed time to formulate what he wanted to say.

"Okay," he said, nodding. "Here goes. Even though we've been living together for a few months now, I still don't know anything about you—where you grew up, what your parents did, do you have siblings, that kind of thing." He shrugged. "I've never been in a relationship where the woman didn't offer up all kinds of details about herself. It puts me in a weird place. People ask me about you and all I do is say I don't know."

"You never asked." Leine shrugged. "I figured it wasn't important to you." The answer was a cop out, and they both knew it. Personal details left her vulnerable—which in her old job could have gotten her killed. She sighed. *Give it up, Basso, or say goodbye to coupled bliss.* "Okay. Here's the condensed version: I was born in California, but didn't spend a lot of time here. I was an army brat. The world was my neighborhood."

"Ah," Santa said, nodding. "That makes sense. So your father was in the service?"

Leine nodded. "Special Forces."

"And your mother?"

"Molecular engineer." Leine stretched her neck, trying to ease the tension that had collected between her shoulder blades.

Santa smiled. "Getting a little uncomfortable, are we?"

"You don't have to be so happy about it, you know." Leine gave him a mock glare. Sharing her past had always been difficult. "Can we do this another time?" She checked her watch. "It's getting late."

He crossed the room, climbed onto the bed behind her, and began kneading her shoulders. Leine leaned back with a sigh.

"You have all day to stop that," she murmured. Eventually his hands roamed lower. He got off the bed and came around the front, pulling her to her feet and into a deep embrace. Leine relaxed into him and raised her mouth to his.

He kissed her slow and deep, and Leine emitted another sigh, unable to ignore her body's response. Or his.

Before she could protest, Santa slid her blouse over her head and unhooked her bra, both of which landed on the floor, momentarily forgotten. He nuzzled her neck and Leine gasped at the chills cascading down her spine. She took a step back, half-heartedly trying to stop him, but when Santiago Jensen wanted something, especially when it came to Leine, argument was usually futile.

"But my flight—" Leine closed her eyes, enjoying the sensation of his lips on her breast.

"I'm a cop with a badge," Santa said, his words muffled. "We'll get there in time." Pausing in his acquisition of her other nipple, he unzipped her slacks and slid them to her ankles.

Leine gave up trying to fight her rising desire and unbuttoned his jeans, pulling them down over his now-obvious erection.

What the hell. Wouldn't be the first time she had to run to catch a flight.

6

S HE LANDED IN Bangkok just after ten in the morning. Suvarnabhumi Airport was an amazing and thoroughly modern structure, rising like a double cross from the surrounding marshlands. Thankfully, there were several ways to get into the city, unlike the old days when there was no light rail and only taxis or *tuk tuks*.

Leine made it through immigration and customs and took the light rail to her hotel in the heart of downtown Bangkok. For roughly the equivalent of sixty US dollars, Lou had put her up in relative luxury: an ultra-modern hotel room on the twenty-third floor with a generous floor plan including a spacious bathroom, flat screen television, free Wi-Fi, and a rooftop pool.

She stowed her carry-on bag in the closet and stopped to check behind the nightstand next to the bed. As expected, she found a package taped to the back. She slit open the wrapping to reveal a 9mm semiautomatic with two full magazines. Slipping the gun into the front of her waistband, she took the elevator to the lobby and headed for the hostel where Kylie had been seen last.

Leine walked into the bright, air-conditioned entrance of the

Happy Day Hostel and was greeted by vibrant green and pink painted walls and dozens of potted tropical plants sprawling across the large picture window. A bookcase overflowing with paperbacks ran along one of the walls, and a huge corkboard sprouted dozens of pushpins holding up business cards, colorful flyers, and handwritten notes.

An older woman with short gray hair and dangly earrings looked up from behind the desk and smiled. "Welcome to Happy Day. May I help you?"

She had a British accent and intelligent brown eyes. Her name tag read *Wilma*. Leine returned the smile.

"Leine Basso. I'm a friend of Kylie Nelson's family. I believe Mindy Nelson told you I'd be coming?"

Wilma's expression turned somber, accentuating the slight etching of crow's feet surrounding her eyes.

"Yes. We've been expecting you." Wilma turned toward the open doorway behind her. "Alak," she called. A young, dark-haired man stuck his head through the doorway and smiled.

"Yes?"

"Would you mind watching the front desk while I take Miss Basso back to look over Kylie's things?"

Alak's smile disappeared and he nodded. "Of course." He looked at Leine, concern evident on his face. "We worry about Kylie. She not be here for many days."

"Thank you, Alak." Wilma came around the side of the counter and motioned for Leine to follow her.

"How long has Kylie been gone?" Leine asked as they walked down a long hallway, past several rooms. Some had bunk-style beds, while others had one or two singles. Everything was clean and bright.

"Since the first," Wilma replied. "Which wouldn't be unusual, except that she left all her belongings."

They passed one room with a heavily tattooed man lying on

a cot. Heavy metal music blasted from a small speaker connected to his iPhone. Wilma rapped on the open door and he glanced up, startled.

"Angus, remember what we talked about?"

Angus nodded, a sheepish smile on his face as he plugged in his earphones, silencing the music.

Wilma smiled and continued down the hall. "We've had a few words with him about the volume of his music. Otherwise, it's quiet here. Our guests are normally quite accommodating and polite."

"How was Kylie before she disappeared?" Kylie's mother had mentioned the young woman's change from a vibrant, witty, smart-aleck to a depressed and sullen loner after her brother died. Leine supposed suicide was a possibility, but the idea didn't feel right.

"Oh, you know. One day she was a complete chatterbox, and the next she would hardly leave her room." Wilma shook her head. "We stayed up talking late into the evening a day or two after she'd arrived. I know about her brother and why she chose to come to Thailand by herself. The day before she vanished she seemed to be doing well."

They stopped near a door marked *Lockers*. Wilma opened it and flicked the light on, motioning for Leine to walk through. The walls of the narrow room were lined with brightly painted metal lockers, each with a padlock. A long bench dissected the room.

"When Kylie didn't return after a week, I gathered up her things and placed them inside a storage bin." Wilma pulled a keychain from her front pocket as she walked over to one of the lockers, inserted the key, and snapped the lock open. Removing it, she swung the door wide and stepped back, giving Leine access. "I went over the security tape for that night a dozen times. Two sisters from New Zealand came

back around five in the morning. There was no sign of
Kylie."

Leine methodically looked through Kylie's things, pausing
when she found something interesting—a postcard of a temple
in Bangkok addressed to her parents, and a small notebook with
several handwritten pages that she assumed was a diary. She
placed everything in a shopping bag Wilma provided and shut
the locker.

"Did she hang out with anyone in particular, or was she
more of a loner?"

"That depended on how she was feeling. The night she
disappeared, she was with the twin sisters from New Zealand I
mentioned earlier, although they've moved on. I believe they left
a forwarding address. I can find it, if you'd like."

"That would be helpful. Anyone else?"

"I believe Charlie was there that night, too. Oh, and of course
Alak."

"Charlie?" Leine asked.

"He's a local tour guide we often recommend. And you met
Alak out front."

"I'd like to speak with both of them, if possible."

"Certainly. Charlie's giving a tour at the moment, but he's
due back in a couple of hours. You're welcome to speak to Alak
right now. The girls from New Zealand mentioned they saw
Kylie leave the bar with him."

Wilma led Leine back to the lobby and introduced her to
Alak. Leine asked him if he'd like to grab a drink and he agreed.

They found a quiet sidewalk café not far from the hostel.
Leine ordered a club soda with lime and Alak ordered a
Singha. Leine made small talk with him until their drinks
arrived, all the while surreptitiously sizing him up. On the
surface, he appeared calm and friendly, but Leine sensed a
jumpy undercurrent. Maybe he was nervous in the company of

strangers, but she didn't think so. He lifted the beer to his lips and his hand trembled. It wasn't much, but coupled with his nervous energy it was enough to take seriously. Leine studied him for more tells and at the same time tried to put him off balance.

"Wilma said you left the bar with Kylie. Where did you and she part company?"

Alak took a long pull of his beer before answering.

"We take taxi back. She got out and I not tired, so I decide to party at friend's house."

"How did she seem to you?"

"What you mean?" he asked. He had another drink and set the bottle down in front of him. His leg jiggled under the table.

"I mean, was she drunk? Having a hard time walking?"

Alak nodded, concentrating on peeling the label off his beer. "She had much alcohol."

"Then why didn't you help her back to her room? Seems it would have been the gentlemanly thing to do." Leine watched him closely.

A flicker of anger crossed Alak's face. "She not ask me for help."

"If she was obviously impaired, I'd think you'd want to make sure she made it back all right."

"She did." Alak glared sullenly at the tiny pieces of foil on the table. "I see her."

"Wilma said there was no evidence of Kylie returning to the hostel. The security cameras only show the sisters from New Zealand coming back around five that morning."

Leine kept her gaze steady. Alak returned the look. This time the anger in his eyes was unmistakable.

"I not know what happen. Like I say before, I go to party at friend's house."

Alak's demeanor had changed to one of suspicion, and his

command of the English language appeared to be degrading. She was beginning to get to him.

"You know what I think happened? I think that you helped her into a taxi with the intention of having sex with her, but when she refused you had the driver stop and then made her get out."

"No," Alak shot back, shaking his head. Tiny beads of sweat appeared on his upper lip, which he wiped away with his shirt sleeve. "That—that not how it happen." He took another swig of his beer and set it down with a little too much force. Foam bubbled over the top of the bottle and dribbled down the neck. He crossed his arms and leaned back in his chair.

"It's what I'm going to tell the police when I file the report. In fact, I'm so convinced that you were the direct cause of Kylie's disappearance that I'm going to offer your name as the main suspect." Leine held his gaze.

Alak broke the stare first, his left leg bouncing as he looked everywhere except at Leine. She slid the gun from her waistband and, keeping her hand under the table, casually aimed it at his groin. His gaze cut to the barrel and he visibly blanched.

His expression was a marquee of emotions as he fought the inevitable—doubt, fear, anger, finally settling on fear. A few minutes passed before resignation took fear's place. His shoulders slumped forward.

"My friend drive taxi..." he said, his voice low.

Leine moved closer so she could hear him.

"He pay me to find girls." He glanced at Leine, a confessor's guilt on his face.

"He pays you to put something in their drink, and then you offer to help them?" *Right into your friend's waiting cab.* Leine inhaled deeply to eliminate the urge to wrap her hands around his neck. And what would choking him accomplish? Nothing. It would create a scene, and he'd need medical attention, delaying her meeting with the taxi driver. Might even involve the police, depending.

Calm down, Leine. He's not worth it.

"I only deliver. I no sell. No illegal activity," Alak said, his conviction obviously genuine.

Leine nodded at the gun in her hand and leveled her gaze at him.

"Well, then, I won't kill you, just shoot your balls off. What do you think? Would that still count as illegal, or do you think I'd get away with it?"

"You can no—"

"Yes, I can. And I will unless you cooperate." She raised an eyebrow as she brought the gun closer. "I need your friend's contact information."

Alak covered his lap with his hands, the whites of his eyes showing. Beads of sweat rolled down the sides of his face.

Leine smiled as she leaned forward and encircled his wrist with her fingers. He tried to wrench free, but her grip proved too strong. His expression changed from anger to fear as he realized that things were going south.

"I need your friend's information. Now," she repeated calmly.

Distress plain on his face, Alak feverishly scanned the café and their surroundings. Finding no one sympathetic to his plight, he returned his attention to Leine. Leine tightened her grip and his hand started to turn white. He stared at his fingers and then at her. Something in his eyes changed, and Leine knew she had him.

"His name Sam. But he not tell you who he work for."

"Oh, I think he will." Leine released her grip and he straightened, rubbing his wrist.

"Then he know it me."

Leine shrugged. "And I care because..."

"Many people die."

"I'm only interested in Kylie. If you give me what I want, then no one has to die."

Alak nodded, and glanced to each side as though making sure no one was within hearing distance. "Sam sell girls to man name Victor Wang. This all I say. I not know where find this man, and Sam no know. I find girls, Sam drive them to arrange place, and someone else pick them up. I no meet Wang. Sam only meet once, when he apply for job."

"Give me your cell phone."

Alak crossed his arms. "Why you need?"

"Give me your phone," Leine repeated, stretching her arm across the table.

By the look on his face he was battling whether to give up his electronic lifeline, not sure what the crazy-ass woman across from him was going to do with it. After a brief pause Alak reached into his pocket to fish out his phone, and laid it on the table. Leine was glad to see it was a well-made knockoff and not a cheap burner phone, easily discarded. She had him tap in his security code and then open his contacts. She jotted down Sam's number along with the numbers Alak called the most often and his contact information. Then she downloaded a simple tracking program and gave it back.

"If anything you've told me isn't true, then I will find you." She stood up and threw a few baht onto the table. "You don't want me to find you."

7

LEINE RETURNED TO her hotel around five and headed to the bar for a drink and a light dinner. Her interview with the guide, Charlie, didn't turn up anything new, and the Kiwi sisters hadn't responded to her calls. Sam the driver wouldn't answer his phone, and Leine didn't bother leaving a message. She'd find a way to contact him if she ran out of options. She powered on the burner phone she'd picked up at the airport, and while she waited for her drink to arrive called a number she hadn't used since the last time she'd been in Bangkok six years before.

"You will find good fortune at the Golden Dragon," a man's voice said in Thai.

"And it rains long in the mountains," Leine answered with the prearranged code in the same language, then switched to English. "Please, may I speak with Kavi if he is available?"

The man on the other end paused briefly. "One moment."

The bartender brought her a Sazerac and Leine signed for the drink. A few moments later Kavi came on the line.

"Is this the dear friend who promised to call whenever she had the good fortune to arrive in this beautiful city of treasures?"

Leine smiled at Kavi's words. He'd been her regular contact whenever she had a job in Southeast Asia, and they'd spent many a night drinking and commiserating in his office overlooking the Chao Phraya River. Kavi was married to a sweet Thai woman named Phan, a diminutive lady with an amazingly fierce temper, which Kavi refused to bait. "I tested her patience once and only once. I will never do so again," he'd said solemnly during one of their many shared meals. His expression had been so grave Leine didn't press for details.

"It is. And is this the most precious friend I had the fortune to meet many years ago in this, the beautiful city of treasures?"

Kavi chuckled. "It is good to hear your voice, my friend. What brings you to Bangkok?"

"I am in need of your services. Is there somewhere we can meet?"

"Of course. Tonight?"

"If it wouldn't be a problem, yes."

"I will text you a location and meet you in one hour, if that will suffice."

"Perfect."

―――――――

KAVI HADN'T CHANGED AT ALL IN THE YEARS SINCE SHE'D SEEN HIM. Apparently, most Thais knew the secret to staying young, even when they'd reached octogenarian status. Kavi was probably closer to forty than eighty, but even if he were the latter, she knew she'd see the same unlined, peaceful face.

Kavi's mouth split into a grin when he saw Leine, and he stood up to greet her, his eyes sparkling. Leine brought her hands up in prayer pose and bowed.

"*Sawadi ka*," she said, greeting him in Thai.

Kavi returned the bow. "*Sawadi kap,*" he replied, waiting for her to take a seat across from him before joining her.

"I took the liberty of ordering for you a Singha." He pushed the beer toward her and had a sip of his own.

Leine brought the bottle to her lips and let the cool liquid slide down her throat. Placing the beer on the table, she felt herself relax for the first time since the flight from LA.

"You're looking well," Kavi observed as he settled back in his chair. He'd chosen the food court of an air-conditioned mall not too far from Leine's hotel. There were several people still shopping at the exclusive stores, which suited Leine.

Safety in numbers.

"I heard you left."

Leine nodded, took another drink of her beer. "My conscience wouldn't let me sleep. Especially after Carlos."

"I, too, have ended my tenure with our former employer," Kavi said, his mouth pulling down at the corners. "There are rumors that it was your hand that ended Eric's life." Kavi watched her intently, his expression unreadable.

"You can't believe everything you hear. My understanding is that he was in the wrong neighborhood at the wrong time." Leine shrugged. Kavi didn't need confirmation that she had eliminated her ex-boss. He probably guessed she had. Besides, his own code of honor would demand the death of one who initiated such a betrayal.

"Either way, it is good that such a man is dead."

Preliminaries out of the way, Leine pushed a photo of Kylie across the table toward him. Kavi leaned forward in his chair and glanced at the picture.

"I'm looking for a girl who was last seen at a hostel downtown. Her family is worried something's happened to her."

Kavi shook his head. "Bangkok is filled with such girls. I will need more information than that."

"I have a name. Victor Wang. Ring any bells for you?"

Kavi frowned. "Chinese."

Leine nodded.

"Triad, then."

"I suspect they are involved, yes. How deeply, I don't know."

Kavi sighed. "I can check with my contacts, although I can't promise anything."

"I realize that. But if anyone can tease a flower from a closed fist, it's you."

Kavi gave her a wry smile. "Finding your Kylie will be like looking for a drop of water in the sea." He paused, focusing on the photograph. "She will appeal to a specific segment of clientele—most American and European men prefer Thai women, so that will narrow it down a little. I will be the essence of discretion so that it does not raise suspicion. It could stir up a nest of vipers, otherwise."

"I have every confidence in your abilities, Kavi. Thank you."

Kavi inclined his head and toasted her with his beer. "For you, my friend, anything."

"How is Phan?"

"She is quite well, thank you. She sends her best."

"What are you doing now that you don't work for our former employer?"

Kavi frowned, shrugging. "Oh, this and that. Not anything exciting, I'm afraid. And you? Are you a friend of the missing girl's family?"

"Yes. But I also work for an anti-trafficking organization called Stop Human Enslavement Now, also known as SHEN."

"Interesting change of pace. Tell me, how did you become involved in the business of finding lost souls?"

"I guess you could say I stumbled onto the opportunity."

"So many are lured into being captured. Like a spider with its prey..." Kavi stared into the distance, seemingly somewhere else. He shook himself and smiled, refocusing on Leine and his beer. "Only good can come when a person like you helps these people. Not many have your talents."

Leine smiled at her old friend. "I think that's probably a good thing, Kavi."

"Maybe," Kavi replied with a shrug. "Maybe not."

8

ARLY THE NEXT morning Leine made her way into Chinatown, before the heat and humidity joined with gridlocked traffic and turned Bangkok into a convection oven, steaming everything by exhaust. She didn't expect to find out much about the trafficker who had purchased Kylie—that information would hopefully come through Kavi's efforts—but she couldn't just stay in her hotel room and do nothing until he contacted her.

The district was busy, with shopkeepers and customers already ensconced in the age-old dance of commerce. Everything could be found for sale here, from cheap knock-offs to fetishes to exotic fare for that night's dinner. There was a huge market for religious statues and talismans made of "certified ivory" although most were not, along with cages filled with exotic and endangered animals for sale. Black rhinoceros horn could fetch upwards of sixty thousand a kilogram and was thought to cure cancer and magically restore men's youthful vigor. It always amazed Leine the extent to which some men would go in order to achieve an erection. Didn't they realize the tongue was mightier than the sword?

Sex was a huge industry in Bangkok. A large proportion of the prostitutes were from rural areas and had been sold into slavery by their families to send money back to support them, but there were many who didn't have familial ties. Leine knew of several non-profits that worked tirelessly to put sex trafficking rings out of business, as did the Thai government, but like most criminal enterprises, when you cut off one head, more grew back to take its place.

Bangkok had always been an interesting mix of modern and ancient that Leine found intriguing. Sleek, massive shopping malls with designer stores and high-end restaurants peacefully coexisted next to three-hundred-year-old temples boasting golden spires and building-sized statues of Buddha. Traffic was horrendous, and for much of the year the city was hot and exhaustively humid, but somehow Bangkok always wrapped itself around her psyche like an eel and wouldn't let go. Even though the city was known for rampant petty crime, Thais were generally such positive and happy people Leine almost didn't mind having her pocket picked.

Besides, they smiled when they did it.

Leine ordered a bowl of *cow pot kai* from a vendor at a food stall and stood off to the side to eat while watching the parade of humanity go by. People of all ages scurried past speaking different languages, accompanied by the clamor of the cars and three-wheeled, gas-powered *tuk tuks*. The colors and sounds, and especially the smells, washed over her as she sized up the neighborhood.

She had just finished her bowl of chicken fried rice and was preparing to go back to her hotel when her cell phone buzzed. She checked caller ID—it was Kavi.

"That's pretty quick, Kavi. What have you got for me?"

"You were right. Your man Wang is involved with one of the local triads. He's directly involved in purchasing women from the US and Canada. Apparently he's a mid-level diplomat based in Tanzania who traffics in ivory and black rhino horns to pay for the women. He then provides them to the highest bidder, often Middle Eastern and Asian traffickers who in turn either pimp them out or sell them to other buyers. Currently, it's more lucrative to sell them to someone than turn them out to work the streets of Bangkok."

"I assume he uses his diplomatic status for smuggling?"

"Yes. My source tells me he makes several trips a year for ivory, and rhino horn whenever his contacts are able to procure it."

"Would your contact be willing to meet with me?" Leine asked.

Kavi paused. "That would be very dangerous. He is an extremely cautious man, and I did not tell him the nature of my inquiry."

"Would he be willing to set up a meeting with Wang?"

"Possibly." Kavi's tone was wary.

"Tell him I'm the representative for a wealthy Saudi buyer who has a penchant for Western women and wishes to remain anonymous. I'll do the rest."

"I'll see what I can do. I trust you remember your Mandarin?"

"Of course." Leine checked her watch. "I'll call Lou to let him know where this is headed. I'll need the usual."

"I'll have it ready for you by this afternoon. Shall we say two o'clock at your hotel?"

"See you then."

As promised, Kavi met Leine at her hotel promptly at two. When he left, Leine had additional ammunition and a suppressor for the nine millimeter Lou had secured, a fake passport with her photograph under a name she'd used during previous visits to Southeast Asia, and another burner phone with pre-programmed numbers for Kavi and his triad contact.

Leine activated the tracking device Lou had given her and then called to check in. The small tracker fit inside the back of her watch and uploaded the information to a satellite to pinpoint her location through her phone. In turn her location was transmitted to a website that could be viewed by anyone with a password in any part of the world. She'd given Kavi a link to the website and his own password so he would be able to monitor her whereabouts.

"I gotta say, I'm not thrilled about you doing this, Leine," Lou said. "You know how unpredictable those guys are. Just when you think they're your new best friend, they split your head open with a cleaver."

"I'm a big girl, Lou. I've dealt with these types before."

Lou sighed. "Yeah, I know. Just like I know what I'm about to tell you is going to piss you off."

Leine stiffened. "What?"

"Your daughter's on the flight to Dubai."

"My daughter—"

"I've got Brigit and Andrew on the same flight, so the tongue-lashing I know you're about to unleash on me can wait. April's in good hands. Besides, she insisted—made a cogent argument citing her ability to get inside the trafficking ring and lead us to the next link in the chain."

Leine took a deep breath and closed her eyes. "What the hell were you thinking?"

"Look, she'll be fine. Like I said, she's in good hands with Andrew and Brigit. They won't let anything happen to her."

"She doesn't have any experience. What if Andy and Brigit lose track of her? You *know* how easy it is to lose an asset, especially if the targets figure out they're being tracked. What happens then, Lou?" Leine's heart rate sped up to match the anger rising in her chest. "This is my daughter we're talking about."

"Look, she's a good kid. She's not going to do anything stupid. She'll be fine." Lou paused a moment. "She wants to be like you, Leine."

The words stopped her cold, the chilling implication of that simple statement breaking through her like a wave.

"She can't." She could never allow her daughter to follow in her footsteps. The nightmares alone would be enough to stop most people from even considering the idea. Eliminating a threat—and, if April continued down the road she was on, killing someone was almost certainly in the cards—royally fucked with a person's psyche—horribly, sickeningly, absolutely *fucked* with your sense of self, your sense of reality. Leine didn't do what she did all those years—working for the agency and assuring April would never be a target—for her daughter to gravitate toward the one thing Leine *didn't* want for her.

"No. You *get her back*, Lou," Leine said, keeping her voice steady. "If anything, and I mean *anything,* happens to my daughter I'm holding you responsible. We both know what that means."

"April will be fine. You have my word." Lou's tone told her he meant what he said. The problem was they both knew good intentions weren't enough.

"That makes me feel *so* much better."

"I told her if she feels threatened to say so and Brigit and Andrew would get her out. She was absolutely fine with that."

"Of course she was, Lou. She's never been undercover before. Just because she can handle a gun and knows a few self-defense moves doesn't mean she's ready for this type of work." Leine rotated her neck until it cracked, her anger at another end run by Lou and April surging to the surface. "You wired her, right?"

"Of course. She posted selfies on FindMe of her and two other girls she was with on the flight before takeoff, and we're circulating their pictures through the proper channels. I haven't seen any more activity on her account, and Brigit confirmed that the girls' phones had been confiscated by their handler prior to takeoff. I notified our contact in Dubai and he'll be there when the plane lands."

"Keep me posted."

"Of course." Lou fell silent but didn't end the call.

"What?"

"You know you have to let April make her own decisions, right? She's over twenty-one, for chrissakes."

"Lou? Lou? Are you still there? Damn. Bad connection. I'll call you back later."

Leine punched the end call button and slid the phone into her pocket. She didn't need Lou or anyone else to tell her that she should let go of April, but not like this. Leine had been what she herself deemed a shitty mother up until a couple of years ago, and now that their relationship was on track to being what it was before Carlos's death, she didn't want things to go sideways. Yes, April traveled extensively and could handle herself, especially now that Leine had taught her self-defense and how to handle weapons, but she was still her daughter. April's entry into undercover work for SHEN was unacceptable. She needed more training.

Tension pushing her, she grabbed the semiauto off the bed and retrieved a towel from the bathroom. She brought everything over to the table, and, with the practiced efficiency of

someone who'd repeated an activity hundreds of times, methodically broke down the gun and began to clean each component.
She needed *something* to take her mind off her daughter and to
keep herself busy while she waited for Kavi's call, and cleaning
weapons relaxed her.

Once she'd finished with the gun she brought up the
Internet and logged into an online language site, accessing the
Mandarin modules to brush up her skills. Relieved to find she
wasn't as rusty as she'd anticipated, after quizzing herself a few
times she lay on the bed and closed her eyes.

Five minutes later she got up and grabbed her phone,
intending to call Santa just to hear his voice, but decided against
it. He'd want to know how the case was going, and would probably be able to tell if she was leaving anything out. There was no
need to worry him. His tone would raise an octave like it did
when he was stressed out—especially if she told him she was
posing as a trafficker and meeting with a member of Chinese
organized crime. He'd go ballistic when he heard what April
and Lou had done.

She sat down at the table and stared out the window at the
overcast, smog-laden sky. Memories of a job she did in Bangkok
years before flooded her mind, and before she could shut it
down, an image from her past hit her full force in the solar
plexus. Her breath caught as the scene unfolded in her head.

The way she remembered it was straight out of a B-grade
Hollywood film from the forties: a dark night on a deserted
street, droplets of water glistening from a recent downpour,
Leine in deep shadow in an alley waiting for a contact.

She remembered checking her watch and growing impatient
for Kavi's predecessor, Bapit, to show. Bapit was fifteen minutes
late, so Leine turned to leave and bumped into him—his lifeless
form hanging from a sign advertising electronics. But a broken
neck wasn't what killed him.

He'd been gutted from breastbone to groin, his intestines wrapped around his neck like a scarf. His eyes were seeping holes, an exclamation above his open mouth, frozen in a terror-filled, soundless scream. The fingernails were gone, the flesh still bleeding.

Eric shut down the operation and called her back to the States, knowing it was too dangerous to continue. She'd never understood why the same people who killed Bapit hadn't tried to kill her. Obviously, they knew she was going to be there or they wouldn't have left the calling card. Bapit had been young and inexperienced, and Leine couldn't shake the feeling of responsibility. She'd been the one to inform his family of his death: a young wife with a new baby on the way and two doting parents whose stoic reaction broke Leine's heart.

She swore after that operation to never work with an inexperienced contact again.

Leine pulled up the Internet and checked her daughter's FindMe page, studying her expression in the photograph from the plane for clues of what she was feeling. Excitement and laughter, but Leine also sensed fear.

Good. She needs to be afraid. She'll be more aware of her surroundings that way.

Fear had been a constant in her work as an assassin. But fear was a good thing more often than not, as long as she didn't allow it to overwhelm her thought processes. Fear kept her on edge, hyper alert to danger and anything out of the ordinary. At the agency, she tended to blow off the operatives who never admitted being nervous when they were in play. Their bravado did nothing for them, and more often pointed to a flaw in their psychological makeup. Many times they'd commit a fatal error that could be traced back to not permitting fear its due. Leine welcomed the feeling, was suspicious if it didn't make an appearance, but never allowed it free rein.

A few minutes later her phone rang. Caller ID indicated it was Kavi.

"The meeting is at five o'clock tomorrow afternoon. I have received confirmation that an American girl is part of Wang's next shipment, although I am not certain it is the woman you're looking for."

"When does the shipment leave Bangkok?"

"Late tomorrow night, so timing is critical. You will meet Wang's associate at the Import Emporium Number Sixty Three in Chinatown, and he will take you to him. You're to come alone, and I suggest you be unarmed. Weapons tend to make these people nervous."

"Not a problem. Thank you for setting this up. I owe you a Singha."

"You will owe me much more than that if the meeting is successful."

"You know I'm good for it."

"Of course. I will monitor your progress, but do forgive me if I remain many miles distant."

Guilt from the reminder of his predecessor's demise carved into her gut. "As you wish, Kavi. Like I said, I owe you."

"Good luck," Kavi replied. "I will say a prayer for you."

"Thank you. I will do the same for you."

Leine ended the call and slid the phone back into her pocket. It was a fifty-fifty chance that Kylie would be on that ship, although the timing certainly worked. Either way, Leine was closer to finding her. She'd have preferred to meet with Wang that evening but knew from experience he would need time to check her credentials, bogus though they may be. The name on the passport Kavi had provided, Claire Sanborn, had a history in this part of the world. The gap in activity wouldn't raise alarms—many times, criminals would either drop from sight after being arrested or would go to ground if incarceration was imminent. The six or seven years between Claire's trips wouldn't be viewed with suspicion.

Leine picked up the phone and ordered an early dinner, opting not to deal with the energy-sapping humidity of late afternoon Bangkok.

There'd be plenty of time for that tomorrow.

9

L EINE ARRIVED IN Chinatown at a quarter of four and made her way through the narrow streets of Sampeng Market, searching for the Import Emporium. The brutal humidity promised a singularly sodden and energy-depleting evening ahead, and the crush of shoppers didn't make progress easy. The store's black and red sign blended well with the rest, and it took her a couple of passes to find it.

She ordered tea from a vendor a few stalls away and sipped it while monitoring activity in and out of the store. An older man wearing dreads shot through with gray and what looked like a bone necklace swept the sidewalk in front of the establishment, his attention riveted to his task. Wiry and tall, he wore sandals and a vibrantly colored tunic over loose, flowing pants, and had an energy about him that seemed unusual given the weather.

The man finished his task and went back into the building. Occasionally a customer would disappear through the doorway, then reappear several minutes later carrying a small paper bag. Curious, Leine finished her tea and crossed the narrow street, dodging pushcarts and the occasional motorbike.

Inside was cool, dark, and musty. Hundreds of ivory statues

depicting Buddhist and Hindu gods, lotus flowers, elephants, horses, and dragons crowded glass shelves, vying for space in the small store. Chinese coins tied with red ribbons hung from the ceiling, along with other good-fortune amulets. There was no one in front. A curtain of multi-colored plastic beads hung behind the register, leading to a back room.

She walked over to one of the shelves to examine the figurines. Most were supposedly made of legal ivory, indicated by a written explanation, paper yellow with age and taped multiple times to the shelf. Leine would bet most of her 401K that the "legal" ivory had been smuggled from East Africa into Thailand, probably by Wang or an associate.

"Good afternoon, madam. I am Abraham. May I help you?"

Leine turned as the man with the dreads appeared in the doorway at the back of the store. The cascading tinkle of plastic beads accompanied his entrance.

"Good afternoon. I'm curious about the price of your statues." She held up a large likeness of the Buddha with gold accents on the deity's head and hands. "And if they truly are legal ivory, as your sign says."

A slow smile spread across his face. "I see you have fine taste, madam." He joined her but kept a respectful distance. He pointed to the old sign on the shelf. "I personally guarantee the origin of each and every piece of ivory in this shop. Should you decide to buy, I will ensure you are able to bring your statue through customs with no ill effects. As for price," he frowned and tapped his finger to his lips. "Since you are one of my last customers of the day, I will give you a reduction."

Leine smiled and placed the Buddha back on the shelf. "Let me think about it. I'm not sure I'll have room in my suitcase." Her gaze drifted to the piece of jewelry she'd noticed earlier. "That's an interesting necklace."

"Do you like it?" He stroked the largest of what turned out to be teeth. "It is from a male lion, my talisman. There is much protection and good luck for those who wear them."

"I see," she murmured, and stopped herself from making a sarcastic remark about how unlucky the lion must have found them. She moved on to another shelf.

"Is this your first visit to Bangkok?" he asked, continuing to stand a respectful distance away, his hands clasped behind his back.

"No. I visited several years ago," Leine said. "I'm supposed to meet someone here in a little while, but thought I'd come early, get some ideas for souvenirs to buy before I return home."

"And where is home?" Abraham's increased interest in Leine was palpable, although the shift in his stance was small.

"Riyadh. I'm here on a buying trip for my employer."

Abraham raised his eyebrows. "Ah. May I inquire as to who your employer might be?"

Leine smiled and continued looking at the statues. "A prince."

"I see." The man visibly perked up at the mention of Saudi royalty. "Then may I interest you in something even rarer than an ivory figurine? Some even say it has magical powers."

Leine put down the statue she was holding. "I might be interested."

Abraham disappeared into the back room. Leine checked her watch to gauge the time until her contact arrived. A few moments later, he reappeared holding an opaque glass bottle. He set it on the counter and Leine moved closer.

"What is this?" Leine asked, studying the label.

"Tiger bone wine," he answered in a hushed voice. "Very rare. Your prince will be quite pleased."

Leine leaned closer. "I've heard it has medicinal qualities, but that the claims can't be proven."

"You have received bad information." Abraham straightened

and emphatically shook his head. "A few drops in your prince's tea, and he will be able to last through the night. It also cures paralysis and other maladies."

"Wow. An aphrodisiac *and* a cure for paralysis?"

"On my honor." Abraham laid his hand across his heart.

"How is it made, may I ask?"

The man smiled and turned on the charm, likely thinking he was closing in on a sale. "Wild tiger bones from throughout Asia —never the lower-quality farmed ones, of course—are steeped for months in a mixture of powerful herbs and rice wine, and then bottled when it is most potent." He brought up his thumb and forefinger, indicating a small amount. "You need but a few drops."

"Just how much do you charge for this rare thing?" she asked, working to keep a neutral expression.

Abraham leaned in, a calculating look on his face. "This quality usually goes for more than a thousand dollars per vial, but I will let you have the entire bottle for a fraction of its worth."

At that moment, someone walked into the shop, cutting short Leine's comment on the efficacy of human bone wine. Namely his.

Detach, Leine. You won't win this fight.

Abraham straightened and palmed the tiger bone wine, the bottle disappearing into the folds of his clothing.

The younger man in the doorway sported a shaved head except for a ponytail that fell past his shoulders. Dressed head to toe in dark clothing, he didn't remove his sunglasses. On his neck was the tattoo of the triad from Kavi's briefing. Leine turned to Abraham.

"It appears the person I'm to meet is here. Perhaps we can continue this conversation later?"

Leine followed the young man out the back door of the shop and into a waiting limousine. He closed the door and the driver edged into traffic, the other vehicles on the street stopping short so the larger car could merge. Expensive cars appeared to be rare in the district, and theirs was given pride of place on the road.

The driver had the same mark on his neck as the man who sat beside her. Leine turned her attention toward her seatmate, who stared out the window.

"How far to the meeting?" she asked.

"Not far." His clipped reply told her he wasn't much for conversation. Leine leaned back in her seat and watched the crush of neon chaos fight with the late afternoon shadows. The congestion of the old neighborhood slowly gave way to sleek modernity and manicured landscaping, the spidery nest of electrical lines above them changing to a more straightforward design.

The limo stopped at an impossibly white building with graceful spears of potted bamboo flanking the glass double doors. Leine and her escort exited the car and walked into the cool, sophisticated lobby with white marble floors and muted silk walls. Ponytail boy moved to the elevators and pressed the button while she took in the huge modern paintings hung throughout the large, airy space. A minute later, the elevator door opened and they stepped inside. He pressed the button for the twenty-sixth floor, and then motioned for her to raise her arms to the side and face away from him. He patted her down and then stepped back, clasping his hands in front of him.

The elevator stopped at their destination and the door slid open to reveal a large foyer.

The entry table held a low stone vase with one delicate pink orchid. A carefully directed spotlight illuminated the perfect flower. Chinese tapestries decorated a section of the massive wall behind her; another wall was faced with an exotic dark wood.

An Asian man of medium height wearing sharply creased tan slacks and a black silk shirt emerged from a doorway on her left. Leine pegged him as early forties.

"Welcome. I am Victor Wang," he said. "Please, come in."

Leine followed him into an open living area. Ponytail boy trailed them, keeping a discreet distance. A sleek bar took up most of the back wall with built-in cabinets made of the same exotic wood as the entrance. Several pieces of black and red lacquer furniture had been grouped in the center of the room. An expensive-looking settee and matching chairs with bright orange and yellow cushions had been grouped together in conversation areas. Floor-to-ceiling windows opened onto a generous balcony the length of the apartment and wrapped around a corner of the building with a sweeping view of the Chao Phraya River. A built-in cooking area and sleek outdoor furniture with matching cushions shaded by market umbrellas completed the magazine-worthy picture.

"May I offer you something to eat? To drink?"

"Some tea, perhaps."

"Of course," Wang said. He turned to an open doorway where a young Thai woman dressed in a blue and green silk sarong had appeared. "Sarai, some tea," he ordered. Sarai bowed and disappeared as silently as she had come. Wang turned back to Leine.

"Shall we sit?"

Leine followed him onto the balcony and picked a chair near a table without an umbrella. Wang had a seat across from her. Muted traffic noises floated up from the street below.

"And how have you found Bangkok, Miss..."

"Claire Sanborn."

"Miss Sanborn. My source tells me you have been to the city before."

"I came here on a business trip several years ago and always meant to return." Leine had to remind herself that small talk and personal stories were the Asian way of doing business, unlike getting straight to the point like most westerners. "The city still enchants, I'm happy to say."

Wang smiled and nodded. "Yes. There is something quite magical about Thailand in general, is there not? I trust you have sampled many of the temples in Bangkok?"

And on it went. Wang asked her questions about her stay and what she'd experienced, and Leine answered in glowing terms, pausing only when Sarai served the tea and a small plate of sweets. Wang asked about her family and Leine told him that work kept her from establishing a more formal arrangement. He nodded in commiseration and switched seamlessly to questions about her employer, which Leine fielded from a memorized script.

After the tea had been exhausted, Leine sensed a shift in tactics. Wang leaned back in his chair, evidently convinced she was trustworthy, and said, "And now, to business. My contact advised me that your employer is interested in hiring several of our domestics for his palace, is this correct?"

"Yes. He's particularly interested in a specific type. I'm sure our mutual friend discussed this with you prior to my arrival?"

Wang nodded. "He did. I am prepared to offer your prince his choice of our newly recruited candidates. Most are from the United States and Canada, with a few from Eastern Europe. I assume he prefers women of the Muslim persuasion?"

"Not really. He isn't averse to such leanings, of course, but considers himself an equal opportunity employer."

Wang nodded and leaned forward, steepling his fingers. "I see. What is your employer's timeframe? Will he want to interview the candidates, or will photographs suffice?"

"The prince trusts me implicitly. I'm prepared to conduct the interviews this evening, if possible."

Wang acted as though taken aback by the idea of rushing things, but his expression told her he was secretly pleased to be able to conclude the business transaction so quickly.

"I will have to ensure enough are available, but yes, I believe what you wish can be arranged."

"Will you be able to secure transportation to the Middle East?"

"Yes. There are several options. If he chooses, your prince may provide his own, such as his private jet. Or, if time isn't critical, there is a boat scheduled to leave for Dammam later next week."

"The prince doesn't use his private jet for domestics." Leine's voice turned icy and Wang's reaction was immediate.

"Of course. I understand. I was merely suggesting this option in case the prince was in a hurry."

Leine smiled coldly. "You guarantee your product?"

"One hundred percent."

"May I see the ship? My employer is quite particular about your transportation methods. It would be a shame to run afoul of the port authorities."

Wang's eyes narrowed. "I'm afraid that would be impossible. The ship is not yet in port."

"Then I'll need to make a phone call to see how or if he wants to continue with the transaction."

"There is a comparable ship leaving tonight. Although it is destined for Dar es Salaam, the accommodations will be similar."

"Excellent." Leine rose from her chair. "Shall we?"

Wang gave her a wry smile as he stood. "Once an American, always an American, eh?"

Leine replied, "Would you expect anything else?"

10

WANG'S DRIVER SHOWED a pass to the guard at the port gate and drove the car through. Victor Wang continued to ask Leine about her family and background, which Leine found tedious. Although polite, she gave him one- and two-word answers, choosing not to expand on her personal life, fictional though it may have been. After one such question, Wang's phone rang and he excused himself, answering in Mandarin. Despite Leine's pretended ignorance of the language, Wang didn't say anything of interest, remaining noncommittal to the party on the other end. He terminated the call and resumed his questioning.

The car continued through the maze of stacked containers until they pulled parallel to a mid-sized container ship tied next to the dock.

"We are fortunate that the ship doesn't leave until midnight. It will give us plenty of time to tour the facilities," Wang explained as they exited the vehicle.

"What's the decoy shipment?"

"Clothing, cheap trinkets for the tourist market, plastic water bottles, that kind of thing."

The vessel was a smaller class of container ship, with two deck cranes. Black marine paint covered the upper half, with the bottom a rust-red. The wheelhouse sat four stories high and looked out over the partially loaded decks. Wang led Leine up the gangway toward the center line of the ship, where containers stacked four high had been secured to the hatch cover sockets. Several bright spotlights illuminated the ship's cargo.

"This is a twin to that which will be used for next week's shipment, so it will give you an idea."

"She's a fairly small ship. How often does she need to refuel?" Leine asked.

Wang shrugged. "Depends on the weather. The crew I will use for your employer's shipment will be an experienced one from the Middle East, so I expect they'll chart their course accordingly. As you can see, this ship has a shallow draft and can take on fuel at smaller ports along the way if the need arises."

They walked over to a container with a large white X painted across the side. Wang nodded at one of the crewmembers to open the door. Inside were dozens of cardboard boxes stacked floor to ceiling with the picture of a water bottle stamped on the side. Wang instructed another crewmember to bring a pallet jack over and remove the boxes from the container, revealing a plywood wall. Wang walked to the wall and slid open a hidden panel near the center. She joined him and looked through the opening.

Leine's heart beat faster at the scene before her. Built as a false wall, the plywood concealed a distinctly human shipment. Packed together inside the small space, several shadowy figures either stood or sat on the floor. Jammed together in darkness, it was hard to tell where one body ended and another began. The occupants remained silent, except for a sharp intake of breath to Leine's left.

Kylie.

The young woman stood against the side of the container, her face illuminated by the sharp beam of the deck light. Before Kylie said or did anything that might alert Wang, Leine stepped away from the wall.

"Room enough for many types of cargo," Wang explained, closing the panel.

"And this is representative of the accommodations?" she asked, keeping her voice calm. Leine needed to conclude the meeting without Wang becoming suspicious so she could contact Lou and the authorities.

Wang nodded. "It is similar to what will be on the ship to Dammam. I have friends in security in both places, so there is no danger of discovery while in port."

"And if the ship is boarded by authorities at some point during the voyage?"

The barest hint of displeasure crossed Wang's face. "Should that happen, I have taken measures to give the impression the ship conforms to all international laws."

"What about the destination port? How do you intend to push the shipment through customs? Dammam is nothing like Dar es Salaam."

A slight tic pulsed near Wang's eye. "I have done this successfully many, many times. Your employer need not be concerned."

At that moment Wang's phone rang a second time. He pulled it from his pocket, glanced at the screen and said, "Please excuse my rudeness. I must take this call." He then turned and walked away, speaking in a low voice.

She checked the impulse to text Lou her findings, deciding to wait until she was clear of Wang and his associates in case he grew suspicious and asked her to hand over her phone. The ship wasn't due to leave for several hours. She had time.

Leine stepped out of the way as the crewmember replaced

the decoy shipment, closed the door, and slipped a container seal onto the handle. After he left, she walked over to inspect the seal. It had been neatly sawed in half, making it easy to open and close the container while still giving the appearance of being intact.

Wang ended the call and rejoined Leine. "Shall we continue? I have one more item to show you."

"I think I've seen enough."

"Please indulge me. It will be of utmost importance to your employer."

Leine had no choice but to follow him down a metal stairway into the hold, past several containers. Below decks the brackish air of the Chao Phraya River gave way to the smell of grease and diesel, along with other, more exotic fare. Leine put her hand to her nose and breathed shallowly as the stench of animal feces hit her full force.

"What else are you shipping? A zoo?"

Wang led her deeper into the bowels of the hold. "You could say that."

He stopped at a watertight metal door with a sign that read *Supplies* near the back of the hold and turned to Leine. "Should negotiations with the prince be successful, alternative accommodations may be possible." He turned the handle and swung the door open, gesturing for her to look inside. Leine stepped forward and at the same time felt a sharp sting in her neck. Staggering, she pivoted, fighting to remain upright as the world tilted and her vision blurred.

With her last bit of strength, Leine lunged forward, driving the heel of her hand toward Wang's face before she collapsed to the floor and the world went dark.

11

L EINE CAME TO with a jackhammer banging inside her head. She opened her eyes to solid darkness and winced as she pulled herself to a sitting position. Her head swam with the attempt and she sucked in air, waiting for a wave of nausea to pass. The air was dank and humid and hard to breathe, and her clothing stuck to her like soggy plastic wrap.

She tried to move her leg and was rewarded with a clank and the weight of hard metal against her ankle.

Where was she? She inhaled through her nose and gagged on the odor of grease and diesel mixed with the ammonia tang of a filthy urinal. Combined with the deep, rumbling vibration below her, she had her answer.

She was on the ship, and it was underway.

Leine wracked her brain trying to remember what was said, what she might have done, how she tripped up in her charade with Wang. Things were going well. He didn't display defensive or abnormal body language, other than annoyance with her questions. There'd been no significant change in his demeanor that she could tell.

Then she remembered the phone call in the car on the

way to the dock. Wang had been noncommittal during the conversation, careful to avoid saying anything Leine might have construed as a warning. Then there was the second call when they were on deck. Somehow, Wang had been notified of her intent to disrupt his plans, although she couldn't be sure how that might have happened. She'd scared the hell out of Alak and Sam, the *tuk-tuk* driver, threatening both with repercussions to not only them, but their families, if they so much as thought about informing Wang of her search for Kylie, so she doubted they were the problem.

Unless...

Kavi's smiling face came unbidden into her mind.

But he was vetted by the agency. Neither of them worked for the agency any longer, and she didn't have access to their current records. She assumed that because of their prior relationship he wouldn't betray her. *You know better than that, Leine.* She felt for her watch but it was gone, as was her phone.

At least they'd left her clothes and shoes.

She was on a container ship on her way to East Africa with a shipment of human slaves and wild animals, and no one knew where she was. Taking into account the size and speed of that class of ship, it would take at least ten days to reach the port at Dar es Salaam, longer if they stopped to refuel.

Good job, Leine. Now what the hell are you going to do? What would happen to April? What if something went sideways during her inaugural undercover case? Leine wouldn't be there to help.

She climbed to her feet and slid her hand along the wall, searching for an opening. Her fingers found the door at the same time the length of chain ran out. She ran her hands along the edges, looking for a handle. There wasn't one.

A plasma torch would come in handy about now. She pounded

on the cool metal with the flat of her hand and kicked against the bottom.

"Hey! Anyone there?" she yelled.

"I already tried that."

Leine pivoted at the sound of a man's voice and dropped to a defensive position.

"Who's there?" she asked, squinting against the dense black.

The man cleared his throat. "Don't be alarmed, now."

The voice grew closer, followed by the sound of metal scraping the floor. Leine tensed, clenching her fists. There was a hollow click and a small flame flared a meter away, illuminating the speaker's face. "Allow me to introduce myself," he said, his South African accent obvious. "My name is Derek."

Derek stepped closer and held out his hand. Large, intelligent eyes stared back at her from an open face. The flame sputtered, followed by an expletive. "Shit, that's hot."

"Your accent. Afrikaner?" Leine asked, still wary.

"Is it that noticeable?" The flame flickered to life, and Derek held it a few inches from Leine's face. "And you, you're American, hey?"

"Born and bred."

Derek extinguished the light, plunging them back into darkness. "Got to save fuel, you know?" He paused a beat before he said, "If you don't mind my asking, what are you doing here? I mean, I know why *I'm* here, but you don't look like someone Wang does business with on a regular basis."

Leine leaned against the wall and closed her eyes. "I'm not sure. I came on board to inspect a shipment and the next thing I know I've been Shanghaied."

That brought a chuckle from Derek. "Yeh. I know what you mean. And you thought that went out with the Barbary Coast, didn't ya?"

Leine turned back to the door and pounded again.

"That won't help. I did try it."

A frustrated groan escaped her as she rested her forehead against the damp metal.

"Why are *you* here?" she asked.

"There's a price on my head and it's a good one."

She heard him slide down the wall and assumed he was taking a seat on the floor. "You know Victor Wang?" she asked.

"Mr. Wang is—*was*—one of my buyers."

"What did he buy?"

"Elephant ivory, black rhino horn, baboon ass. You know, the usual."

"You're a poacher."

"I like to think of it as big game hunting without the bad shooting."

"And there's a price on your head in Dar?"

"Yeh. That's about the size of it. I'll probably be sold to the highest bidder. I have a lot of enemies."

"You don't sound very concerned."

"Why should I? If I'm meant to die, then so be it."

"That's a bit defeatist, isn't it?" Leine remained on her feet, keeping her distance. He acted friendly enough, but if the crew had orders not to feed them, she figured things could get ugly, fast.

"Eh, I've had a good life. Maybe it's my time, you know?"

"Sounds like you've given up." Leine slid her hand around the seams of the door, searching for a possible weakness. "How long do you think we'll be at sea?"

"Well now, that's a fine question. I'm not sure. Could be we'll go straight to Africa. Could be we won't. Wang's not one for being predictable. Another reason he's been able to do this so long without getting caught." Derek snorted. "Along with paying the right people." He flicked on the lighter once more and peered at her. "You never did tell me your name or why you were here."

"Claire. And I don't know, exactly. Wang brought me on board to see what type of ship he used for transport. My employer asked me to check it out for him. He's very particular. Wang was in the process of giving me a tour and I woke up in shackles." There was no point in telling the truth. Maintaining her innocence would be difficult if Derek decided to offer the crew information about his new roommate in exchange for leniency. Wang didn't need a plant to tease a confession out of her—he'd already acted as her judge and jury as evidenced by her floating prison. Why he didn't have her killed was a question she'd like answered.

"I'm surprised your employer, whoever he is, would send a lady like yourself to do a man's job. Seems a little off, you ask me."

Leine let the comment slide as she continued to study the room through her fingertips. "How did you get into poaching?"

"I started out as a tracker helping hunters bag the big five— you know, lion, elephant, rhino, leopard, buffalo. I got to be known for successful tracking, you check? On one of those hunts, some mad tourist asks if I can smuggle him out some ivory, says he'll pay me triple the going rate." Derek whistled. "From that point on, I was everybody's go-to for ivory. I expanded into whatever the market would bear and haven't looked back."

"Why would Wang want to take you out of commission? Seems to me he'd be more interested in keeping you on the procurement end of things."

"*Ja, ja.* Well, you know, I got a bit greedy. Started holding some back for myself. Wang and the other interested parties I worked for didn't take kindly to me helping myself, so here I am."

"Imagine that." Leine stopped herself from making a snarky comment about karma being a bitch, preferring to keep on Derek's good side for the time being. She'd readily admit she was pissed off at herself for having ended up a prisoner on a container ship in the middle of the Indian Ocean, and it was messing with her mood.

There was no way she'd be able to be there for April if she needed her. And really, how rusty was she? She'd thought the inspection would be just that: a simple walk-through before supposedly reporting back to her employer regarding shipping conditions. Kavi, or someone, had put a wrench in that proposition. If it was her old friend, he'd cleverly lulled her into letting down her guard, which she had never allowed to happen in the past.

But she'd been trying to leave that all behind, to forget. She wouldn't relish going back to the old way of doing business. She liked her life with Santa and her daughter. Hell, she was even getting used to living in LA again. She'd hated being continually paranoid to the point of never trusting anyone. Always expecting a bullet or a knife in her back. Yes, she learned to live in the moment, but she *never* felt safe, never had the opportunity to put down roots and have anything familiar to hold onto.

Had she chosen to work for SHEN because in some twisted way she missed the lifestyle? *No,* she thought. She chose to work for SHEN because she believed in the mission, believed she was doing the right thing.

She'd felt the same way working for the agency.

That had turned out so well.

Kylie's presence in the container made Leine's situation even more untenable. If she didn't get off the ship, she'd be no use to her. But if she did manage to escape, and that was a big if, how would she track Kylie? Africa was a massive continent. Wang could send her anywhere.

Not finding anything worthwhile in her exploration of the room, Leine took a seat on the floor and leaned her head back. She'd resume her search in the morning when there was some daylight.

"Given up trying to find a way out?" Derek asked, amusement lacing his voice.

"For the time being. Tomorrow's another day."

"You're right about that. Whatever happens, we've got a few thousand miles of ocean to work on it. I suggest we try to get some sleep. I promise you don't need to be concerned about me."

Leine folded her arms across her chest and shifted her position so she could doze sitting up.

"I'm not," she said. *You have more to worry about than I do.*

12

L EINE SNAPPED AWAKE as the door screeched open. Derek clambered to his feet, blinking against the weak, gray light filling the room. The fresh air from the open door was short lived as the stench of animal feces Leine noticed the night before hit her full force.

She stood, raising her arm in front of her eyes to block the light and squinted at their visitors. A solidly built, dark-haired man with a straggly goatee pointed an AK-47 at them while a small, wiry man placed two bowls of rice, a rusty lantern, and a container of water just inside the door. Leine looked past the men into the hold, but she couldn't tell if there was anyone else nearby.

"How long until we arrive in port?" Derek asked the men in Swahili.

The smaller of the two, the one who delivered their food, answered, "Maybe two weeks."

"Can't we make a deal?" Derek asked. "I can get you money, my brah. I'll pay if you let me off the boat before we pull into port."

The smaller man smiled and shook his head. "Wang pays us more than you."

"How do you know? Have I given you a price?"

Derek was all charm, reminding Leine of a money lender she'd met in Morocco, although his cropped blond hair and accent placed him squarely in the Dutch South Africa camp. The two crew members just laughed and walked out. Derek stepped past the bowls of rice and wedged his free foot in the opening. When the door failed to close, the smaller man peered at the threshold, a puzzled look on his face. Realizing what Derek had done, he yelled for the other man. With a shout, his counterpart wrenched the door open and shoved the barrel of the machine gun into Derek's face.

Leine remained quiet, certain the wild-eyed man holding the AK-47 would pull the trigger, splattering pieces of Derek across the room. Beads of sweat appeared on Derek's forehead, and his Adam's apple bobbed as he licked his lips.

No one moved as the two men glared at each other. Leine held her tongue, acutely interested in how events would pan out, recalculating her options if she had to make the voyage alone.

Time crawled and the tension in the small space crackled. Finally, Derek broke the silence.

"Now wait a minute, my brah," Derek said, keeping his hands in the air as he inched his foot away from the door. "I meant no disrespect."

A few heartbeats later, the man with the gun released his finger from the trigger and stood down. He narrowed his eyes at Derek, who let out a breath and lowered his hands.

"You must not ever do this again," the smaller man scolded him. "I am not responsible for my brother."

The two men exited the container, slammed the door closed, and locked it.

"That went well, don't you think?" Derek's voice echoed in the small room.

"Well, at least now we know they have machine guns." Leine felt for the lantern and popped the switch. A bright white glow illuminated the space. Battery operated. They'd have to conserve.

"I noticed you didn't react when he pointed that thing in my face," Derek said. "Aside from your obvious disregard for my well-being, that kind of composure is rare."

"Why is that?"

"Well, you've got to admit, most women would be a sobbing mess confronted with that kind of threat."

"You think so? You must not know many."

"What kind of shit is that? I know a lot of women."

"I see." Leine rolled her eyes. *Great. I'm stuck with an idiot for a travel partner. Two weeks?*

"I *do*." Derek's voice rose an octave, obviously irritated. "Piss off. You think what you want. I know what I know."

Leine didn't reply, preferring to let him de-stress from the incident with the gunman. She assumed he was crashing from the adrenaline dump. A person could get testy when that happened. She scooted one of the bowls of rice toward Derek while taking the other for herself. The rice was tepid, but at least it meant their captors were interested in keeping them alive.

"What are they going to do with you, I wonder?" Derek asked between mouthfuls.

Leine had been trying to work that out. Worst-case scenario, Kavi hadn't just betrayed her reason for being in Bangkok—he could have told Wang who she'd been in her former life, giving him unlimited marketing options. "I honestly don't know," she said.

"Will your employer pay a ransom to get you back? Wang's a greedy bastard."

"Maybe." Leine finished her rice and set the bowl on the floor. She'd resigned herself to being at sea for the foreseeable future. There had to be some way to either bribe or overcome the crew. She'd have plenty of time to plan her escape. For now, she contented herself with the task of making Derek an ally, which appeared to be her best bet for getting off the ship.

"I gathered by your interaction with our guards that the three of you have worked together."

"A time or two."

"Tell me about the two brothers. The smaller one seems less inclined to follow orders."

"You'd be right about that. Sefu, the big one with the machine gun, has something to prove, whereas his brother Kibwe isn't such a bad guy."

"Could be a way to leverage that, don't you think?" she mused.

"*Ja*, definitely."

"I noticed they weren't too interested in your bribe. What's Wang like when things don't go his way?"

Derek gave her a rueful smile. "He can be a ruthless shit when money's involved. Obviously, a reward has been offered for my safe delivery to interested parties."

Leine could work with greed. At least it was something. She wiped the perspiration from her forehead with the back of her hand. The hot, muggy space was like being locked inside a dirty humidifier. Thankfully, they weren't above decks. The temperature in their little prison could have been much worse.

"Since we have a bit of time, let's get to know each other," Derek suggested. "Maybe I'll be able to figure out why they've decided to keep you locked up in here with me." Derek folded his arms across his chest and studied Leine. "I'll go first. You've been around guns, obviously, and not just your normal, everyday handguns. I'll venture a guess you were in some kind of military unit at some point in your life, yeh?"

Leine shook her head. "Nope. My turn." She held his gaze. "There's more to your being here than just skimming a little off the top."

Derek's attention shifted to the floor for a second and then back to her.

"I'm right. What's your great sin? Did you betray Wang?"

Derek shrugged, paused. "He might look at it that way."

Leine leaned her head back. "Ah. Then it's even more important we escape before pulling into port. Betrayal is a worrisome accusation when the aggrieved party has triad connections. Things don't normally end well for the accused." For all of Derek's earlier bravado, the look in his eyes telegraphed his concern.

"How do you propose we do that?"

"I haven't figured that out quite yet, but I will. Are you interested? Because if not, I'm fine going it alone."

A look of annoyance crossed Derek's face. "Well, of course I'm interested. Jesus, I knew I should've skipped that meeting with Wang."

"Tell me about poaching. What's your motivation, other than money?" Leine asked. "You say you have plenty. With the exception of career criminals, I've met very few wealthy people pursuing a way of life that could land them behind bars or face down in a ditch somewhere who were solely in it for the money. At least, very few who are as successful as you say you've been. The luster of gold wears off, while the challenge dies with achievement."

"I live for the hunt."

"Not good enough," Leine shot back. "Not much challenge locating game in a helicopter now, is there?"

Derek nodded. "When I first started, poaching was hard

work. Dangerous work. It took skill and gave game a fighting chance. I only took what I needed to fill orders." He gazed past Leine at some far-off memory. "Nowadays, they track them by air and use machine guns. No skill in that. And no way to replenish the herds, either. Shortsighted bastards."

"And this is how Victor Wang operates?"

"Yeh. He's got a traveling safari camp and uses a helicopter to scout game for his clients. Some of 'em actually prefer hunting from the air."

"Pretty tough to outrun a chopper."

"You could say that."

"And you decided to stop doing things his way, is that it?"

He shrugged. "That's part of it."

"Not only did you skim profits, but you attempted an end run around Wang with one of his clients. Am I close?"

Derek smiled. "You must have a crystal ball. I figured I could work things better than Wang. His business practices aren't what I'd call sustainable."

"Greedy without a view to the future."

"That's Wang in a nutshell. As soon as one commodity's depleted, he just moves on to the next, like a wave of locusts."

"'*There is no torrent like greed*'."

He grimaced. "Yeh. A lot of good changing tactics did me. Here I am headed for the auction block, just one more of Wang's commodities."

"What does he do with the girls?"

Derek's gaze cut to Leine's. "What girls?"

"The girls he's transporting on the ship."

He shook his head, shifting in his seat. "I don't know about any girls."

"Sure you do." Leine raised an eyebrow.

"There's a word for it, you know."

"Yes, I know. Wang already trades in illegal ivory. Why stop there? Human beings are lucrative. And he needs domestics for his camp, as well as entertainment for his clients."

Derek narrowed his eyes. "Why are you so keen on whether or not Wang's into slaving? Unless you're here at his request, to see if I'll sell him out." He shook his head. "No such luck, Claire. I'm in deep enough shit. Go look somewhere else. I've already said too much."

"You're right. I'm sorry. And why would Wang plant a spy in here? According to you, your fate is already sealed, right?"

"Good point," Derek conceded. "I tend to be a bit paranoid. Professional hazard."

Leine paused, thinking about what he'd said. Time to change tack. "Ever think about working in a conservation capacity?"

"Like helping save the elephants?" Derek laughed. "Yeh, that'd go over well."

"I'd think the conservationists would welcome your expertise. Why not use your abilities to conserve what's left?"

"It's not that easy. Anyone who comes between a smuggler and his clients winds up dead. Life is cheap in Africa."

"Then how about working on the demand side? Give talks. Educate. Tell people that their taste in ivory trinkets and belief in the magical qualities of powdered rhino horn is misplaced and damages the larger picture."

"Same argument."

"Don't do it in Africa. Do it in other countries where they buy the stuff."

He studied her, his expression unreadable. "You sound like someone who's been on both sides of an issue yourself. Am I right?"

"Astute observation."

"And which way did you choose?"

At that moment, the door rattled and opened with a screech.

Sefu and his trusty AK stood to one side, the barrel of the gun pointed at both of them, a wary expression on his face. Kibwe stepped into the room and held out his hand.

"I'm here to empty the bucket," he said.

Derek moved to the back of the dank room and picked up the five-gallon plastic bucket they'd been using as a toilet. He returned and handed it to Kibwe with the cover on.

"I wasn't kidding about being able to pay you," Derek muttered to Kibwe, out of earshot of Sefu. Leine caught the bribe, but didn't react. Any seed planted in Kibwe's mind had potential, although she didn't trust Derek to include her in any of his escape plans. Yet.

Good thing she was a light sleeper.

13

S EVERAL DAYS LATER, Leine and Derek had managed to forge a wary friendship. They saw Sefu and Kibwe twice a day, once for their daily ration of food and water, and once to empty the bucket. Each time, they engaged the two crew members in conversation, lulling them both to the point of carelessness. Sefu was the last to let down his guard and now wore his gun over his shoulder, looking bored whenever the other three exchanged words.

Leine and Derek had worked out a schedule of sorts, where they would engage one or the other guard in harmless banter. Leine had gotten Sefu to admit he had a girl back in Dar es Salaam whom he missed dearly, and she'd even made him blush, once, when she asked him about her. After each conversation, Leine and Derek would compare notes, parsing what was said and figuring out how to burrow deeper into their psyches, teasing out more personal information which they intended to use once they sailed closer to port.

The next morning, Kibwe came by to deliver breakfast. It was Leine's turn to work on Sefu while Derek would have a friendly chat with his brother. But Kibwe had come alone.

"Where's Sefu?" Derek asked, taking a bowl of rice.

Kibwe shrugged. "He has more important things to do. You will speak only to me from now on."

"I will miss your brother, but I'm glad we'll have more time with you, Kibwe," Leine said with a smile. Kibwe smiled back, but then checked himself as though he remembered whom he was talking to.

"Sefu has big plans. He wishes to climb higher in Wang's organization so he can stay in Dar with his girl."

"And you? What do you want?" Leine asked.

Kibwe frowned. "To become a doctor. I have some money saved, but not enough."

Leine and Derek exchanged looks. Derek cleared his throat.

"You know, Kibwe, if you help us, we will help you."

"This is not possible," Kibwe replied, shaking his head. "I like you both very much, but Wang is a dangerous man. If he found out I helped you escape, he would kill me and my brother, maybe even our family."

"Then we need to make it look like it isn't your fault," Leine said.

At the suggestion, Kibwe's eyes widened and he stepped backward. "No."

"You know that you're sentencing us to die, don't you?" Derek said, his voice low. Kibwe, clearly afraid of where the conversation was headed, glanced behind him before he took another step backward and started to swing the door closed.

"You will be responsible for the death of two innocents," Derek repeated.

"You are no innocent," Kibwe murmured to Derek. He glanced at Leine. "I do not know why you are here, but there must be a good reason." He walked out and slammed the door shut.

Leine paced the small area that the chain allowed her,

excited by the progress they'd made with Kibwe. "It won't be long now."

"What the fuck are you talking about? We just set ourselves back a week. He'll never trust us now. We don't have enough time," Derek said, scowling. "I shouldn't have pressed him so hard."

"I disagree. Sefu no longer feels the need to shadow Kibwe. That's huge progress. Of course Kibwe's going to react with fear when one of us suggests escaping. That's entirely normal. But you've planted a seed." She turned to face him and crossed her arms. "You continue to lead him on with promises of money, but what happens when he finally capitulates and expects to be paid? If it were me risking my life and the lives of my family, I'd turn in the asshole that made a promise of money when he didn't deliver."

"*Ja, ja,*" Derek said, waving away her concerns. "Don't worry. If he 'capitulates' as you put it, I can pay." He let his gaze travel along her body and back up to her face, where he arched a brow. "I'm not sure what we're going to do about your predicament."

Leine rolled her eyes. "Don't flatter yourself. I can't pay anything now, but I will guarantee your safe passage to anywhere you choose."

"I'll believe *that* when I see it," Derek scoffed. "At least we agree you're going to owe me." He cocked his head and smiled. "I think I like that idea."

THE DAYS MARCHED ON, AND EACH TIME KIBWE VISITED THEM HE kept his comments brief and noncommittal, even though Leine and Derek continued to work him.

The two prisoners passed endless hours teaching each other

their respective talents; Leine demonstrated fighting moves from various martial arts disciplines and Derek taught her about the movement of elephant herds and lions, and ingenious ways to track prey. His was an encyclopedic knowledge of the animals he tracked, and he probably knew more than most scientists conducting observations. Little by little, Leine developed a grudging respect for the poacher. The feeling appeared to be mutual.

"You know," Derek said one afternoon after describing the way the light played on the acacia trees at sunset, "Africa's a massive place with a lot of potential. You and me, we could go into business together, make a name for ourselves."

Leine gave him a look that said she thought he'd gone off the rails, and he hurried to explain.

"No, no. I am aware of your disdain for my former trade, believe me. I was thinking we could go into the export business, but not game or ivory. Imagine this." He spread his hands wide, describing a marquee sign in the air. "Derek and Claire's African Fabric Emporium." He grinned, his teeth glaringly white against his newly sprouted beard. "We could include jewelry and other handmade stuff, yeh?"

Leine shook her head. "Not even remotely interested. But thanks for thinking of me." She allowed herself a brief longing for Santa and April before she turned her attention back to the present. From Derek's suggestion, she surmised that a kind of trust had been established between them, although she wasn't naïve enough to believe it would last given the circumstances. Still, it was something.

Hurt showed in his eyes but quickly disappeared. "Your loss," he said with a shrug.

"I don't judge you, you know," Leine said.

Derek leaned his head back. "Why not? I do."

"Because I've finally gotten to a point in my life where I realize it doesn't matter what you've done. It's what you do."

Derek didn't say anything for a long moment. Then he nodded, slowly. "I was right," he said, his voice a quiet echo in the room. "You have been there."

Leine closed her eyes. "More often than you can imagine."

14

L EINE WOKE TO something warm touching her ankle. She sat up quickly as Kibwe, flashlight in hand, released her from the metal cuff. Finger to his lips, he made his way to Derek's sleeping form and tapped his shoulder. Derek started to say something but Kibwe cut him off.

Once he freed Derek, Kibwe slipped past Leine and out the door, gesturing to them to follow. They moved furtively through the hold, past the container that Kylie was in with the large X painted across the side. At least Wang had moved the box off the upper deck and out of the sun.

Unless there was more than one.

Leine slipped around to the back of the forty-foot box. Derek and Kibwe waved at her to follow but she ignored them. She leaned in close and gently rapped her knuckles against the metal wall. Hearing nothing, she tried again. A few seconds later, there was a faint tap. Leine knocked again, this time louder, certain that the rumble of the ship's engines would cover the sound to anyone nearby. A louder, answering knock came back. Derek had eased up behind her and put his hand on her shoulder.

"We have to go. Now, Claire."

"There are people inside this container." Leine stood motionless, her mind racing for a way to overpower the crew and hijack the ship, knowing he was right and they'd have to leave. She stared at Derek, searching his face for a hint of compassion. Derek blinked, revealing nothing.

He let out a frustrated sigh. "What are you going to do? We can't take them with us."

"No," Leine said, an idea beginning to take hold in her mind and growing. *But you can track them.*

She noted the positioning of the X on the side of the container before following Derek back to where Kibwe waited, pacing nervously. The three stayed in the shadows until they reached the metal stairwell Leine had used when Wang first led her below decks.

Kibwe leaned in close and said in a low voice, "There are two crewmen in the pilot house, but I know they are not watching the deck."

"How do you know that?" Derek asked.

Kibwe shrugged. "They have discovered a magazine someone left near the captain's chair by mistake."

"Ah." Derek lifted his chin. "Naked ladies to the rescue, once again. Where are the rest?"

"Most are asleep. We have been at sea long enough now that the captain is slack in his orders, so only a handful of us are on watch."

"Where are we? Is there land nearby?" Leine asked. Being stranded in the middle of the Indian Ocean didn't sound like much of an escape plan.

"That is why you must leave tonight. We are only a day's journey from Dar es Salaam. We will dock late tomorrow night."

"How do we get off the ship?" Derek asked.

"The lifeboat. There should be enough fuel to reach land."

"But doesn't a lifeboat need someone to launch it? How will you explain your way out of that?"

"I will suggest to the captain that you allowed Claire to escape in the lifeboat, while you climbed down the side of the ship. They will think she picked you up once you reached the water. I will drop a line over the side to make it look convincing."

"Why the change of heart?" Leine asked.

"I thought about how long it would take me to save enough money to become a doctor and realized it would never be. God has provided another way." Kibwe's expression turned serious as he shifted his attention to Derek. "I will make it look like you overpowered me and took the key for your manacles." He handed him the key. "We don't have much time. You have money, yes?"

"Yes," Derek replied.

"Good. Follow me."

They climbed the stairs and sprinted across the deck, threading their way through the shadowy rows of containers toward the stern. Kibwe paused in the darkness to allow a crew member to pass, and then continued on to the lifeboat.

"You will find food and water as well as a compass inside," he said. "There is also a first aid kit. In calm seas, the boat will travel at six knots. That should place you near the mainland by late evening." He looked at Derek expectantly.

"Oh, right." Derek patted his pockets. "Could I bother you for a knife?"

Kibwe frowned and handed his rigging knife to him.

"You may want to turn away," he said to Leine. "This won't be pretty."

Derek dropped his pants, twisted around, and using the tip of the knife, carved into the side of his buttocks, gritting his teeth as he did so. Blood surged through his fingers and down his leg and he used the bottom of his shirt to stanch the flow. A few moments later, he straightened and wiped something off with a clean section of shirt. Then he instructed Kibwe to hold out his hand and dropped an object into his palm. Kibwe held it up, squinting. The diamond's facets sparkled in the deck light.

"That oughta pay for a year or two of medical school, eh, my brah?" Derek said, wincing as he slid his pants over the wound.

Kibwe nodded, his mouth gaping in surprise. He clamped his lips closed and blinked. "Thank you," he managed. "God is great."

"Small payment for saving our lives, eh?" Derek replied. "Shall we?"

Leine and Derek climbed up the platform and made their way into the enclosed lifeboat, closing the watertight door behind them. The small boat itself had seen better days, but still had the webbing to hold them in place during the launch. Leine sat in front at the controls. Grimacing, Derek maneuvered himself into the seat across the aisle from her and they buckled themselves in. After a slight pause, there was a loud clunk and the lifeboat rumbled down the rails. Seconds later, they were airborne and weightless, rushing toward the dark ocean.

Leine braced for impact as the bow split the water, plunging beneath the surface. The force threw her forward but the straps kept her from slamming into the console. The boat leapt upright and bobbed like a cork, seawater streaming across the windows. She started the engine and steered away from the ship, the lights on the upper deck fading into the ink-black night.

"How's your ass?" Leine asked as she unbuckled the safety strap and started searching under her seat for supplies.

"It's been better." Derek released himself from his seat and limped down the aisle, checking the rest of the lifeboat for the same. "Aha," he said, holding a first aid kit in the air. "I'll just be a minute."

While Derek cleaned and bandaged his cut, Leine kept the

little boat on course, headed in the direction Kibwe had told them to go. Images of the container with the X on the side continued to crowd her mind. She needed to convince Derek to help her track Wang's shipment.

Derek returned and placed a canvas bag on the floor, then gingerly lowered himself into his seat.

"In addition to the first aid kit, we've got several liters of water, a hatchet, a flashlight, and a knife. There's a signal mirror and a couple of ropes, too."

"Any food?"

"Just these." Derek held up a handful of individually wrapped energy bars.

"Better than nothing," she said, helping herself to one. She took a bite and stretched her neck to release the tension. "I hope the crew doesn't notice the lifeboat missing too soon. I would assume there's a transponder somewhere on board."

"Yeh, but I'll bet the captain delays telling his boss about our departure. It's not like he can turn the ship around and come after us. I imagine Wang's going to be very unhappy."

"Remember the container marked with an X?" Leine asked. "The one with the human cargo?"

When Derek didn't say anything, Leine repeated her question. He studied her for a moment before replying.

"Wang marks the ones with live cargo so they're easier to spot and unload."

"I thought you said you didn't know anything."

"I lied." Derek leaned forward, his forearms on his thighs. "Look, I didn't know you, and besides, it's not a business practice I agree with."

"I'm looking for someone."

Derek stared at Leine. "That's why you were on the ship. You think the person you're looking for was part of Wang's shipment?"

"She is. I confirmed it before Wang sidelined me. She disappeared from a hostel in Bangkok. I received information linking her disappearance to Wang's latest shipment. An associate set up a meeting, and I saw her inside the container."

Derek crossed his arms. "Is there even an employer?"

"In a manner of speaking."

"So now we're even. We both lied."

"You can help me find her."

"How do you know Wang isn't going to just auction her off?"

"I don't. But when you told me about Wang's floating safari camp for wealthy hunters in Tanzania, it clicked."

Derek shifted in his seat, trying to get comfortable. "And if I decide to help you, what's in it for me?"

"Like I told you earlier, I can ensure safe passage anywhere you want to go."

"Nah. You need to give me more than that. I'll be risking my life getting that close to Wang's people after fucking up his little plan to sell me off to the highest bidder."

"I'm sure we can work something out." Leine watched him closely. "The girl I'm searching for witnessed a drug dealer gun down her little brother. As if that weren't enough, she's been kidnapped and shipped halfway around the world, to be used as a slave. You know Wang and can find his camp. My gut tells me she's being delivered as part of the entertainment."

"Add in a hefty payment and I'll think about it."

"I'll see what I can do." Leine held out her hand.

After a brief hesitation, he extended his and they shook. "What the hell am I doing?" Derek let out a frustrated sigh before he got up and limped to the forward hatch.

"Mind if I open this for some fresh air?" he called back to Leine.

"Go ahead."

Derek unlatched the cover and heaved open the hatch.

Warm sea air and the sound of gently lapping waves filled the cabin. "I'll be back to relieve you in a little while," he said before climbing out through the opening.

Leine peered through the window at the brilliant stars, thousands of shimmering diamonds like the one Derek had given Kibwe.

She'd been so close to rescuing Kylie. She took a deep breath and let it go, feeling the weight of all the victims out there who needed help.

Needed her help.

Stop it, Leine. It's not your job to save the world.

Didn't Santa tell her that once? He was right, of course, but for Leine the weight of the guilt she felt—for all of the targets she hit, no matter who she'd killed, for all of the women and children she couldn't save—that guilt clung to her like a massive anchor tied around her neck, dragging her under.

She'd have to tread carefully with Derek. Without him, she wouldn't stand a chance.

15

K YLIE CLOSED HER eyes and leaned her head against the wall. For what seemed like months she'd been squashed inside the small space alongside the other women with barely enough food and water to stay alive. She'd lost all sense of time and place, only knew they were still at sea. She yearned for the sun on her skin, a good meal, and a soft bed. If it wasn't for the filtered light that came through slits near the roof, the women would be in total darkness, unaware if it was day or night.

Sapphire had been singled out during the transfer from the van to the ship, and Kylie hadn't seen her again. Nor had she seen the little boy, Jaidee, since he'd been taken from the cell. The only hope she'd had was days—weeks?—ago, when she thought she'd seen her mother's friend, Leine. But no one had come for her. Leine would have found a way to rescue her; she was certain of it.

Now, she wasn't sure whom or what she'd seen that night before leaving Bangkok.

Two dozen women of differing ages and ethnicities sat huddled together in the back of the container. The walls were covered in Styrofoam and other noise-canceling material, as was the plywood separating them from the rest of the shipment. Dirty, threadbare blankets, not nearly enough for all of them, had been neatly folded and stacked in the corner, waiting to be shared. The women had taken to sleeping in shifts, the small space and hard floor less than ideal but better than nothing. Several jugs of drinking water had been lashed to one side with bungee cords. The throb of the ship's engines became the droning background music to their tiny world.

Modesty soon took a backseat to survival, especially when it came to the five-gallon bucket they were expected to use for relieving themselves. The days stretched on, unbearably hot and stagnant, filled with dull monotony punctuated by short, terror-filled moments.

Except for when someone tapped on the outside of the container. Certain it was a trick by one of the crew, none of the women had tapped back. After the third time, Kylie moved to the spot where it had come from and, heart in her throat, tapped back. Whoever it was had knocked again, once. Kylie tried a few more times, but there was no reply. Convinced it had been a cruel joke by a crewmember, she pushed it from her mind.

The women inside that small room had come together in solidarity in an attempt to buoy each other from the crushing degradation of being at the mercy of the crew. On countless occasions when one of them delivered their food or emptied the bucket, he would pick out a woman and drag her, screaming, from the small compartment, to be offered as entertainment to the rest of the crew. Kylie had been relieved to learn from another woman who spoke English that the crew's interest did not extend to her, as she was considered an infidel, and they were afraid she carried HIV. Although beyond grateful for their ignorance, her heart broke each time they brought one of the women back, shoving her through the opening as though worth no more than her ripped and bloodied clothing, a vacant stare replacing the human being who had once lived inside.

The longer they were at sea the more terrified Kylie became, not knowing what would happen to her when they reached their destination. The English-speaking woman offered no insight. Unaware of the identity of her kidnappers, she'd been bundled into a van and driven away as she walked to the market for the day's groceries. She didn't know why she'd been targeted. According to her, most of the women's stories were similar.

After several days, the taste and quality of the air changed, growing incrementally different than what she'd come to expect in Thailand. It felt drier, less verdant, although the briny sea air still overpowered everything else.

How far had they gone? Would she ever be able to return home? The last time she saw her father, they had a fight. He tried to forbid her from going on the trip by herself, citing her impulsiveness and politically liberal naiveté. After enumerating the myriad dangers that a young woman traveling alone in Southeast Asia would encounter, he stated bluntly he didn't think she'd survive.

Like a pressure cooker at its limit she'd exploded, accusing him of failing to understand her, of telling her what to do, of his own bad judgement in choosing to eat at a restaurant in a bad section of town, where Brandon had been killed. The hurt in her father's eyes still haunted her. What she wouldn't give to take back the words she'd thrown at him. Yes, their views on politics and religion were vastly different, so much so that she often wondered whether she'd been adopted, but he'd been a good father, and she loved him in spite of it, as he did her. She missed her mother the most. Her calm demeanor and loving acceptance went a long way toward keeping the peace between them.

The women had finished their allotted bowls of rice when the ship's engines slowed, followed by shouts from the crew.

Kylie turned to her friend sitting next to her and asked what was happening.

"We're stopping," the woman said. "I think we are coming into port."

Heart in her throat, Kylie crossed her arms and hugged herself. During the endless days and nights she had imagined every horrific scenario, which she tried to offset with more positive ones, like meeting someone who could help, or Leine finding out where she was and swooping in to rescue her. What was it that her mother always told her? How nothing would ever be as bad as what she could imagine.

She hoped she was right.

16

KIBWE HAD BEEN partially right about the amount of fuel in the lifeboat. Twelve hours later the little craft's engine sputtered, coughed once, and died. Leine was sitting outside on the bow in the relentless tropical sun when it happened. Land was still miles away, tantalizingly close yet too far to swim.

"Claire—" Derek called from inside. "I need your help."

She dropped through the hatch. With no power, they'd be subject to the whims of the prevailing currents, drifting toward the busy shipping lanes leading to Dar es Salaam. Thankfully, the weather was cooperating with a slight wind from the northeast and calm seas.

Derek was near the stern. Oars from an equipment locker lay at his feet.

"Here," he said, handing her one. "You prefer port or starboard?"

"Starboard."

"I'll take port." He handed her several rations of water. "You'll need these."

Leine grabbed the compass from the steering station, and

they both climbed through the hatch. Oar at the ready, she knelt on the right side of the bow. Derek did the same on the left.

"I'll call the strokes," he said, and waited until they'd both hydrated themselves. "Now row."

Leine carved her oar into the water, matching his stroke.

They continued for twelve strokes, and then rested for a few moments before rowing another twelve. Leine relaxed into the rhythm of paddling followed by short rest periods. The lifeboat crept through the glare of sun on the water's surface, headed for the shimmering continent.

They made landfall several hours later. Exhausted from the grueling workout, wind- and sunburned, they left the lifeboat where she ran aground. Checking on their supplies, Leine grabbed as much water as they could comfortably carry and shoved a couple of energy bars into her pockets. They bandaged the worst of their blisters before setting off down the white sand beach.

"We're going to need money," Derek said. "I've got a bit back at my place, but if the ship's already in port, then Wang's found out we escaped. It won't be safe."

She gazed at the lineup of ships on the water, waiting their turn to pull into port. "I assume his ships are able to bypass the line?"

Derek shrugged. "I wouldn't doubt it. Grease the right palms..."

"I can send a message to my employer to wire funds."

"You'll need a passport."

"Not if they wire the funds to you." Leine figured Lou would be able to find her a passport, but it could take days. They didn't have days. She could go to the embassy, fill out the paperwork to get an emergency passport, but she didn't have time to go through the red tape and long lines, and Derek had mentioned that Wang had friends who worked there.

Derek nodded. "All right, then. Cyber café it is."

He hooked a sharp right and led the way through palm trees and heavy vegetation to a dirt road where they began to walk. The sun had just dropped below the horizon and everything was bathed in a dark orange hue. The dust of the road rose to greet them, settling on Leine's skin like a fine talc.

Derek waved at an ancient, overloaded *dala dala* as it chugged past them. Its sole brake light blinked on and the rusty, derelict bus slowed to a stop. Derek jogged to the open door and spoke rapidly to the driver. He turned to Leine and nodded at the roof.

"He says we can ride into Dar on the top of the bus for free if I promise to help his cousin."

Leine cocked her head but didn't say anything. She grabbed hold of the metal bars on the open-air bus and climbed to the roof. Derek followed close behind, flopping onto his back on top of a large canvas bag.

"I have the feeling the man's cousin is going to be disappointed," Leine said.

He grinned at their fellow passengers and winked.

"Fuck it. It's Africa."

Traffic in Dar es Salaam was purported to be some of the worst in the world, and that evening's slow crawl into the city did not disappoint. It didn't take long before Leine had enough of diesel exhaust and sweat, mixed with the steady honking of impatient and hostile drivers. As soon as she spotted a sign advertising Internet access, she signaled to Derek she was getting off. He followed her into the small store, complaining loudly that she had gotten off too soon.

"I'm done, Derek. I can't take the slow pace. We can walk

faster than that. Besides," she said, indicating the crowded café, "this should work nicely."

"And just how the hell are we going to pay for access? Did you happen to pick up a few shillings?"

Leine glanced at his backside and arched an eyebrow. Derek shook his head and stepped away.

"Oh no, no, no. There's nothing left back there. I gave Kibwe all I had."

Leine shrugged. "You'll figure it out," she said, heading to a recently vacated computer. "Use your charm."

Still grumbling, Derek walked to the counter and engaged the clerk in conversation. A few minutes later, he was back and handed her a slip of paper.

"Here's the code. You've got twenty minutes."

"Let me guess. You're going to help his sister?"

"Just send your message. Use this bank." Derek scribbled a name on a piece of paper.

Leine logged into a secure chat room and sent a message to Lou, detailing that she'd found Kylie, what had happened since Bangkok, and why he hadn't heard from her, adding a line asking about April. It was before dawn back in LA, but Lou was an early riser and tended to check his email first thing. Then, she sent a note to Santa, letting him know she was all right and not to worry.

Yeah, she thought, *that's gonna happen.* The man sitting at the computer to her left stood and walked out of the café, his screen showing several minutes remaining. Then the woman to her right scowled at her and did the same. Leine scanned the room, searching for the reason they'd left, but didn't notice anything unusual. Was it something she said?

A few minutes later, Lou replied, confirming the amount and the bank's address. He added that one of his old contacts in the city should be able to get her a passport quickly. His answer regarding April was frustratingly vague. Leine glanced at the clock on the wall behind them to see how much time they had left. Five minutes. Derek walked over to speak with the clerk in order to give her some privacy.

Deciding to pursue Lou's non-answer about her daughter once she had more time and resources, she replied that she'd lost Kylie, who was now most likely on her way to Wang's camp somewhere in Tanzania. She sketched out her plan to use Derek's help to find the camp, mentioned that he asked for payment, and that she'd offered to get him out of the country. She waited for a reply, but Lou didn't respond right away. Derek returned and now it was his turn to get antsy. He started agitating for her to end the session since their time had almost run out. Leine ignored him.

"He'll reply," she said, hoping she was right. Every time she cut off communication with her handlers in her former profession, it was like severing an umbilical cord. Once she broke contact she was literally on her own, and if she fucked up, anyone associated with her or her mission would disavow all knowledge.

Granted, this time wasn't quite the same, but it was still like being cut loose.

Another glance at the clock told her they had less than a minute remaining. The clerk was giving them a dirty look. Derek crossed his arms and tapped his foot. Leine moved the cursor to close out of the chat room when a message from Lou popped up on the screen. She allowed herself a sigh of relief and read it.

"He says a passport can be expedited. It'll be ready tomorrow afternoon."

Derek whistled. "He's got some kind of connections. That usually takes days."

"Former life," she said, by way of explanation. Lou also gave her the go-ahead to track the container and pay Derek. He added that he'd contact Kylie's parents with an update.

She wrote down the address where she was to pick up the passport and logged out of the program. "Where do you suggest we spend the night?" she asked, standing. "Your place won't be safe, and neither of us has any money."

"I know just the spot," Derek said.

17

L EINE FOLLOWED DEREK up three flights of stairs in the well-lit block building, then down a long hallway to the third door on the right. Although it was obvious that he'd been there before, perhaps many times, there was no number or letter signifying that it was a separate residence.

Derek rapped on the door two times, followed by three short knocks. Leine stepped back in an attempt to get downwind of him, but then sniffed her own underarms.

And gagged.

Jesus. No wonder the people at the cyber café had gotten up to leave.

The door opened and a stylish, statuesque woman who would have looked at home on the cover of *Jet* or *Vogue* appeared, expectation bright in her dark eyes, a delighted smile on her full lips. The smile dissolved when she caught sight of Leine. With a frown, she pushed the door open with her foot and stood aside, arms crossed. Ignoring her scowl, Derek walked into the apartment and leaned in for a peck on the cheek. She sniffed and waved at the air. Wary of the woman's displeasure, Leine followed him in.

The clean, sparsely furnished apartment had been decorated in bright colors: a cheery yellow print covered a futon resting against one wall. A brilliant red and black tablecloth covered a wooden dining table with matching chairs next to the small kitchen area. Similarly bright fabric had been used as wall hangings. All in all a cheerful place—and in direct contrast to the woman's current mood.

"Who is this?" the woman asked Derek in Swahili, nodding at Leine. Hostility radiated off of her, her expression practically shredding Leine where she stood.

Leine made a mental note to sleep with the knife from the lifeboat if they stayed.

Derek turned, smiling, and held out his arm in an expansive gesture. "A friend I met on my trip over from Bangkok." He stepped closer to whisper in the woman's ear. Whatever he said, it did little to break the tension. "Claire, I'd like you to meet Nia. Nia and I go way back. She's very special to me."

Somewhat placated, Nia let her arms fall to her sides and lifted her chin in a defiant gesture.

"It's good to meet you, Nia. Derek's told me so much about you," Leine said.

Derek ignored the sarcastic remark but Nia brightened somewhat, apparently thinking Derek had been talking about her. Although she didn't smile, judging by her posture she'd relaxed a bit.

"Welcome," she said, stepping closer to Derek. Though he was easily six feet, Nia was taller than Derek by several inches. "How long will you stay this time?" she asked him.

He cupped her chin in his hand and gave her a longing look. "Only one night, my love."

Leine had to stop herself from rolling her eyes. Nia's expression softened, and she took him by the hand, leading him across the small apartment toward a door that apparently led to the bedroom.

"First, you need a bath. Then, we can greet each other properly."

Derek hung back. "Nia, I'm afraid I won't have nearly enough energy unless I get something to eat. I'm happy to go out, if you'd like."

Nia sighed dramatically and dropped his hand, obviously annoyed. "There is a tin of fish and some biscuits in the cupboard. You'll find olives in the icebox."

Derek gave her a grateful smile and walked over to investigate the contents of the cupboards. In a matter of minutes, he'd created a passable meal for the three of them, and they sat down at the table. Nia ignored the fish and had only one biscuit, but brought out two bottles of lager, one of which she split into two glasses to share with Leine. The other she gave to Derek.

As they were eating, Nia's gaze trailed down Derek's torso to the rust-colored bloodstain saturating the left rear section of his pants. She glanced at Derek, concern etching her face.

"Have you been injured?" she asked.

Derek shrugged. "A bit of minor surgery. Nothing to worry about. I might have you take a look at it, though. See if you can do a better job with a bandage."

Nia leaned back in her chair. "How did the two of you meet?" she asked, nibbling her cookie and sizing up Leine.

"We were on the same ship and ran into a slight problem," Derek said.

"You have been quite generous under the circumstances, Nia," Leine added. "Thank you for your hospitality. I will leave if my presence in your home makes you uncomfortable."

Nia studied her for a moment before she got up and walked to the sink with the dishes. She came back and stood behind

Derek, placing her hands on his shoulders and leveling her gaze at Leine.

In a voice reminiscent of a queen, she said, "Your friend may sleep on the futon."

Derek smiled and nodded, patting her hand. "Thank you, Nia."

THE NEXT MORNING, LEINE WAS AWAKE AND READY TO GO BY THE time Derek made it out of the bedroom. She'd woken repeatedly during the night due to the rantings of an upstairs neighbor, an apparent insomniac who enjoyed yelling at himself. In contrast, Derek sported a relaxed yet irritating "just had mind-blowing sex" smile. Along with the tousled bed-head, he appeared supremely happy, giving Leine a sharp pang of Santa-longing.

Shrugging it off, she glanced at his bush pants, expecting to see the bloodstain. It wasn't there.

"Change of clothes?" Leine asked, wishing she had something, as well. The quick shower she took earlier didn't help much, since she still had to wear the same clothes. She was damned sick of smelling herself.

Derek nodded. "I'd ask Nia if you could borrow something, but I think that might be pushing it."

"No problem. After the bank there should be time to pick up a change of clothes before we get my passport and head out of town."

"Sure, sure."

Derek avoided her eyes and appeared distracted. Leine wondered if he'd changed his mind about helping her find the camp.

"So what's the plan?" she asked.

"While you're picking up the money, I'll check with a couple of contacts, get an idea where Wang's camp might be."

"What if Wang's gotten to your contacts and they know there's a price on your head?"

"Yeh, that's the only problem. I'm not sure who I can trust at the moment. Only money speaks here."

"That's true everywhere," Leine said. "May I suggest setting up a meeting with whoever you think you can trust, and wait for me to join you? There's safety in numbers, and I can act as point."

Derek studied Leine for a moment before he nodded. "That's a sound plan. There's one more thing. We're going to need tools."

"You're talking about guns and gear, I take it?"

"Yeh. Even if we do find the camp, we won't be able to accomplish much without some kind of serious persuasion."

"And that means going to your place."

Derek nodded. "I guarantee Wang will have someone there watching. He doesn't take kindly to looking the fool."

"I've had some experience in surveillance and can help you check things out before we go in." Leine walked to the tiny kitchen sink and filled a glass with water. "We'd be better off waiting until dark, although it wastes precious time. Could we purchase the tools we need, rather than risk a trip to your home?"

"I'd rather not. Once word gets out that I'm in the market for weapons, they'll be on us like jackals." Derek shook his head. "No, we need to get into my place, grab what we need, and get out. Besides, there's a Range Rover in the carport. Beats taking the bus."

"Good point," Leine conceded. "Do you know how Wang transports his girls once they're off the ship?" she asked.

"Trucks them out in the containers."

"How long do you think it will take for them to offload?"

"The ship has to clear customs, but Wang's got connections so it doesn't normally take long. I wouldn't be surprised if they were on the road in the next twenty-four hours. That's if the ship's here. The way Kibwe was talking, they'll be in port by now. Probably last night."

Nia emerged from the bedroom wearing a short silk robe and rubbing the sleep from her eyes. "Tea?" she asked.

"None for me, thanks." Derek grew silent for a moment, thinking. "Would you be willing to do me a favor, Nia? It won't take long. You can complete it before you go to work."

"That depends. What is it?"

"I need you to check on a container shipment for me."

Nia considered Derek for a long, slow moment. Then she turned to Leine. "You are unable to do this because Wang is looking for you, too?"

"Yes." Surprised Derek had told her that much, Leine didn't go into detail. The less she knew the better.

"I can pay you." Derek kept his eyes trained on Nia. That was probably a good thing, since Leine was watching him with a bemused expression. She knew the type. As long as it was someone else's money, he was more than willing to pay.

Whatever gets me closer to finding Wang's camp.

Nia glanced at the clock hanging on the wall over the futon. Six thirty. "I can give you two hours," she said.

"Great. Here's what I need you to do."

18

An hour and a half later, Nia reported that Wang's containers had indeed been offloaded from the ship and most had been dispatched by truck. When she asked the security guard if the container with a large white X on the side was one of them, he'd become cagey and told her he wasn't aware of any with that specific marking.

After a late breakfast paid for with cash from Nia, they set out through an older section of Dar toward the address Lou had given Leine for the passport. The city was an eclectic mix of African, Arabian, Indian, and German architecture, with shiny new high rises dominating the Central District.

"I used to live down here," Derek said, "but the fucking rents skyrocketed with all the growth. Most of the residential apartments are gone, taken over by businesses. Now you'd be lucky to find something under three thousand a month. It's like losing the soul of the city."

Several blocks later, they turned up a quiet side street into a residential neighborhood. An advertisement for a soft drink adorned the top of an open-air market, with cardboard boxes stacked several high in front, creating a backdrop for a half dozen five-gallon bottles of water. Most of the older buildings surrounding it had fallen into disrepair.

Derek double checked the address and stopped three doors down from the market.

"This is it," he said, and stepped through the darkened doorway. Leine glanced up and down both sides of the street and, satisfied they hadn't been shadowed, followed him in.

The burning incense didn't even remotely mask the bizarre odors wafting about the small space. Unable to identify even one scent, Leine took shallow breaths. Where had Lou sent her? As her eyes adjusted to the dim light, she had even more reason to wonder.

Glass shelves and cases lined the walls of the shop, most containing vials and plastic bags with mysterious substances. Resting beside several white boxes containing dark, shriveled, unidentifiable objects were hand written cards identifying each item. One read *Genitals, lion.* A vial next to it read *Blood of baboon, male.*

Leine glanced at Derek and raised an eyebrow. He checked out a few more of the shelves' contents and leaned in close.

"Witchdoctor," he said in a low voice.

At that moment, a tall, imposing man pushed aside a heavy curtain at the back of the store and entered the room. "May I help you?

The dark print dashiki and several gold necklaces set off the man's luminous eyes. There was something unusual about him, but in the dim light Leine was unable to put her finger on exactly what it was.

"I'm here to pick up a passport for Claire Sanborn," Leine said.

The man nodded. "Yes. It is almost ready. One moment." His clipped British accent didn't match his appearance and surroundings. "Please, make yourselves comfortable." He disappeared into the back of the shop, leaving them alone.

Derek continued to peruse the shelves while Leine crossed her arms and leaned against a glass case.

"I take it this is legal?" she said.

"He's considered a healer by most." Derek shrugged. "I doubt the police would waste their time harassing him unless someone complained. Your friend Lou certainly knows interesting people." He pointed to a set of bones behind a glass case. "Leopard. The claws and teeth are supposed to give the wearer the strength and hunting ability of their original owner."

"And baboon blood?"

"They're fierce as hell. Bravery and agility, most likely."

Leine shook her head. "So you're trying to tell me LA Fitness wouldn't go over too well here?"

Derek snorted. "Yeh. Africans are an interesting mix of modern beliefs and old superstitions, you know? It's in their blood to believe in the spirit world and magic. With a continent this massive wide swaths of the country survive without the Internet. The old beliefs are strong, especially in rural communities. In some places they still banish people thought to be witches. All it takes is some fetish priest with a bone to pick, if you'll excuse the pun, and the person is branded a witch and sent to live among outcasts. At least most of the general population has abandoned the idea of killing them."

"What is it about him? There's something I can't quite put my finger on," Leine said, nodding toward the curtain where the man had disappeared. They were standing in front of the delicate skull of some luckless animal, killed because someone thought its spirit remained attached to its body at death.

"Did you catch the amount of makeup the guy was wearing?" Derek shook his head. "He makes a transvestite look like a kid playing dress up."

"That must be it. I wasn't close enough to see."

"Could be an albino." Derek shrugged.

"Why would he feel the need for makeup?"

"Because there's a good chance he'd be killed."

"What?"

"Some believe the body parts of an albino are strong medicine and will bring good luck and prosperity," Derek explained. "Traditional healers have been known to use the arms, legs, genitals, whatever they can whack off with a machete. Lately, though, it's children who are being targeted." He crossed his arms. "Children have always been targeted, albino or not. Either they're sold to the highest bidder, or they're abducted and hacked to death. It's believed the body parts of the innocent will bring power and position. Especially during an election cycle."

"And that sex with a virgin will cure AIDs."

Derek nodded. "Yeh. And yet there are beautiful homes and fine restaurants here, and some of the better medical services on the continent. Like I said, Africa's an interesting blend."

A moment later the shopkeeper reappeared through the curtain. In his hand was a British passport. He gave it to Leine, and she flipped through the pages. Her picture had been secured and stamped, and there were entries to several other countries in the pages that followed. All in all, a superb forgery. Leine closed the passport and slid it into her back pocket.

"Thank you. I trust Lou took care of this?" she asked.

The man nodded. "Yes. There is nothing more you need do, unless you've found something you'd like from my cases?"

Leine shook her head. "Not really my cup of tea."

He shrugged and glanced at Derek. The air in the room stilled and the man's eyes gleamed in the dim light before they rolled back in his head. Leine tensed, eyeing the exit, and took several steps back.

"You have been the hunter," the man said, his voice a monot-one, "but are now the hunted."

Startled, Derek said, "Wait a minute, now—"

"Death is no stranger to you," he continued, his voice growing louder. "You have wielded the power only gods are allowed, and the spirits cry out for justice." His chest heaved, his breath coming in short bursts. Leine's fingers closed around the knife in her pocket.

"Death will continue to stalk you." His voice dropped to a murmur and he gripped the edge of the counter. "The spirits demand atonement. If you do not do as they wish, Death will claim its payment and you will cry for mercy."

The witchdoctor closed his eyes and drew in a prolonged breath, letting it go with a loud *ahhh*. Then he opened his eyes and stared at Derek. Leine half expected him to hold out his hand and demand payment, but he remained still. Derek stayed rooted to the spot as the two men stared at each other. Derek broke the spell first by shaking his head as he backed away.

"Time to go, Claire." He turned and strode toward the door. A muffled expletive escaped him as he clipped the corner of one of the glass cabinets on his way out.

"Thanks for the passport," Leine said before she stepped through the door and onto the sidewalk, blinking against the blinding sunshine. She found Derek doubled over next to the building taking deep breaths, his hands on his knees.

Leine leaned against the stucco wall next to him.

"You all right?" she asked.

Derek straightened and plastered a weak smile on his face, obviously trying to cover his reaction.

"Never better," he replied.

Perspiration ran down the side of his face and his upper lip glistened. She didn't think it was from the heat. A woman walked past them wearing a brilliantly colored *kitenge,* using one hand to balance an immense basket on her head. The ability had always amazed Leine.

"You're taking what he said seriously." It was more a statement than a question.

"Nah," he said, shaking his head.

Leine gave him a sharp look. He avoided her gaze. Leine crossed her arms.

"Okay," Derek admitted. "Yes. I take what he said seriously." He stared into the street, not focusing on anything. "I grew up here, remember. The things I've seen." He nodded behind them, apparently indicating the rest of Africa. "Strange goings on. You wouldn't believe me if I told you."

"Probably not." Leine stepped away from the wall. "Either way, we should go. It's getting late, and I have to get to the bank."

He squared his shoulders and wiped the perspiration from his forehead. "I'll give you directions. There's something I need to do in the meantime."

19

L EINE SLID THE money into a grocery bag, thanked the teller, and exited the air conditioned bank. Surrounded by modern office buildings with myriad street-level storefronts, Dar es Salaam's central business district was a bustling enterprise, choked by too many cars carrying too many people traveling in too many directions. Slightly less humid than Bangkok, nevertheless the two cities were twin sons of a different mother: chaos reigned, albeit in a more *laissez faire* style, and the energy of the downtown core was palpable.

Derek waited for her at a coffee shop one block over. From there, they would hire a taxi to Derek's home in the Mikocheni District, about fifteen minutes away. If luck was with them, they'd be able to store whatever weapons and gear they'd need in his Range Rover and leave that evening.

Leine stepped into a narrow alley and quickly pulled a small amount of cash from the stack of bills in her bag, which she placed in her front pocket. Carrying around several thousand dollars in a grocery bag wasn't ideal, but until she purchased a backpack or bag of some kind it would have to do. She retraced her steps and continued down the boulevard, headed north toward the coffee shop.

Half-way down the block, a window advertising clothes and gear caught her eye, and she veered into the small business.

Deciding against anything too colorful in order to blend, Leine picked out a long-sleeved shirt and a pair of khaki bush pants with side pockets, several pair of underwear, socks, and a hat with a brim. The clerk showed her to a fitting room where she changed into the new clothing and distributed the money between pockets. Her filthy clothes went into the now empty grocery bag.

Leine chose a multi-tool with a five-inch, spring-assisted knife; a compass; and a small container of waterproof matches. Redundancy never hurt on an operation. Especially if Derek didn't stick around. She paid for her purchases and left.

Back on the street, Leine tossed the bag of filthy clothing into a nearby trash can and continued down the boulevard and around the corner, headed for the coffee shop. She made one more stop at another store, this one with dozens of handbags and backpacks hanging on a rack outside on the sidewalk. Leine chose a leather messenger bag, and continued on to her meeting with Derek.

She spotted him as she neared the tables situated on the sidewalk outside the café. He was talking animatedly to a barrel-chested man with a swarthy complexion standing next to his table. The man smiled, although it looked as though Derek wasn't happy to see him. Leine slowed her pace and scanned the area. Two tables near Derek were occupied; one by a young couple with a small child, the other by an older man intent on a thick book spread out before him. Neither appeared to pose an immediate threat. The man near Derek, however, crossed his arms over his chest and shook his head, no longer smiling.

Noticing Leine approach, Derek turned toward the man and

said something with a head nod in her direction. The other man looked her way and narrowed his eyes. He uncrossed his arms and said something to Derek. Derek stood up, dug in his front pocket, pulled out a wad of something and shoved it at him. The man accepted whatever Derek had offered him, glancing at it before throwing it onto the table. Leine was close enough to hear the anger in the man's voice, although she didn't catch his words. He shouted something else and then stalked off.

Leine joined the poacher at the table, keeping an eye on the man who'd just left.

"Who's your friend?"

Derek grimaced and took a drink from the glass in front of him, setting it down hard enough that beer sloshed over the rim.

"He was no friend." He cleared his throat. "He was, as are most of my contacts in this godforsaken shit-hole of a city, acutely interested in what I can pay him for his continued silence." He shaded his eyes with his hand and squinted at her. "Looks like Wang's already gotten the word out. If things continue as they are, I'll run out of money soon. I've already given out a half dozen IOUs." He picked up the cash the other man had thrown onto the table and tucked it into his pocket. "It won't matter, anyway. Someone will tell Wang or his thugs I'm in town. Most of my acquaintances aren't what you'd call the honorable type."

"Then we'd better get moving." Orange-tinted cumulonimbus clouds had begun to build ominously to the north, indicating an approaching storm.

"Yeh. We'd better. Looks like the weather's changing." Derek slid his chair back and stood. "Have any trouble with the money?"

"No. There should be enough for whatever we need. The faster we move, the sooner we'll find Wang's camp. I don't want the trail growing cold."

"You know, that diamond was a big chunk of my retirement," he said, eyeing the messenger bag. "If it wasn't for my generosity, you'd still be on that ship, headed for an uncertain end."

Leine considered him for a moment. "Duly noted. Help me find the camp and we'll discuss compensation."

"How do I know I can trust you?"

She shrugged. "You don't."

Twenty minutes later the taxi pulled to the side of the road two blocks from Derek's house. Derek paid the driver, and the car sped off in search of another fare. A light rain had begun to fall, tamping down the dirt road. The atmosphere was redolent with ozone and damp earth and electricity, portending a steady build to the approaching storm.

"We should go in through the back—the alley behind the house leads to a gate that opens onto the courtyard where the Rover's parked. There aren't many places to hide, so we should be able to see if anyone's waiting there. My guess is that Wang's stationed someone at the front of the house and another covering the back. If we can take out the guy in back, then we should be able to get what we need without alerting the one watching the front."

They crept along the dirt-track alley behind stately white- and tangerine-painted stucco homes, most of them cordoned off behind high block walls. A wicked breeze kicked up out of nowhere and slashed at the palm trees, the shadows cast from the sodium yard lights dancing a macabre tango. A few houses down, a dog whined.

Leine wiped a damp strand of hair from her face and tucked it behind her ear. She squinted at the dark shapes near the walls they passed, alert for unwanted guests. Fat drops splatted against her like a wet dog shaking its coat after a swim. Though solid in her hand, the extended blade of the multi-tool didn't give her the same confidence as a side arm.

About halfway down the alley, Derek stopped near a solid metal gate with a large padlock guarding a stucco wall.

"This is it."

The backyard light was burned out, which worked in their favor. The neighbor's light from across the alley didn't reach Derek's gate, leaving them in shadow.

He bent down, turned over a flat rock near the base of the wall, and retrieved a key. "Doesn't look like it's been tampered with," he muttered, inspecting the lock.

Leine kept watch as he opened the padlock with a crisp *snick*. He quietly removed it and hung it on the hasp before easing the gate open just wide enough for them to squeeze through. With one last scan of the alley, Leine followed him into the courtyard.

They paused by the wall, taking in their surroundings. The curved brick driveway was bathed in darkness, except for a small area where a next-door neighbor's dim light encroached. A windshield glinted in the carport, the rest of the Rover a large black mass.

The storm intensified, pelting them with cold rain. The runoff flowed past them in a muddy river, searching for escape through the holes at the foot of the wall. Leine followed Derek across the driveway, narrowing her eyes against the wind as it whipped past, kicking sand and gravel up into her face. They took shelter in the alcove near the back door.

Derek leaned in close so he didn't have to shout over the sound of the driving wind. "Looks like we're clear."

An instant later, a round slammed into the wall beside Derek, sending pieces of stucco flying. Leine dropped to the ground and rolled to the other side of the alcove, coming to her feet in a crouch, her back flat against the wall. Derek dove beside her.

"Where the hell did that come from?"

"Shh." Leine held her finger to her lips. "Can you make it through the door?"

Derek took a deep breath and glanced at the entry. "I think so."

"Go."

In a crouch, he shadowed the wall to the door and eased his hand over the doorknob. Two more shots went wide, tearing into the side of the home. Sections of stucco and concrete exploded into the entryway. Derek turned the handle and swung the door open. Leine waited until he cleared the entrance, and then sprinted inside and slammed the door shut behind them, locking it against the muted pop of gunfire. The staccato thump of bullets peppered the wood outside, but the door held. Glass shattered as the gunman scored a direct hit on the outside light.

Leine stood in a short hallway that opened onto a large living room. Immediately to her right was the kitchen; the LED clock on the microwave glowed green. A staircase leading to the second floor stood several feet forward and to the left. A faint glow from a streetlamp outside massive clerestory windows at the front of the house spilled across the living room, partially illuminating the interior. The oversized front door appeared solid, similar to the back entrance.

Should give us a short window of time, Leine thought.

"Fuck me," Derek muttered, and moved past the kitchen. Leine followed him, keeping distance between them in case someone was inside the house.

"Think he has a radio?" Leine asked.

"Probably. If there *is* another guy out front, we're screwed."

"Oh, come on. Don't give up so easily."

Derek snorted. "You're right. I'm not used to being the prey, you check?"

"Yeah, I check," Leine replied. "Where's the equipment?"

"Upstairs," he said, nodding toward the staircase. Three steps led to a landing before the stairs took a sharp left turn and ran the rest of the way to the second floor. The main threat was the floor-to-ceiling windows dominating the living room. They'd be like sitting ducks in a shooting gallery if a gunman was sighting on the front of the house.

"We need to move before they have a chance to get into position," Leine said. She dropped to the floor and field-crawled across the tile toward the stairway. After a moment's hesitation, Derek did the same.

Leine reached the bottom step and sprang up the three stairs onto the landing. Just as Derek reached the bottom, there was a muted *pop-pop-pop* and one of the massive front windows shattered, a thousand glass shards splintering across the floor.

"Go, go, GO," Derek yelled and Leine sprinted up the stairs with Derek close behind her.

They reached the landing on the second floor and Derek took the lead, racing down the long corridor, past a bathroom and several bedrooms to the end of the hall. He reached above the frame for the key, unlocked the door, and kicked it open.

Inside the room were gun cases, gun safes, and boxes of differing sizes. Plywood covered the window at the far end. Sightless eyes stared down at Leine from above; mounted heads of long-dead predators and prey decorated the walls. She took a step backward and bumped into what she thought was a piece of furniture. She turned and caught her breath, startled by a fully stuffed, life-size lioness standing behind her, glassy eyes glinting in the dim light of the closet. Body poised at the moment of attack, its fierce expression was frozen in a perpetual snarl, claws extended as though ready to strike.

Leine shook it off and approached Derek, who was in the process of flinging open boxes and safes. He tossed her an MP5, along with two full magazines. She slid one mag into the gun and pocketed the other. Derek did the same.

"Since when does a poacher need a submachine gun?" Leine asked, slipping on a shoulder holster. "Not that I'm complaining."

"Since poaching became so lucrative." Derek handed her several boxes of ammunition, a 9mm semiautomatic pistol, and a canvas bag to which he added two torches, two knives with wicked-looking ten-inch blades, and more matches. "I've seen them use AK-47s, grease guns, grenades, whatever gets the job done."

"Good to know."

The rapid *pop-pop-pop* of a machine gun erupted outside the front of the house.

"Shit. There goes my good neighbor award."

"Got a plan?" Leine asked.

"No plan, but thanks for asking." Derek threw an aerosol can into the bag. "Bug juice," he explained.

"I'll need the gun," Leine said, nodding at the M21 sniper rifle next to him.

Derek handed it to her. "You know how to work one of these?"

Leine nodded. The rifle was surprisingly light. "It's been a while. Anything I should know about it?"

"Only that it's accurate as hell."

"How many ways out of here?"

"Just the front and back doors," Derek replied. "I guarantee the guy in back's covering the Rover."

"What about roof access?"

"Down the hall to your left. The master bedroom has a balcony that overlooks the neighbors. A big acacia obscures the view from the street. You're going to have partial exposure from the back, though. Depends on where he's set up."

"Any lights?"

"None that I can think of."

"Good. I'll climb onto the roof, see if I can take out the shooter in front, then come at the guy in back."

"It's gonna be slick." The wind outside howled as if to punctuate his words.

"Tile?"

"Composite. Only looks like tile, but bad enough."

"I'll just have to contend with the wind and driving rain, right?" Leine scanned the closet. She spotted a dark-blue windbreaker and reached for it. She turned to Derek. "You mind if I take this?"

He shook his head. "Be my guest. The bottom half's behind it." He picked up the canvas bag and slung a second rifle and both MP5s over his shoulder. "I'll run a torch near the windows in a couple of the rooms at the other end to get the shooter's attention. Should give you enough time to set up."

"Good. Give me a few minutes before you start to work your way to the Rover. I'll need you to draw the guy out. He'll give away his position when he shoots. Should be easy to spot with the scope."

"Yeh. Easy." Derek shook his head. "Like I said, I'm not comfortable being prey."

"Consider it a training exercise."

Leine shrugged into the windbreaker and pants, slung the rifle over her shoulder, and moved to the master bedroom. She slipped the hood over her head and opened the glass door, ignoring the wind and driving rain.

20

N O FIRE CAME at her from either direction. Leine assumed the shooter wasn't covering her side of the house. The acacia tree was as large as Derek had said and obscured the view from the front. The rear of the house hid the balcony from most of the backyard. She slung the M21 over her shoulder and climbed onto the railing, then turned and faced the house, leaning her head back to gauge the distance to the edge of the roof.

A burst of gunfire erupted near the front, followed by the sound of Derek returning fire from an upstairs window. She flexed her legs and jumped, hooking both hands onto the edge of the eaves, her lower body dangling in space. Derek had been right about how slick it would be. She lost her grip with her right hand and for one heart-stopping moment thought she was going to fall.

Leine managed to grasp the edge of the roof with her finger-tips, securing her position. She kicked until she was able to hook her heel over the eaves and then pulled herself up and over. Lightning pulsed overhead, followed a few seconds later by the deep rumble of thunder.

Pausing to take a breath, Leine worked to slow her galloping heart. Sporadic gunfire continued in the front, blending with the thunder. She lifted her head and scanned the area. The roof had three sections. The left and right sides jutted out like wings, giving her good cover from a majority of the backyard, although she would be exposed, briefly, when she moved into position.

With a deep inhale, she low-crawled to the apex of the roof, expecting to feel the hot bite of a bullet with each meter gained, or, alternatively, the hair-raising buzz and crack of a lightning strike. The storm hadn't yet washed away the dirt and dust on Derek's roof. The resulting slurry made progress even more challenging.

She reached the top and removed the rifle, then released the bipod, setting it up so only the tip of the barrel cleared the roofline. She lay on her stomach, flipped up the front and rear dust covers on the scope and sighted on the house across the street. Her body relaxed into the most efficient position naturally, as though it hadn't been years since she'd done this. Muscle memory was a powerful thing, especially after spending hours upon hours learning a specific weapon.

Part of her missed the familiarity. This was something she was good at.

Leine scanned the area across the street through the night scope, pausing at the positions she might have chosen, but didn't notice anything out of the ordinary. She wondered where the police were, or if anyone had called them. The neighbors had probably confused the crack of gunfire with the sound of the storm.

She kept coming back to a dark area near the house across the street. All she could make out at first were two garbage bins. She scanned the bushes next to them.

A shadow near one of the bins moved. A man in a dark shirt

and pants broke away from the house and headed across the street in a crouch, a machine gun in both hands.

Leine inhaled and seated her cheek securely against the pad on the butt stock of the gun. Sighting just above his shoulders, she released her breath and squeezed the trigger. The man's head snapped back, and he dropped where he stood.

One down, one to go.

Leine closed the dust covers on the scope and rolled onto her back, taking the rifle with her. She pitched forward and headed for the section of roof over the entryway at the back of the house. The rain was falling harder now and obscuring her view. Traversing the muddy, synthetic tiles in heavy wind was an exercise in balance and calculation. Purported to be all-terrain, she doubted the manufacturers of her footwear had this particular scenario in mind when they wrote the advertising copy. She stopped to assess her position but at that moment a strong gust of wind pushed through and she lost her footing, landing with a thud on the rifle stock.

She picked herself up and slung the weapon back into place, wondering how badly the fall had screwed with the rifle's accuracy but unable to stop to find out. In minutes, Derek would be a target.

If he wasn't already.

Leine dropped to her belly and crawled to the tip of the roof closest to the back entrance. She set up, wiped the rain off the scope and peered through the downpour, searching for the second gunman.

Nothing.

This time she didn't have a feeling one way or another. There were only a couple of positions she would have taken if she were the shooter, and there wasn't anyone visible in either.

Had he gone into the house? Was Derek inside, right now, fighting the second shooter? She listened for gunfire below her but heard nothing. Leine continued to scan the area, searching for some kind of tell.

There.

She tracked back across the alley to the roof of the neighbor's garage, where she noticed a pile of palm fronds fluttering in the wind. Several palm trees surrounded the home, so the debris wasn't unusual. Leine stared through the scope as the rain beat a monotonous chorus on her windbreaker. The wind howled through, whipping at the trees. Shadows danced across the roof, messing with her view.

She had just wiped the rain off her face and was about to clear the scope again when she caught movement in the pile of vegetation. She tightened her focus and zoomed in. Nestled in the chaotic pattern of fronds was a perfect circle, similar in size to the circumference of a rifle barrel.

Leine's finger hovered near the trigger, waiting for the gunman to move, wishing she and Derek had taken the time to grab radios.

She assumed the shooter wasn't paying attention to the roofline, or that little circle would have been pointed at her instead of trained on the back door.

All she had to do was wait, and hope neither of the two gunmen had called in reinforcements.

A few minutes later, the fronds moved again.

Derek must be in view.

Leine released her breath and waited, finger slowly taking up slack on the trigger until it was tight.

The palm fronds levitated, like something was pushing them up from underneath. Leine sighted in and watched the mass of leaves transform into a man's face, partially obscured behind a scope.

She fired. The rifle was off and the bullet clipped a tile next to him. The man dropped to the roof.

Cursing under her breath, Leine corrected her aim and fired. At the same instant a flash erupted from the other man's rifle. A tile exploded in front of her, hurling bits of composite into her face.

Heart racing, Leine sighted again, but a bright light erupted from the back of the house near the shooter. A man's silhouette appeared in the doorway.

"What's going on out there?" the man shouted.

The shooter swiveled toward the man, leaving himself open for an instant. Leine took the shot. The gunman slumped forward onto the roof.

"*Shit.* Margery—*get back inside.* Someone's fucking shooting out here," the man yelled and slammed the door closed.

Leine sighed with relief. She waited a beat, expecting return fire, making sure the shooter didn't move.

Nothing.

"Derek?" She called out, the wind and rain stealing her words. "Derek?" she called again, this time louder.

No answer. Was he hurt?

Leine closed the dust covers and inched backward, taking the rifle with her as she made her way to the balcony side of the house. She collapsed the bipod and slung the M21 over her shoulder before climbing down to the master bedroom. Then she sprinted along the hallway to the stairs and descended, taking two at a time, headed for the back door.

Easing the bullet-riddled door open, she followed the wall until she could make out Derek's dark form crouching near the Rover.

He was all right. Leine relaxed her grip on the gun and made her way over to him.

"Any movement?" she asked.

"None that I could see." He handed her a pair of night vision binoculars. Leine took them and scanned the roofline of the neighbor's carport and surrounding area. She didn't see anything.

"We'd better get out of here," Derek said. "Jim and Margery aren't going to let this slide. Won't be long until the police are crawling all over the place."

Leine helped him stow the weapons and ammunition in a false compartment under the cargo area and then jogged through the pouring rain to open the gate. Derek drove through, and she closed it behind him, replacing the padlock. She climbed into the passenger seat and they sped away.

21

DEREK DIDN'T TURN on the lights until he was well clear of the alley. He didn't say anything as he drove. The adrenaline began its slow retreat from Leine's system, leaving her drained. Derek appeared to be exhausted, too, so she relaxed back in her seat and watched the storm rage on through the steady beat of the windshield wipers.

They drove past neighborhoods and small community markets, all shuttered against the storm. Not a soul walked the streets. A cardboard box flew out of nowhere, smacking the windshield and whipping up and over the roof.

Soon the terrain shifted to just plain dark, uninterrupted by streetlamps or the glowing windows of houses or storefronts. She assumed they were traveling through the countryside now and wouldn't encounter a large city for several kilometers.

They drove in silence for the better part of two hours. Leine couldn't help dozing off and on. When she woke, she checked the odometer. They'd covered half the normal distance. The Rover's headlights illuminated barely a meter in front of them; sheets of rain obscured anything beyond that. The road was fast becoming a river, but Derek seemed unconcerned.

"Would you like me to take over? You've been at it for quite a while."

"No," came the short reply.

"Do you think we should stop somewhere until the storm blows over?" Leine didn't want to end up buried to their axles in mud, having to dig out after the storm.

Derek didn't answer.

Leine fell silent, wondering if he was having a hard time concentrating. She sensed an undercurrent that hadn't been there before, and tried again.

"Is something wrong?"

Dodging a tree branch, Derek turned onto a road riddled with potholes. He shook his head. "I was thinking that it's a damned shame I'll never be welcome in that neighborhood again. I sure as hell can't go back. Not anytime soon."

"Do you think Wang's going to continue to watch your place?" she asked.

Derek shrugged. "Don't know. Maybe. That isn't what I'm worried about. My neighbors prefer peace and quiet. Cocktails at seven and dinner parties on Friday." He hit the steering wheel. "Damn. I worked hard to make myself into an upstanding member of society. Now I'm fucked."

"I'm going to ignore the obvious irony here, and just suggest that you live somewhere else where no one knows you. Like I said, I can make sure you're able to go anywhere you want, within reason." Leine leaned her head back. "Besides, that kind of lifestyle sounds awfully boring if you ask me. Especially in light of what you've done for a living."

"You don't get it." He glanced at Leine. "I can't leave. Africa's in my blood. It's my home. What else am I supposed to do?"

"How about import-export? Remember your invitation to go into business together?"

Derek gave her a lopsided smile. "Yeh, I didn't really expect you to go for it. It was just an idea to pass the time."

Leine raised an eyebrow. "You mean you weren't serious about Derek and Claire's Fabric Emporium? I'm devastated."

"*Ja, ja*. Devastated," he said, grinning. "That's a good one." He glanced at her and shrugged, then looked out the windshield. "It's hard to imagine myself anywhere else."

"Africa's a big place. Why not cross into Kenya or Botswana? With your knowledge you'd make a great addition to a safari company."

"Yeh. Maybe...." His voice trailed off. "What if I talk to your boss? He obviously has reach. I don't know many people who can work up a passport as fine as yours in twenty-four hours."

"I wouldn't really call him my boss. We used to work together in another lifetime. He still has the contacts he established back then. Comes in handy with the work we do."

"If I didn't know any better, I'd say you and he were members of a criminal enterprise." Derek said, watching her for a reaction.

Leine smiled. "Some people might feel that way, but technically, no. We were legit." She didn't tell him the jobs the agency and its operatives were involved in often stretched the definition of lawful and reasonable.

Often? Hell, most of the time.

"Hmm. Well now, that sounds mysterious enough to warrant further discussion—"

Derek's words died in his throat as he slammed on the brakes and steered hard to the right. The Rover skidded to a stop.

"Shit."

The headlights cut through the driving rain and dropped off, illuminating a large swath of swift-moving water streaming over the road.

"How deep?" Leine asked, eyeing the mud-filled chasm between them and the rest of the road.

"A meter, maybe more." Derek squinted at the water. "It's the 'maybe more' that worries me. We could be digging out in Kenya in the morning." The joke did little to lighten the mood.

Derek shifted into low gear and inched forward, frowning in concentration. Leine gripped the door handle and craned her neck to look out the side window. The muddy water rose first to mid-wheel and then fanned out over the tire as they moved forward into the washout. She scanned the floorboards for seepage as Derek pushed through the deepest part.

"Are you sure we're going to make it?" Leine asked.

"Of course we'll make it. I modified this beast a while back for such occasions. She's been through a lot worse."

Derek's bravado had a hollow ring, but Leine bit her tongue and held on.

Midway across the impromptu river, the back end of the Rover skidded to the right. Leine caught her breath as the rear wheel slid into a void with a loud *thunk*. Derek ignored it and gunned the gas, forcing the four-wheel-drive forward, and then back, spinning the wheels and trying to rock the vehicle. The water rushed past, splashing Leine's window. On the third try, Derek punched the accelerator. The Rover rocketed out of the hole, climbing out of the water and onto the other side.

Derek drove a safe distance away and parked.

"Haven't failed me yet, have you girl?" Derek said, patting the Rover's dash.

"Good job." Leine looked back at the ruined roadway. "How long do these downpours usually last?"

Derek shrugged. "They're normally just a squall. It'll be blue skies and sunny days tomorrow, I'll wager."

Clearly covered in mud, the headlights projected a weak

beam maybe a foot in front of the grill. Derek reached into the backseat to retrieve a hooded raincoat and shrugged it on.

"Hand me that, would you?" he said, pointing to a dirty T-shirt on the floor by Leine's feet. She gave it to him and he got out, proceeding to the front of the vehicle. Still wearing the slicker he'd lent her earlier, Leine tore off several paper towels from a roll in the backseat and joined him, cleaning the lenses as well as she could. Derek inspected the undercarriage for damage and, finding none, they climbed back into the Rover and continued on.

"You asked me earlier where we'd be stopping," Derek began. "That's up to you. In good weather, the drive to where Wang likes to set up his traveling sideshow takes about nineteen hours from Dar—nine hours to Arusha, and then about ten more after that. Now, we can bust our asses to make it there by tomorrow night, which, by the looks of that wash doesn't seem likely, or, we can drive until we're tired, camp for the night, and resume our trip in the morning. Up to you."

"I'd like to get as far as possible," Leine replied, "but you know the terrain. I defer to your judgement."

Derek's eyebrows shot up. "I didn't expect that answer from you."

"I know when I'm out of my element. It's called being prudent."

Derek let out a chuckle. "Well, I'm not known for being much of *that*."

"I gathered." Leine closed her eyes and sighed, wondering if it was too late to attempt finding Wang's camp on her own.

22

L EINE WOKE WITH the sun the next morning. They'd driven to the town of Arusha, where they stopped to fill up the Rover and the four jerrycans lashed to the back. Derek drove for another couple of hours before pulling over to rest, preferring to take a northerly route to the Akili Game Reserve during daylight. Guttural snores coming from the front seat told her he was still asleep. Grateful he let her have the back where there was more room, Leine yawned and stretched, then quietly opened the door and got out.

Derek had been right—the storm passed over them in the early hours and the day looked promising. A verdant expanse of savannah stretched in all directions with no buildings or towns or remnants of civilization to mar the otherwise peaceful scene before her. Mount Meru jutted skyward back the way they'd come, anchoring the terrain. A smattering of graceful, flat-topped acacias punctuated the green, along with a vast herd of wildebeest munching contentedly in the distance.

Egrets circled the herd, swooping in to rest for just a moment on the backs of the tolerant before launching themselves into the air in graceful arcs. Other birds she didn't know the names of sailed above her head, serenading her as she retrieved Derek's single-burner stove and filled the tea kettle. She searched for and found a tin of breakfast tea and two travel cups, along with some matches, which she used to set the kettle to boil.

She was sitting on the roof of the Rover, dangling her feet over the racks and sipping her tea when Derek scrambled out of the front seat, disoriented, his hair sticking out in all directions. He noticed the makeshift table Leine set up with the tea kettle and stove and staggered toward it, acknowledging her with a grunt. He poured himself a cup of tea and, yawning, scratched his chest, gazing out at the wildebeests.

"It's migration time, you know," he said, his back to her. "Although, not *the* migration. The rain brings them back to the valleys. Predator, prey. The dance of life and all that."

"You sound like an advertisement for *The Lion King*," Leine said with a laugh.

Derek swiveled to look at her and grinned. "Yeh. I guess I do." He turned back to the massive herd of animals slowly moving north. "God, I love this place. It gets in your blood."

"I can see why."

They sat in silence, watching the peaceful scene and enjoying each other's company as they sipped their tea. Derek produced a package of jerky he swore was the best he'd ever had, and offered her some. When she asked him what kind of meat he'd used, Derek's answer was vague.

"Let's just call it bush jerky."

As they cleaned up breakfast, Leine glanced back the way they'd come and noticed a tiny white speck in the distance. She retrieved the binoculars from the Rover and trained them on the speck. An SUV with official-looking emblems was headed their way.

"Derek." Leine nudged him and handed him the binoculars, nodding at the approaching vehicle.

Derek shaded his eyes and squinted through the glass. "Shit." He threw the rest of their things into the Rover and slammed the back shut. "Get in. We're leaving."

"Won't that look suspicious?"

"Probably, but they're too far away to check my plates. Besides, if they catch up with us, they're only going to want money. I'd hate for you to lose more of that stash."

"Less for you, right?" Leine offered. Derek shrugged, smiled.

"You know me well."

They climbed in and Derek hit the gas. The back tires spun, finally caught, and the Rover lurched forward.

Derek drove with one eye on the road in front of them, and one on the rearview mirror, trying to keep a good distance from the other vehicle. Leine trained the binoculars out the back window. There were two people in the front seat.

"They're getting closer," she said.

Derek nodded. "Yeh. I know. I just need to get over this next hill..." He stepped on the accelerator, and the Rover screamed forward, zigzagging wildly as Derek steered clear of potholes and chunks of road washed away by the downpour.

They crested the rise and dropped down, headed toward a dense thicket of brush in the midst of acres of towering grass. The Rover left the road, flushing a flock of doves as they drove across the flat and into the grass, not stopping until they were deep in the thicket, obscured behind a wicked-looking thorn tree. Derek turned off the ignition and got out. Leine slipped on her shoulder holster and followed him through the tall grass to a lookout where they could watch for the approaching car.

He glanced at the gun in her holster as she came up beside him. "I don't think we're going to have to kill them," he said, his voice low.

"This is for the fauna," Leine replied.

Derek's eyebrow twitched upward. "That nine won't do you

much good if you're charged by an elephant. Or a lion, for that matter. You'll learn. We'll make a poacher out of you yet."

"That's not exactly what I was hoping for—" Leine fell silent at the sound of the vehicle coming over the rise. The car slowed as it crested the hill, pausing near where they'd left the road.

"Our tracks will be obvious from last night's rain. Let's hope they decide it's not worth the effort."

The vehicle with the official markings crept along, its front windows down. The passenger leaned out the window, watching the ground.

"What happens if they decide to follow us?"

Derek shook his head. "They aren't going to want to work that hard. Unless—"

"What?"

"It could be they're looking for *my* vehicle, specifically. That little exchange of gunfire we had at the house was major activity for my neighborhood. Violent crime isn't normally a problem in that area. Knowing my neighbors, the police are going to be stirred up hotter than a termite nest and looking for results. I guarantee they'll be after whoever did the two gunmen. My place was obviously the target." He shook his head. "It's not like it'll be hard to guess who's responsible."

"This is a long way from Dar. Would they really come after you here?"

"It's possible that they put out a description of the Rover so they can bring me in for questioning."

The vehicle stopped and Derek fell silent. The passenger opened his door and got out. Tall and thin wearing a white, short-sleeve shirt with epaulets and dark slacks, the man started toward them, following the Rover's tracks. Leine and Derek stayed where they were.

"Turn around, now," Derek whispered to him. "Don't come any closer."

The man took several steps forward, and then stopped. The driver, now outside and leaning against the vehicle, called to him, urging him to continue. The passenger paused for a moment before a strange look washed over his face, and he turned and quickly walked back to the car. When he reached the vehicle, the driver shook his head and climbed back behind the wheel. The passenger got in and slammed the door closed. The car hacked a U-turn and sped back the way they'd come. Derek let out a low whistle.

"Did you see that guy? It's like he sensed something bad would happen if he came any closer."

"I'm relieved he didn't. We don't have time to dick around with the police." Leine wasn't sure she trusted how Derek might react in a stressful situation. Would he have shot the two policemen? How could she know? She'd only just met the man a couple of weeks ago. Not for the first time, Leine wondered if she'd made the right decision to work with the poacher.

Derek waved the insinuation away. "Nah. He wouldn't have walked any farther. See this?" He grabbed a handful of the straw-colored grass. "Lion habitat. It's great cover. He didn't look like he had a gun on him. Probably just thought better of walking through high grass without his side arm."

Leine stiffened at the mention of lions, her hand moving reflexively to the gun in her holster. She quickened her pace and scanned the terrain.

They were three-quarters of the way back to the Rover when Derek stopped and drew his forty-five. Leine slid her gun free, despite what Derek had said about the smaller caliber weapon not being effective against larger predators. At least it was something.

"What?" she whispered, nerves tingling.

Derek remained motionless for a few more seconds, then

relaxed and slid his gun back into his holster. "Nothing. I thought I heard something."

"You thought—" Leine glanced at him, catching his smile before he looked away. She rolled her eyes. "Okay. I get it. Freak out the American who's never been on safari." She shook her head and slid her gun back into her waistband. "You want predators? Come to LA and I'll show you predators—the kind that shoot back."

Derek laughed. "Sorry. Couldn't resist."

They headed back to the Rover and Derek stopped again.

What now? Leine stepped past him to see what had brought him up short this time and froze. On top of the Rover lounged an impressive looking lioness, her huge front paws draped over the roof, tongue lolling to the side. Sharp, intelligent eyes studied Leine as if the large feline were contemplating a morning snack. Her breath caught at the sight of the impressive animal, and she reached for her weapon. The small movement caught the interest of the lioness. Her tongue disappeared as she tracked Leine's hand.

"Don't. Move." Derek muttered under his breath. Leine checked at his words, her fingers inches from her gun.

The big cat kept its gaze riveted on Leine and rose to all fours. Powerful muscles contracted and shivered beneath her pelt as her tail twitched. A low growl emanated from deep within her chest.

"*Shit,*" Derek said, his voice tight. Leine attempted to swallow, but her throat had gone dry.

Was this it? Her last hurrah? Former assassin, Leine Basso, mauled by a lion while traveling through Tanzania, carrying a phony passport, in the company of a notorious poacher.

Not the kind of death she would have chosen.

Something crashed through the brush toward them and the lioness turned her head. Leine and Derek drew their guns as an enormous male lion, brown mane flowing like a living head-dress, barreled through the grass toward them with a tremendous roar. Before either one could fire a round, a rifle blast thundered through the trees, flushing a flock of birds from the understory. The male skidded to a halt, flipped around, and loped away. The female leaped off the Rover and disappeared into the high grass behind him.

Derek's mouth gaped open in surprise.

"Where did that come from?" he asked, searching the area for the source of the blast.

"I don't—"

"That was close." A man with a rifle stepped from the grass behind the Rover.

The man was clean-shaven and appeared to be in his mid-forties. Easily six feet tall, maybe more, and close to two hundred pounds, his dark brown eyes looked as though they missed nothing. He wore a park ranger's uniform.

"There is plenty to eat out here. I'm not sure why they picked on you," he said, his gaze tracking the lion's exit. He turned to them and cocked his head when he noticed Leine's gun. "A nine millimeter won't do you much good out here." He squinted at Derek, studying him. "Do I know you?"

"Doubt it," Derek replied. He stuck out his hand. "I'm Derek. And thank you. I don't usually go into the bush without my hunting rifle."

"Naasir." Naasir shook Derek's hand and studied him for a moment longer before directing his attention to Leine. She stepped forward and offered her hand.

"Claire. And that was my first encounter with a lion."

"Welcome to Africa, right?" He shook her hand and laughed. It was a big, booming laugh that flushed the last of the doves from the trees surrounding them.

"Thanks," Leine said, glad the standoff was over.

"What are you two doing out here?"

"Claire hasn't ever been on safari, so I thought we'd head into the reserve, show her some of the wildlife."

He nodded behind them. "Ngorongoro Crater is that way."

"I wanted her to experience the wilderness."

Naasir slung his rifle over his shoulder. "She will see that. Although, I'd suggest visiting the crater. It's an amazing place, and the roads are better." He eyed the gun in Leine's holster. "You know how to fire your weapon?"

"I'm licensed to carry in the States, why?"

"Just like to know whether you two will need my services again. Wouldn't want you to end up as a meal for a hungry predator," he replied with a smile that didn't quite reach his eyes. Naasir paused for a moment, obviously sizing them up, and then smiled, breaking the tension. "Well, have fun, but be careful. You never know what could jump out at you."

With that, Naasir disappeared in the same direction as the lions.

"I wonder where he came from?" Derek frowned as he opened the door of the Rover. "He wasn't what I'd call a typical park ranger. Besides, I know quite a few of them. There aren't many that work out this far."

"Good thing he was close by," Leine said. "I think we should do what he suggested and leave."

Derek smiled. "Before those two cats decide they lost out on a good snack, you mean?"

"Exactly."

23

SEVERAL HOURS LATER, Derek pulled off-road and parked in the shade of an acacia tree. Leine helped him haul out a camp table and two chairs, and put water on to boil. When the water was hot enough, he reconstituted a couple of freeze-dried dinners in their pouches. Leine chose the beef stew and stood up to eat, enjoying the reprieve from the Rover.

Leine had been fascinated throughout the drive. They'd passed herds of zebra, impala, and buffalo and had to wait for a family of elephants to cross the road in front of them. Giraffe sightings became almost routine, and they'd spotted a pride of lions. She marveled at the diversity of wildlife, wishing Santa was there to see it all.

After lunch, Derek pulled out a cigar and offered it to Leine. She shook her head. He shrugged and lit the end with a water-proof match.

"We're getting close to the region where Wang likes to set up camp," he said, a cloud of smoke encircling his head.

"I assume we're talking about a large area?"

Derek nodded. "Yeh, it's large, all right. A few thousand kilometers."

"A few thousand," Leine repeated, unsure she'd heard correctly. "Then we'll need a plan. I'd rather not waste time driving without some idea how to find the place." She didn't like winging it, not when there were lives at stake. Improvisation had its place. Just not at the beginning of an operation.

"Don't worry so much. I've got a plan," Derek assured her.

"Were you going to let me in on it, or do I have to guess as we go along?" Her cheeks grew warm, a sure sign her blood pressure was on the rise. *Calm down, Leine. Derek just approaches problems from a different angle than you do.* She inhaled deeply and waited.

"*Ja, ja*. See," he leaned forward and picked a twig off the ground. "Here's Wang's natural habitat." He drew a rough rectangle in the dirt. "And here," he tapped the upper left quadrant, "is where he likes to be. The wildlife is abundant, and the few park rangers who patrol the area are known to accept bribes." Derek leaned back. "So, all we really have to do is find a willing ranger and pay him more than Wang."

"Fine. Say we find the camp. How do we get inside without Wang's knowledge? He knows us both. I assume it's billed as the ultimate experience, right? Where servants are at your beck and call, no request too outrageous? Won't they alert Wang if we're recognized?"

"We won't have to worry. Wang hates the rainy season. He only visits in early fall and occasionally in December. Bangkok's more his style, although he has been known to come out looking for trophies, so in theory, anything's possible. I thought we'd pose as a married couple looking for an 'authentic' experience. The ranger will contact the camp for us. The trick is finding the right ranger. Not all of them are corrupt, although in that area they are more often than not."

"Have any idea who you're going to ask?"

"Don't worry."

"Let me guess. You have a plan for that, too."

Derek smiled. "Why yes, I do. Thank you for asking."

She groaned inwardly. "Can we please just do this?" After so many years of being a free agent, Leine found it difficult to work with someone else. Especially a person like Derek, who was apparently more concerned with fitting into his exclusive neighborhood in Dar than rescuing people who'd been trapped for days inside a shipping container.

Derek sighed and stubbed out his cigar. "I guess we'll be on our way, then."

"I guess."

THEY DROVE FOR TWO MORE HOURS BEFORE DEREK STOPPED outside a village of mud huts and thatched roofs. Men and women wearing brightly colored clothing regarded the Rover with mild interest. A number of goats ambled through the village staying just out of reach of a young boy.

"Maasai," Derek explained. "A friend of mine lives here. He has his ear to the ground and might know where Wang's camp is."

Derek exited the vehicle and walked toward one of the buildings. Leine did the same, and several of the younger children crowded around her, laughing and vying for attention. The older children kept their distance, mimicking their elders.

One of the villagers, a younger man with finely braided, ochre-hued hair and dressed in a brilliant red *shuka,* broke free of the crowd and walked up to Derek. The younger man's expression was anything but happy, and Derek let his arms fall to his sides, his friendly smile replaced by uncertainty. They walked a short distance away from the rest of the village to speak to each other while Leine played with the children, letting them lead her around the village.

After a short conversation, Derek and the young man returned to where Leine was admiring one of the women's elaborate beaded collars. The young man broke off from Derek and pulled a satellite phone from the folds of his *shuka*. Derek joined Leine.

"Your friend doesn't look happy," Leine said.

"*Ja*, well, it's just a little misunderstanding." Derek waved it off. "It seems that one of my investment recommendations didn't go over very well with the elders."

"Does he know where Wang's camp is?"

Derek nodded. "He said he saw it last month, although Wang likes to change things up a bit. I don't think his camp has stayed in one place longer than six weeks. My friend wasn't sure how long the compound had been there when he ran across it."

"Did you tell him why we're looking?"

"Don't worry. He hates Wang. In fact," Derek nodded at the villagers, now going about their business, uninterested in Derek and the *mzungu* woman. "Everyone here hates him. Last year he burned down their village to get access to Maasai land for his camp. My friend is quite happy I no longer work for him."

"And nothing happened to Wang for doing that?"

"Couldn't prove it was him, although everyone here knows it was."

"I'm surprised they haven't retaliated. I always thought the Maasai were renowned as warriors. Or has that changed with the times, too?"

"Oh, believe me, they have done, but Wang's well connected. All retaliation is met with the same or worse. Usually it's worse."

"A tyrant, then?"

"You could say that."

"Then it'll be doubly satisfying when we find his camp and rescue the men and women he kidnapped."

Derek raised his eyebrows. "I think I'm beginning to like you, Claire Sanborn."

They paid their respects to the village chief and Derek left packages of gum and jerky with the children.

"They invited us to stay overnight, but I politely declined. Didn't think you'd want to sleep in a mud hut on cow skins."

"I've done worse," Leine replied.

"Yeh, but have you ever slept on a layer of dried cow shit? They claim it keeps the mosquitoes away."

"I'll bet." Leine shifted in her seat. Another night in the back of the Rover was going to hurt. "I don't suppose there are any lodges between here and our destination?"

"You know me."

"You have a plan?" Leine asked.

Derek nodded, grinning. "Yeh. I do at that."

They bounced along the pothole-filled road for an hour, something Derek referred to as an "African massage," and created each other's backstory for when they infiltrated Wang's camp. Derek would be an adventurous, wealthy businessman who'd sold his company to a software giant, and Leine would play his long-suffering girlfriend who hated hunting, which would allow her to remain in camp while everyone else went on safari. Besides, Leine doubted she'd be able to stand by and watch a group of spoiled billionaires firing automatic weapons at terrified animals from a helicopter without wanting to shoot one of the billionaires.

Derek was in the middle of recounting an amusing story about a time when he shot at what he'd thought was an impala but was actually the rear end of one of Wang's clients, when they rounded a bend and Derek stopped talking. He stepped on the brakes, bringing the Rover to a halt, and stared out the window.

Leine followed his gaze to see what had interrupted the story. The breath left her body.

"Oh, my god."

Dozens of elephant bodies lay strewn in front of them—some large, some small, some in the middle of the road, with others off to the side and facing away, as though caught trying to escape.

"Fuck." Derek stared at the carnage.

Leine's throat constricted as she tried to pull in a breath. She had a hard time reconciling what she was seeing now compared to the peaceful, turf-eating families of pachyderms they'd passed earlier.

One of the larger victims had a gaping, crimson hole where its face had been sawed from its skull. Many of the others were missing the lower half of their jaws, making tusk removal easier for the poachers. Some had their feet cut off at the knees, leaving bloodied stumps.

Leine's chest squeezed tight, stunned at the scene before her. "How—?"

Without saying a word, Derek opened his door and exited the Rover. He walked first to one, and then another of the dead, his grim expression conveying conflicting emotions of sorrow and anger. Leine climbed out of the vehicle and moved between the gigantic beasts in silence, tears pricking her eyelids.

Derek squatted near one of the larger elephants who was missing its face, and pointed to several bullet holes pockmarking its side.

"Machine guns and machetes."

"My god. I had no idea..." Leine couldn't finish. No stranger to blood and death, what she saw in front of her was a scene she would never forget.

"Poachers used to use poison arrows." Derek shook his head and stood. "This is why Africa is losing her wildlife."

Leine remained quiet, opting out of reminding him of his former trade. He cut his gaze to hers and lifted his chin.

"I know what you're thinking. You believe I had a hand in creating this" —he glanced at the bodies lying at his feet— "this slaughter mentality. But I didn't. I was one of the good guys. The one who did what needed to be done, but in a sustainable manner. Besides," he continued, his tone hardening, "if I didn't supply Wang and the others, someone else would have."

"You can't excuse yourself from being a part of this, Derek," Leine said. "You were. Just like everyone who buys a trinket, or piano keys, or religious icons made of ivory is an accessory. Doesn't matter if it's certified or not. Poachers won't stop until the demand disappears. It's simple economics." Her gaze settled on one of the smaller of the dead, its ears brutally sliced from its skull. "But it's a vicious circle. How can the demand disappear if ivory continues to be available?"

A pained expression crossed his face. Closing his eyes, he bowed his head.

"Remember what I said before?" Leine added. "It doesn't matter what you've done. It's what you do."

Derek opened his eyes and squared his shoulders, turning to look at the bodies scattered along the road.

"Come on," Leine said, her voice quiet. "I'm sure there's someone you can notify about this, right?"

Derek nodded.

"Let's go," Leine said gently.

He paused for a moment longer as though to commit the scene to memory. Then he turned and walked back to the Rover. They both climbed in and Derek started the engine.

Leine glanced at the bodies lying on the ground in front of her.

Whatever it takes.

24

THE LATE AFTERNOON sun cast elongated shadows across the pockmarked back road, bathing the surrounding terrain in a dusky hue. Leine lifted the hair off the nape of her neck and fanned the air. The weather had cooperated and no billowing clouds marked the horizon indicating an approaching storm, although the dampness from the heat and cloying humidity made it feel like she'd been caught in a downpour.

Derek turned onto a dirt track, driving past a metal sign printed with a machine gun surrounded by a red circle and a line drawn through it, and the words "Rafiki Conservation Center" stenciled above it.

"Alma and Hattie are friends of mine," Derek explained. "We'll be able to stay here for the night in proper beds."

"And just how did a poacher become friends with a pair of conservationists?" Leine asked.

Derek shrugged. "I used to bring them the babies."

She didn't ask him to elaborate.

They continued along the dirt driveway, through cooling

shade cast by a thick canopy of trees crowding the roadside—a welcome relief from the incessant sun. Derek maneuvered the Rover around rain-soaked potholes, missing the worst of them.

At last, they broke through the trees and came upon three, one-story thatched-roof buildings. Derek parked in the dirt lot and they followed a wooden walkway over a small stream and entered the largest of the structures.

Once inside, Leine's eyes adjusted to the cool, dark interior, allowing her to study the space. One side of the spacious room held a desk on top of which sat a large calendar filled with hand-written notes. A long couch, low table, and two chairs created an intimate seating area on the opposite side, while the back of the structure was open to the outdoors. There didn't appear to be anyone around.

Derek walked over to the desk and glanced at the blotter.

"Looks like it's feeding time," he said. "Shall we?"

Leine followed him through the open doorway at the back of the building and down a narrow, wood-chip path toward a paddock situated at the bottom of a hill. The acacia-trunk fencing surrounding the corral was at least twelve feet high and reinforced with chain link. Two women, one with gray hair pulled back in a bun, the other with dark, shoulder-length hair, stood beneath a roofed enclosure feeding a half dozen lion cubs. In the distance, near a group of trees, an elephant trumpeted.

Derek continued around to one of two gates and opened it.

"After you," he said.

The woman with the gray hair glanced up from the cub she was feeding and shaded her eyes as Derek and Leine walked inside the paddock.

"Don't forget to close the gate," she said and rose to her feet, dusting off her khakis.

As they neared the group, a curious cub broke away from the dark-haired woman and bounded over to check them out. Leine bent down and held out her hand, which the cub immediately rubbed with its head. A quiet rumble emanated from its chest. She scratched the little feline behind the ears and the vibration grew louder.

"It's best if you don't interact with them too much. We don't want them to become habituated to humans," the older woman said. Leine stopped petting the small feline and straightened.

"Alma, this is Claire."

Alma wiped both hands on her shirt, and, smiling, extended her right, which Leine shook.

"It's good to meet you, Claire," she said.

"Alma's the founding member of the Center."

"Nice to meet you, too," Leine said.

"And the ugly one over there is Hattie," Derek said with a grin. The younger, dark-haired woman gave him a look that said she thought Derek was about as funny as a heart attack and extended her hand.

"You must be a special friend. Derek doesn't usually bring anyone to the Center." Hattie gave him a mischievous look.

"Colleague, Hattie. Get your mind out of the gutter," Derek chided her.

Hattie was younger than Alma by at least three decades and had lovely brown eyes, a slender physique, and delicate features. Leine studied Derek for signs he was interested in the stunner, but all she got was a sibling vibe from both of them.

"So, what brings you here, Derek? Have any more babies for me?" Alma asked, peering past him.

Devoid of makeup, Alma's complexion spoke of years of sunsets and the wear and tear that accompanies them. She wore faded khakis with a worn chambray shirt over a red tee with the Center's logo in white. Her leather hiking boots were one shoelace short of total disintegration.

"No, no babies. I told you I'm done with that."

Alma's face lit up. "You mean you actually meant it? Hallelujah." She clapped her hands. "When are you going to come and work with us, Mr. Hunter Man? We could really use your expertise tracking down the orphans."

Hattie leaned toward Leine to explain. "Most of the time when the poachers kill the families, they try to catch the babies to sell them to breeders or on the black market. Every now and again they escape and have no way to fend for themselves." Hattie nodded toward Derek. "That's when someone like him would come in handy. He could bring them back here where we care for them until they're old enough to be reintroduced to the wild." She paused. "Unless they're too young, or maimed in some way. Then we keep them here so they can live out the rest of their lives."

"I think that's a great idea, don't you, Derek?" Leine smiled at the former poacher's discomfort.

"*Ja, ja.* Whatever," Derek said, scanning beyond the enclosure. "Where's Zara?"

Alma's mouth set in a firm line.

"She's gone."

"Gone?" Derek cocked his head. "What do you mean, gone? I thought this was her life."

"They came more than a month ago," Hattie interjected, giving Alma a nervous look.

Derek stilled. "Who's they?" he asked, his gaze cutting from the older woman to Hattie.

Leine sensed Derek's rising anger and wondered what kind of relationship he had with Zara. Alma sighed, worry lines etching her face.

"Assad and his men came by again. I ordered them off the property, but of course they refused. They made themselves at home, eating our food, drinking our beer, shooting off their wretched guns. Zara ran herself ragged trying to calm the babies." She shook her head and held Derek's gaze, her eyes moist. "The next morning they'd gone, along with several of our lion cubs. We haven't heard from Zara since. I can only surmise they took her with them."

A muscle throbbed near Derek's clenched jaw. "Why didn't you contact me? There are things I can do, people I can talk to."

Alma nodded at the pair of curious cubs play fighting near her feet. "We'd just gotten these sweet babies and one of them had been sick, which took all the money we had in reserve. No money, no way to push Zara's case to the front of the line. Besides, I contacted the police and they did a cursory investigation. The gunmen left a message two days later." Unable to hold the tears at bay, Alma wiped at her cheeks, concentrating on the cubs.

Hattie took up the narrative, stormy emotions playing across her face. "They killed the sick cub and left a note next to its body warning us to leave Zara's disappearance alone or more deaths would follow." Hattie wrapped her arm around Alma's shoulders in a protective gesture. "Zara's a huge loss to us personally and to the Center, but we can't risk making them angry or they'll destroy everything we've worked for. Zara wouldn't want that."

His body clearly spring loaded, Derek paced the paddock. The lion cubs tumbled over themselves, trying to keep up with his feet.

"I know how you feel about Zara, Derek, but you need to be careful," Alma warned. "These are not your usual militants. They have equipment like I've never seen in these parts. The DRC, sure. But here? Machine guns, shiny new side arms, brand-new four-wheel-drive vehicles. Even their uniforms match."

"Why are they here?" Leine asked. "Is there some kind of rebellion going on?"

"I haven't heard of any unrest." Alma shook her head. "Most folks are content with the government."

"Then it's even more important that we find the assholes." Derek stopped pacing. "Zara *would* want that."

25

DINNER WITH ALMA and Hattie consisted of coconut bean soup, a salad of greens and tomatoes, and *ugali*, a kind of dough made from cornmeal. Afterward, Alma built a fire outside of the guest building where they gathered to share a drink.

Against the backdrop of impossibly brilliant stars, the maniacal laughter of hyenas, and the occasional roar of a lion, they drank lukewarm beer and shared stories. Alma and Hattie entertained them with tales of successfully reintroducing into the wild several of the animals they'd cared for through the years, of working to make the center self-sustaining by using wind power and installing solar panels, and growing their own produce, which they traded for other necessities like batteries and beer.

Leine spoke of her fascination with Tanzania's wildlife, and of the near-miss with the pair of lions earlier that day. That brought on several stories of close encounters by the other three, each citing instances of what they assumed would be certain death but having something happen to save them in the nick of time. Derek swore by always having a six-pack of beer at the ready.

"One time, I was alone in the bush taking a piss and a lioness got a little too interested. My rifle was too far away to grab and all I had with me was a beer. So I shook it up real good and let it fly." He laughed. "She didn't like the spinning bottle, or the fizzy stuff that came out of it. Diverted her attention just long enough for me to go for my gun."

"African Karma," Alma said with a knowing look. "If you're lucky enough to get out of that kind of situation alive it means you owe something."

"To whom?" Leine asked.

"Ooh, she's talking about the African spirits." Hattie wiggled her fingers in the air and made a face, smiling as she did.

"Don't you go dissing what you don't understand, Miss Hattie," Alma said, wagging her finger at the younger woman. "I've been living on this dark continent for a lot longer than you have and can't begin to explain some of the goings-on around here."

Hattie rolled her eyes and smiled affectionately at her mentor. "You keep telling me that, but I have yet to experience what you're talking about."

"Be glad, missy. You don't want to be beholden to any spirits down here. They tend to go overboard in their demands."

Eventually, talk turned to poaching and Leine and Derek described their encounter with the massacred elephants. Alma nodded, the lines around her eyes deepening.

"The official number's over ten thousand elephants killed each year in Tanzania alone, but I'm certain it's more than that. Illegal kills have risen to sixty-five percent of the population across Africa. At this rate, experts predict extinction within our lifetime. Maybe within the decade."

"Economics are driving things again," Hattie added.

"What do you mean, again?" Leine asked.

"Poaching was a huge problem back in the seventies and

eighties," Alma replied. "Supply far exceeded demand. We fought hard to save what was left, even enjoyed a twenty-year lull. But now things are ramping up again due to the rise of an elite economic market, the newly rich." She let out a heavy sigh. "We'll fight this one, too."

"It's not all doom, though. There are a couple of bright spots," Hattie said. "There's a push to educate wildlife rangers in the hardest hit areas, which appears to be helping. And a group of scientists and conservationists are using drones with night vision capabilities to track both poachers and elephants."

"What about the legal or educational side of the equation?" Leine asked. "Reduce demand by strengthening laws against buying ivory and educate people on the cost of doing business as usual. Supplying the ivory won't be as attractive."

"For what it's worth, the Chinese have begun a re-education campaign, but it's not enough. Pardon my pun, but the punishment for buying non-certified ivory has no teeth." Derek shook his head. "Look at Wang. The big smugglers will figure out how to slip illegal ivory through, especially with the amount it's worth now. There's always someone who's willing to look the other way for a price. Believe me, I know."

"It goes much deeper than just supply and demand, Claire," Alma added. "What we need are more living-wage jobs. Eradicate the crushing poverty of the Tanzanian people and I guarantee the number of poachers will decline." Alma leaned back in her chair. "Most people will do anything to feed their family. I can't blame them."

"But how do you explain the massacre we saw today?" Leine asked. "Dozens of elephants were slaughtered with automatic weapons. That's a huge amount of ivory being moved for someone who only wants to feed his family. This looked like a concerted effort by a well-armed group of people. Efficient and ruthless."

Alma and Derek exchanged looks.

"There've been rumors that terrorists have moved into the region and are slaughtering the elephants. They sell the ivory to fund their jihad," she said. "Could be one reason we're seeing more militant activity. Where there's money..."

"If that's the case, Africa's fucked." Derek folded his arms, eyes blazing with anger.

"Don't be such a nihilist, Derek," Alma scolded. "The possibility isn't good, obviously, but if the Chinese take the rumors seriously, they just might do something about it. They don't want to lose 'their' ivory to a pack of terrorists."

"Knowing Wang, I'm certain he'd figure out a way to do business with them," Derek muttered.

"As long as people are starving, there will always be a black market. At least we can try." Alma focused her attention on Derek. "Now it's your turn. What are you two doing here? And don't tell me you're on holiday and you wanted to take Claire on safari."

Derek shifted in his chair, obviously uncomfortable. Leine answered the older woman.

"I'm looking for someone's daughter, and Derek has agreed to help me find her."

Alma shifted her glance from Derek to Leine. "And you've tracked her here?" she asked.

"We're pretty sure she was sold to a man named Victor Wang to work in his camp."

Hattie frowned. "Wang is not someone you want to deal with, believe me."

"You know him?" Leine asked.

"Oh, yeah. We know him." Hattie sat back and crossed her arms. "He's supposedly starting up a rehabilitation center. Right."

"Wang's never helped anything or anybody other than

Wang," Alma added. "He has a few key politicians in his pocket and can push through most anything he wants, including killing endangered species with impunity. It's why his place is known as Camp Kill."

"He stole our grant." Hattie spat out the words.

Derek raised his eyebrows. "The one from SWI?"

Alma nodded. "That's the one."

Derek turned to Leine. "Save Wildlife International is a huge umbrella non-profit dedicated to preserving wildlife around the globe. If Wang was able to detour the grant promised to Rafiki, then he has more pull than I thought."

"More like his friend does. He's the head of their African division." Alma shrugged. "We don't have the resources to fight him."

Hattie added, "We don't have the resources, period."

"All this talk of Wang and his shady business practices has made me tired." Alma stood up and rubbed her back. "It's well past my bedtime, ladies and gentleman. Hattie will show you where you'll be sleeping tonight." She pulled her wrap closer and gave Derek a wistful smile. "Think about what I said, Derek. We could use your expertise here at Rafiki."

She turned to Leine and bowed, her hands in prayer pose. "I wish you peaceful dreams, Claire. Thank you for being here." With that, she walked toward the larger building, the inky darkness swallowing her whole.

LEINE ASKED TO BORROW THE CENTER'S SAT PHONE AND WALKED out to the Rover for some privacy. It was close to noon Santa's time, and she hadn't contacted the homicide detective since she'd sent the message from the cyber café in Dar. The events of the day produced a powerful need to check in with him.

"Jesus, Leine, where the hell are you?" Santa's tone wasn't what she would call happy. In fact, he sounded angrier than the time she called him after being shot in Tijuana.

"Shh, Santa. Everything's fine. I'm fine. I just wanted to hear your voice."

Leine tamped down the emotion rising in her chest. Between the lack of a good night's sleep and the scene with the slaughtered elephants, not to mention almost being lunch for a couple of lions, she was emotionally and physically drained.

Santa's tone changed to one of concern. "Are you all right? You don't sound so great."

Leine smiled. Leave it to Santa to switch from raging bull to mother hen in an instant. Living with someone able to change direction on a dime was disconcerting to be sure, but never boring.

"Like I said, everything's fine. I'll talk to you about it all when I get back."

"Lou told me you found Kylie and you're going after some triad's business."

Great. Thanks, Lou.

"Victor Wang. Apparently he supplies women to clients at an illegal hunting camp he owns here in Tanzania. We're close."

"*We're* close? Who's with you?"

"A former poacher named Derek who crossed Wang. Wang was transporting him on the same ship and was going to sell him to the highest bidder."

"A poacher? Nice. You couldn't leave the guy to his fate?"

"Not really. It's a long story. Let's just say we needed each other to escape. He's been useful—he knows the area, and Wang, well."

"Watch him, Leine. Poachers aren't normally what you'd call trustworthy."

"You know, I wasn't aware of that. Could you enlighten me

further, oh wise one?" Leine tried to keep herself from laughing but failed miserably.

"Okay, fine. I deserved that." Santa chuckled. "God, it's good to hear your voice. This being apart is *no bueno*."

"Agreed. Have you ever been to Tanzania? It's an amazing place, even given the circumstances. And heart wrenching."

"Haven't had the pleasure. Why heart wrenching?"

"We rolled up on an elephant massacre today. They used machine guns. Mowed down an entire family just for the ivory."

"That had to be hard to see," Santa said. "Sorry, L."

"Rumor has it terrorists are behind it. All to fund a jihad doomed to failure. What a waste."

"Yeah." Santa paused a few beats. "Just so we're clear, you're not thinking about going after the jihadists, right?"

Leine almost burst out laughing. "No, Santa. I'm here to find Kylie. Nothing more."

"Okay, good." The relief in Santa's voice was palpable. Leine smiled.

"I love you, Santiago Jensen. Remember that."

"I love you, too, Leine Basso. Come home soon."

Leine ended the call and returned the phone. She walked back to the fire, thinking about Santa and her daughter, missing her life.

26

KYLIE FINISHED DRYING the last kettle and placed it behind the curtained cupboard in the tent that served as the kitchen. It was late, and the guests had all retired for the evening except the owner and his friend, who, rumor had it, was a billionaire with a capital B.

The camp was luxurious. The guest's quarters had been erected on top of wooden platforms and each had its own *en suite*. The sheets, which Kylie helped wash, were high thread count and the nicest she'd ever seen. One tent was dedicated to wine, with two temperature-controlled chillers—one for red, one for white. Guests had their choice of high-end liquor and Cuban cigars, dined on fine china, and drank from delicate crystal. Everything Kylie and the rest of the workers did was behind the scenes. They were warned to never show themselves—obviously to reduce the possibility of any of them seeking help, either by escaping or sending a message to a family member.

Earlier in the evening, Kylie had been asked by another worker to deliver a bottle of wine to the two men sitting at the blazing campfire, sipping cognac and smoking cigars while they talked. The owner, a well-dressed Chinese man named Victor

Wang, had become angry and grabbed Kylie by the arm, dragging her back behind the kitchen to where Ghanima, head of the kitchen staff, was prepping for the next day. Wang screamed at the woman to keep her staff away from the guests, making Kylie a new enemy. In retaliation, Ghanima put Kylie on pots and pans duty, and gave her the most arduous chores she could find.

At first, Kylie had been relieved to be assigned domestic duty when she arrived at the camp rather than being put into service in other ways. But that relief was short-lived. From sunup to sundown, she worked until her fingers bled and her vision blurred; otherwise she risked painful retribution. Punishment could take many forms, from having her ration of food taken away to actual flogging, depending on the infraction. The first time she witnessed someone tied to a tree and beaten, Kylie had to stop herself from running at the person holding the whip. The prison camp, as most of the workers referred to the place, was an unrelenting *Groundhog Day*. Only things didn't get better like in the movie. They got worse.

Kylie untied her apron and hung it on a hook next to the massive grill. That night guests had feasted on gazelle, water buffalo, and rhino, although Kylie was pretty sure the last dish was considered an endangered species. Although tempted, she didn't bring up the legality of serving something about to go extinct. Ghanima would be only too happy to have a reason to tie her to a tree and slice her back to bloody strips.

At least the nights weren't cold. Most of the women were locked in a hut, crowded together until morning with only a thin blanket between them and the uncompromising dirt floor. The crowded conditions acted as efficient insulation, although this time of year was warm, even in the evenings. The other people in the hut gave Kylie some comfort every time she heard a lion's roar or screaming baboons. No way would she venture into the dark alone. The wilderness around them was an effective escape deterrent, at least for Kylie.

There were other dangers. One night Kylie had awoken to a hand over her mouth as one of the male laborers, who wasn't even supposed to be inside the hut, tried to take off her clothing. Terrified, Kylie had reacted by kicking him in the groin as hard as she could. The next day, the man was nowhere to be found. Kylie didn't ask where he'd gone. Now, she rarely slept more than a few minutes at a time.

She signaled to the guard that she was ready to go and started down the wooden path toward the sleeping hut, with him following close behind. They passed a newly built enclosure, and Kylie ran her hand along the solid wood walls. Strange sounds could occasionally be heard behind the fence, but it was hard to tell what they were.

Kylie had been at the camp long enough for the mental cotton of self-delusion to wear off. Each day she clawed through the despair and depression now taking its place, trying to keep the tiniest thread of hope alive. But there was no one to go to for help; no cops, no lawyers, no recourse, and the illusion of seeing her mother's friend, Leine, on the ship was just that—an illusion. One man ruled this small corner of the world, and did so without regard to its inhabitants. Before, she couldn't imagine a place this miserable.

She could now.

AFTER BREAKFAST DISHES THE NEXT MORNING, UBAYA, THE GUARD assigned to the kitchen, ordered Kylie to gather together a box of food and several containers of water and take them to the new enclosure. Eager to see more of the camp, Kylie piled the provisions on top of a small cart and set off along the gravel path. Another guard named Lek followed behind her.

The walls were several feet high and made of rough, dark wood. Kylie followed the wall, eventually arriving at a barred, metal gate secured with a padlock. On the other side of the bars was an arena with a straw-covered dirt floor. Lek produced a ring of keys and unlocked the gate, allowing Kylie through.

"Don't take too long," he warned. "I'll be right outside." Unassisted, Kylie muscled the cart inside, and he swung the gate closed.

A young woman with long, dark hair sat on the straw in the middle of the arena, surrounded by five or six lion cubs, all vying for her attention. The woman held something up with her hand and they tumbled over themselves trying to be the first to get at whatever it was.

Forgetting herself for the moment, Kylie giggled at the cubs' antics. The young woman turned toward her at the noise. Kylie smiled. The woman gave each cub something to eat before she climbed to her feet and walked over.

"I didn't think they let anyone walk freely here," she said.

"They don't. A guard is outside." Kylie waved at the supplies on the cart. "Where would you like these?"

"Over there is fine." The woman nodded toward a small enclosure. She helped Kylie roll the cart closer, and started to unload the items.

"The cubs are adorable," Kylie said. "What will happen to them?"

The woman stiffened and turned away, wiping at her eyes.

Kylie's insides twisted at her reaction. She put down the bag of rice she was holding and offered her hand. "I'm Kylie."

The other woman gave her a wary smile as she shook it and answered, "Zara."

"Do they ever let you out of here?" Kylie assumed Zara was a prisoner like herself but refrained from mentioning it.

"They let me out at night." She looked down at her bare feet. "But I can only walk freely while I'm in here. They wrap my ankles in heavy chains otherwise."

"Where are you from?"

The ghost of a smile crossed Zara's lips. "I was working at a wildlife conservation center before...before I was brought here. We took care of sick and abandoned wildlife, reintroducing them into the wild when we could."

"That's so cool. Did you get to work with babies like you do here?" Kylie asked, nodding at the lion cubs.

"Yes." Zara turned to watch them play fighting with each other.

"Will they let those little guys go, too?" She couldn't help asking, even though Zara's initial reaction suggested the answer wasn't good.

"He says he will, but I don't think so."

"You mean Victor Wang?" Kylie asked. One of the cubs crouched low, preparing to attack a piece of straw sticking up out of the ground.

Zara nodded. "Wang's only interested in money. Rafiki, the center I worked for, relied solely on donations, and even then we had to cut corners. Wildlife rehabilitation is not a money-making enterprise." She cocked her head. "Where are you from?"

"Arizona." Kylie's chest contracted. *Home.*

The gate clanked open, and Lek poked his head in. "Hurry up," he said, his annoyance obvious.

"Almost finished," Zara called. She and Kylie quickly put away the rest of the supplies.

"I hope I can come back to see you," Kylie said.

"Me too."

Kylie wheeled the cart to where Lek waited. He locked the gate behind them and followed her back to the kitchen area. Ghanima was waiting for them. The expression on the older woman's face told Kylie she wanted nothing more than to wrap her hands around Kylie's neck and squeeze until the breath left her body. Ubaya stood behind her, a smug look on his face.

His manipulation was clear. Lek lost no time hustling out of the tent. Kylie's stomach did a flip at his abandonment, and she lowered her gaze to the ground, hoping her look of contrition would help to alleviate her punishment.

"Who give you permission to leave?" Ghanima's voice shook with suppressed rage.

"He did." Kylie glanced at the man standing behind her accuser. Ubaya glared at her, his eyes resembling two black holes.

Ghanima stepped forward and gripped Kylie by the arm.

"You *not* take orders from anyone but me. Ever," she said, her voice dripping menace. "Come." She yanked Kylie after her and Ubaya followed.

They walked past the outskirts of the camp to another, smaller section of tents. The main camp may have been beautiful, but this was extraordinary.

Three large, colorful canvas tents with rich, dark wood floors stood at the center of a clearing. A small grouping of curtained huts about the size of beach cabanas were scattered throughout, each with two or three comfortable-looking chairs in front, grouped around a raised fire pit. Discreet solar lighting hugged several of the trees, and a soothing fountain bubbled in the background.

Ghanima shoved Kylie up the steps of the largest tent, stopping just outside of the entrance. Deep, rich Persian rugs covered the floors.

"Mistah Wang. It is Ghanima from the kitchen."

The older woman was breathing heavily from the forced march and perspiration slid down her face and onto her neck. Kylie lowered her gaze to the ground, not wanting to court her wrath. The two women waited while Ubaya stood sentry a few feet away. There was movement inside the tent, and a few moments later Victor Wang appeared wearing a white terry cloth bathrobe with a large W embroidered in black across the chest.

"What is it?" he asked, his tone conveying his unhappiness at being disturbed.

Ghanima bowed and lowered her gaze. "Mistah Wang, please forgive me for bothering, but this girl" —she nodded at Kylie— "is bad trouble. This girl no listen to what Ghanima say and go wherever she want. Ghanima ask permission to punish this girl."

Wang studied Kylie for a moment, sucking on his teeth as he did so. "Maybe she'll listen when you put the chains on her."

Ghanima smiled and nodded, her gaze still lowered. "Yes, sir, Mistah Wang. Beg pardon, but can Ghanima ask one more favor?"

Wang sighed. "And that is?"

"Ghanima would like to stake this girl."

"As long as it doesn't interfere with running the camp, you can. Now, leave." Wang walked inside the tent and pulled back the curtain surrounding the bed. Sapphire was lying on her side, and their gazes met. Kylie blinked in surprise at the woman who had been with her in the cell in Bangkok. Before Kylie could say anything, Ghanima gripped her by the arm and dragged her off the platform and down the stairs, headed back to the main camp.

27

L EINE WALKED TO the outdoor cooking area and helped herself to a cup of hot coffee. Alma was back from feeding "her babies" and was in the process of making breakfast for everyone.

"How'd you sleep?" she asked Leine as she poured scrambled eggs into a hot skillet.

"Very well, thanks. Your beds sure beat the Rover."

Alma chuckled. "Ain't it the truth? Good mattresses were the first things I made sure we had here, once we built the pens." She turned, wiping her hands on a towel. "A miserable night's sleep and aching back don't help when you need to take care of things."

Derek appeared, looking well rested. He grabbed a cup of coffee and sat at the counter separating the cooking facilities from the eating area.

"Where's Hattie?" he asked.

"She's up at the main building, talking to Captain Hugh and checking in supplies."

"Captain Hugh?" Leine took a sip of coffee and glanced toward the big building.

Alma scooped up the partially scrambled eggs and flipped them over. "Captain Hugh's been delivering supplies to us since the beginning. He runs a hot air balloon company outside of the park. Takes visitors on the ride of a lifetime, from what I hear."

"You haven't gone?" Leine asked.

Alma shook her head and chuckled. "Not me. I'm a big chicken when it comes to heights."

Just then, Hattie walked out of the main building and headed down the path toward them. A man dressed in a long-sleeved shirt, cargo pants, and a bush hat followed her to where the others were sitting.

"You must be Captain Hugh," Derek said when the two reached the counter. "I'm Derek, and this is Claire."

"Guilty." Captain Hugh smiled and shook Derek's hand, then did the same with Leine. "Good to meet you."

Leine could've sworn his sky-blue eyes twinkled. A few inches taller than Leine, the affable pilot's calloused hands and broad shoulders suggested someone who worked physically for a living.

"Along with the feed you ordered, I left batteries, milk, a case of your favorite beer, and some chocolate up there." He felt his pockets and pulled out a handwritten list, placing it on the counter in front of Alma.

"Thank you, Hugh. I appreciate it. Can you stay for breakfast?"

Hugh's face lit up. "Why, yes, ma'am. Be happy to."

During breakfast, Hugh regaled them with stories of flying his balloon over the Serengeti with all types of passengers, from a retired director of the NSA to a wizened Italian mobster who wanted to commemorate his ninetieth birthday.

"I was sweating bullets on that flight, let me tell you," he said with a shake of his head. "I didn't want *la cosa nostra* paying me a visit because I damaged their capo."

"How did you get a ninety-year-old into the basket?" Hattie asked. "I mean, he couldn't have been that spry, right?"

"There was a big, muscle-bound dude with him who picked him up and set him inside. The guy handled the old man like he was a baby chick. He was right there when we landed, too." Hugh finished his plate of eggs and pushed away from the table. Holding his coffee with both hands, he leaned back in his chair. "Besides visiting Alma and Hattie, what are you two doing here?" he asked, nodding at Leine and Derek.

"We're looking for someone we think is staying at a temporary hunting camp near here," Derek answered. "Have you seen anything like that on your flights?"

Hugh considered his question and shook his head. "I don't normally fly this area. The only camps I know of are the ones that have been here for years. What's the owner's name?"

"Victor Wang," Leine said.

Hugh glanced at Alma. "I wasn't aware he'd come this far north."

"You know him?" Derek asked.

"Everybody knows Victor Wang. He's the king of canned hunts. If it wasn't for the politicians in his pocket, he'd have been run out of Tanzania by responsible hunting groups years ago."

"Canned hunts?" Leine asked.

Derek cleared his throat. "*Ja, ja,* that's where the hunters and the animals are contained in a small pen."

"You said hunters, with an S."

Hugh nodded. "There's usually more than one, and that's with charging thirty-five thousand a pop. I've seen five shooters go after one lion with high-powered rifles. It's appalling."

"Maybe Wang will end up being killed by one of the endangered species he likes to hunt," Hattie said.

"One can only hope," Hugh said.

"So I take it canned hunts are legal here?" Leine asked.

"At this juncture, yes," Alma said. "They aren't as prevalent in Tanzania as they are in South Africa, but the practice is growing. The cost to hunt a lion in the wild here is at least twice that of what a canned hunt costs. Wang has jumped on the bandwagon and is exploiting amateur hunters who can't afford a 'real' trophy." Her cheeks grew pink. "The government looks the other way. It's a blatant case of money over conservation."

Hattie placed her hand on the older woman's arm. "Take it easy. It looks like your blood pressure's going through the roof."

"I know, I know. It's just so upsetting." Alma leaned back with a sigh. The conversation continued, but on a more somber note.

After breakfast, Derek and Leine walked Captain Hugh back to his Land Cruiser.

"Just how involved is the government?" Leine asked.

"No one knows exact numbers, but interest is growing. A general was arrested not too long ago for allegedly working with poachers." Derek sighed. "Government types are most at risk for taking bribes. The wages aren't exactly wealth-inducing, and their jobs ensure that they come into contact with the poachers. These guys don't just look the other way. As long as the money's good, they're actively participating."

"You know," Hugh said when they reached his rig, "I don't have any flights scheduled tomorrow morning. If you're interested in going up to see if you can spot that camp you were talking about, I'm available."

"That would be really helpful," Derek said. "What time and what do you need from us?"

"It'll be early, like five thirty. Still interested?"

"Sure. We're more than happy to pay for the propane as well as your time," Leine added.

Hugh waved her offer away. "Don't worry about it. I'm glad to help."

28

K YLIE REPOSITIONED THE metal cuff attached to her ankle and wiped at the trickle of blood. Ubaya had slapped them on her that morning and didn't seem concerned when she told him how the sharp metal cut into her skin. Now past eleven, the raw sores oozed pus and blood. Infection had set in fast. The sharp pain reminded her to keep her head down and not draw Ghanima's ire.

Bone-tired and looking forward to her thin blanket on the ground in the sleeping hut, Kylie waved at Ubaya to let him know she was ready to go. After making sure the pots and pans were put away and the grill was turned off, she removed her apron and hung it next to the towels. She shuffled out of the tent and down the path, the chain clanking noisily with each step. Ubaya followed close behind her. When she turned toward the door of the sleeping hut, he hit her between the shoulders with the butt of his gun.

"Keep going. You will not sleep here tonight."

The pain from the hit was nothing compared to the chill that slid up her spine at his words. Was he going to rape her? Was this part of her punishment? The chains grew heavier, so much so that she found it difficult to continue. At one point, she tripped over a wooden slat and would have taken a header into the walk if he hadn't grabbed on to her to keep her upright.

They continued past the end of the camp where the worker latrines were, and out into the dark bush beyond. Ubaya flicked on his flashlight and trained it on the ground in front of them. Insects buzzed in the dark, and mysterious grunts emanated from the world beyond the small beam of light.

Eventually they came to a wire fence with a gate. Ubaya opened it and pushed her through. The night sounds she'd been able to ignore in the sleeping hut were now close. Very close. In the distance, a hyena's maniacal laugh echoed in the darkness. Kylie shivered, her skin erupting in goose bumps.

He closed the gate behind them and walked Kylie to the center post where he bent down and picked up the end of a long chain. He reached for the short length of metal between her ankles.

"No!" Kylie jerked her foot from his hand and stepped backward, forgetting for a moment she was chained. With nowhere for her feet to go she fell, landing on her hip with a heavy thud, the pain shooting to her shoulder.

He crouched next to her and connected the chains, testing the bond by pulling on the longer of the two. Kylie grabbed on to his hand, panic closing her throat.

"What are you doing? You can't leave me out here alone—"

He wrenched his hand free and stepped back, a cruel smile on his face.

"You should not make Ghanima angry." He scanned the enclosure. The roar of a lion shattered the still night air. Close.

Kylie pushed herself onto her knees and lunged for the man's legs. He moved out of the way and she fell to all fours, skinning her palms in the rocky dirt.

"Please—" she said, hot tears sliding down her cheeks.

When he didn't respond she sank to the ground and pulled her knees up, wrapping her arms around them. The gate closed with a screech and the guard's footsteps faded, leaving her alone and tethered to the pole in the dark.

HOURS LATER, KYLIE WOKE FROM A FITFUL DOZE, DISORIENTED and afraid. Something had woken her, and her imagination went into overdrive with visions of hungry lions and hyenas, ready to tear her apart. She held her breath trying to quiet the pounding of her heart, and strained to hear.

The footsteps came closer, accompanied by clanking. Kylie exhaled with a sigh. It wasn't a wild animal stalking its prey, but she was still wary of the late-night visitor.

"Kylie?" A woman's voice.

"Zara?" Kylie cleared her throat and peered into the darkness, trying to make out the woman she'd met earlier. The clanking paused as the gate opened and closed, then resumed before Zara materialized. She knelt down next to Kylie.

"How did you know I was out here?" Kylie asked.

"I heard Ubaya laughing about how frightened you were when he left you alone. Here—" Zara reached into her pocket and pulled out a folding knife, which she handed to her. The metal blade glinted in the moonlight. "It's the only thing I dared take. Hopefully they won't miss it. You can hide it under your clothes when they come to get you in the morning."

Kylie's shoulders slumped as she felt the weight of the knife in her hand.

"What's wrong?" Zara asked. "I know it's not much, but at least you'll be able to protect yourself if something gets in."

"No. Of course, thank you." A tear slid down Kylie's cheek

and landed on her wrist. "It's just that I was hoping you were here to bring me back."

Zara put her hand on Kylie's shoulder. "I'm sorry. If anyone found out I was here with you I'd be punished. The guard, Lek, gave me the key for the gate, and I have to make sure I get it back to him, soon. I wanted you to know someone other than Ghanima knows you're out here."

Kylie glanced behind Zara to make sure no one else was there. "I haven't been able to sleep more than a few minutes at a time. Whenever I drift off, something wakes me. Most of the time it's some animal noise."

"You're going to be fine. This is the monsoon season. With all the rain, there's plenty of food to go around. You're not a predator's favorite meal, anyway." Zara tilted her head back and looked at the sky. Kylie did the same. "Isn't it gorgeous?"

Zara was trying to get her mind off of her situation, and Kylie willingly played along. Watching the brilliant dance of stars above her with Zara nearby gave her new hope that she'd see morning.

"I saw one of the girls from Bangkok," Kylie said. "Wang's using her as his—" She searched for the right word to describe Sapphire's situation. "She's staying in his tent."

"She goes by the name of Sapphire, right?"

"How did you know?"

"Victor brought her to see the cubs." Zara paused for a moment. "She didn't look very good."

"I know. I saw her a couple of times." Kylie shook her head. "He's hurting her, isn't he?"

Zara nodded and looked back up at the stars. "There was a young boy with them. I think his name was Jaidee."

Kylie's heart skipped. "He's here? Was he okay?" A spark of protective anger bolted through her at the thought of anyone hurting him.

"He was when I saw him." Zara gave Kylie a quick smile. "I think Wang likes having him around. Looks like it, anyway. He brings him things, like his paper or his lunch."

"Like a dog." Kylie's voice was flat.

Zara nodded. "Like a dog."

The two women sat together in silence, listening to the wild night sounds and staring at the stars. Kylie couldn't keep her eyes open and soon nodded off. When next she woke, Zara was gone and the sun had just begun its ascent.

She'd survived the night.

29

H UGH AND ONE of his crewmembers, a young Tanzanian named Rashid, rolled up at five twenty in a four-door pickup pulling a flatbed trailer with the balloon and basket. Leine and Derek climbed into the backseat and they headed down the drive in the dark, turning left when they reached the main road. Half an hour later, they parked near a flat area devoid of trees.

While Derek and Rashid rolled out the massive fabric envelope, Hugh and Leine removed the gas-powered fan from the back of the pickup and stationed it near the mouth of the balloon. Derek ran back and helped Leine hold the mouth open as Hugh turned on the fan, aiming directly into the balloon. As air inflated the envelope, Rashid stood near the crown, holding on to a rope connected to the top. Once the balloon was fully inflated, Hugh took control of the burners and fired, shooting hot air into the multicolored fabric. The envelope lifted gracefully into the air, a giant behemoth come alive, dragging Rashid across the ground toward them until he let go of the rope. At Hugh's instruction, Leine and Derek climbed into the wicker basket while Rashid sprinted over and jumped on to help weigh them down. The balloon hovered a few inches above the ground, straining to fly.

"Okay, Rashid, time for lift off," Hugh said. Rashid hopped off the basket onto the ground, and the balloon began to rise as the earth dropped away. Rashid and the pickup grew smaller until they looked like miniatures.

Except for the occasional blast from the burner, the flight was quiet and serene, with no sense of movement. The rising sun bathed the terrain in a crisp, yellow-orange glow. A hush fell over the landscape punctuated by early morning birdsong. Leine leaned against the edge of the basket and took in the scenery, keeping an eye out for Wang's camp. At one point, the sound of the burner flushed several *dik diks* from the brush below them.

"Do you have any idea where the camp might be?" Hugh asked Leine.

"Not really. The last known location was approximately ten kilometers northwest of here."

"Why? Can you steer this thing?" Derek asked.

"In a fashion. Remember that little black balloon I launched earlier? That told me which way the wind was blowing at different levels. So, when I want to head that way," Hugh pointed over Derek's shoulder, "I climb or drop to the level with the wind direction I need and let nature take it from there."

"What happens when a storm comes up?" Derek asked.

"This time of year's tricky because of the monsoons. If I see clouds building up anywhere nearby, I'll land."

"Glad to hear it," Leine said.

Hugh steered to the northwest, flying over trees and grassland. A herd of zebra scattered as the balloon approached. As soon as they flew past, the animals regrouped and resumed their grazing. Derek spotted several objects in the distance and asked Hugh to maneuver them closer. As they neared the spot, the objects in question turned out to be a Maasai settlement with mud huts and fenced-in cattle, so they continued on. The landscape gradually changed from straight savannah to an intermixed, wooded terrain.

About an hour into the flight, Hugh warned, "I only have enough propane to fly another twenty minutes." He radioed Rashid that they'd be landing soon. Rashid, who had been following them in the pickup, acknowledged the transmission and continued to track them.

Just then, Leine caught a glimpse of several colorful objects nestled in a wooded area.

"Look. Over there." She handed Derek the binoculars.

He nodded. "Promising."

Hugh changed course and they floated toward the spot in question. This time it wasn't a Maasai settlement, but a small group of brightly colored tents next to an even larger assemblage of tan ones.

"I think we found it," Leine said.

"Sorry, guys, but I gotta land."

As they neared the ground, the wind kicked up and pushed them toward a thorn tree. Hugh blasted the burners, raising the balloon to a calmer wind level, then tried again. This time they dropped gently toward the earth.

Rashid caught the rope Hugh threw overboard, and guided them to an open area. Hugh opened the vent at the top of the balloon, allowing the hot air to escape. The envelope and basket sank gracefully.

"Thank you, Hugh. This was just what we needed," Leine said. She climbed over the edge of the basket and dropped to the ground. Derek followed.

"My pleasure, guys. I hope you find whoever you're looking for. And," he added, "I hope to hell you mess with Victor Wang. A lot of people would be grateful."

Leine turned to say something to Rashid when a burst of gunfire erupted behind them. Hugh's head snapped back, and his body crumpled to the basket floor. Rashid froze, staring in horror at his mentor.

"Get down!" Leine ran at Rashid in a crouch and connected with his midsection, propelling him behind the basket. Derek followed seconds later. The gunfire intensified. Leine and Derek drew their weapons, each taking a corner.

"This wicker won't stop much," Derek said, his breathing heavy.

"No kidding," Leine replied.

Eyes wide, Rashid attempted to stand. Keeping her attention on the three visible gunmen moving through the trees, she shoved the younger man to the ground.

"Stay down!"

"Get to the truck. I'll cover you both," Derek said, nodding to where Rashid had parked several yards behind them.

Leine pushed up to a crouch and Rashid did the same, the whites of his eyes visible. She held up her fingers and mouthed, "*One, two...*"

On three, the two sprinted toward the truck, staying low, the sound of gunfire exploding behind them. Rashid tore around the front of the truck to the driver's side while Leine wrenched the passenger door open and dove onto the floor. He slammed the truck into gear and stood on the accelerator. For a sickening moment the wheels spun, spitting rocks and dirt, trying to gain traction. The truck's tires finally grabbed hold and they rocketed toward Derek.

It looked like they were going to overshoot the balloon, but at the last minute Rashid gunned the motor, spun the steering wheel, and hauled on the emergency brake. The truck skidded alongside the basket, kicking up a cloud of dirt and almost jack-knifing the trailer.

"Get in!" Leine shouted, holding the door open. Derek emptied his magazine at the remaining gunmen and launched himself into the truck. Leine dragged the door closed and Rashid punched the accelerator to the floor.

Bullets pinged the trailer and truck bed as they careened through the tall grass. Seconds later, they bounced onto the dirt road, the trailer fishtailing behind them. Rashid kept driving and stared straight ahead, his knuckles blanched white on the steering wheel.

"Holy shit," Derek said. "What the hell was that?"

Leine turned to look out the back window. Her heart thudded in her chest with the familiar rush of an adrenaline spike. She glanced at Rashid to see how he was holding up and noticed tears streaming down his face.

"We must retrieve his body." Rashid's voice was barely loud enough to be heard over the engine.

"We will, Rashid. I promise," Leine answered.

Derek shook his head. "Not bloody now, I can tell you that. I only knocked down one of the fuckers. The other two just kept coming."

"Did you see how they were dressed? In military gear," Leine said.

"They were serious, that's for sure. Looked to me like the militia group Alma was talking about. Weapons, fatigues. Matching caps. The lot. Glad they were far enough away. I doubt they would've missed, otherwise."

Rashid kept his eyes on the road and didn't comment. Leine touched his arm. He continued to stare through the windshield.

"Look, I realize Hugh was your friend. I'm sorry it happened. But we can't change the fact that he's gone."

"He was teaching me to fly," Rashid said in a quiet voice. He grew silent for a moment before he asked, "Was this man whose camp you are looking for responsible?"

"I don't know. Probably." Leine sighed. She was getting tired of Wang and people like him. Of his belief that he had the right to take whatever and whomever he wanted for his sole profit, damn the consequences.

Too bad Wang wasn't in Africa. She'd have liked a shot at him. One less asshole to contend with.

Forty-five minutes later, Rashid dropped them off at the Center. He refused Leine's invitation to join them, insisting instead that he wanted to see his family, especially his children. Unable to talk him into staying, Leine and Derek wished him well and warned him not to go back to the site.

"In fact, Leine and I were planning to pick up the body tonight, when it's dark."

Leine nodded. "We'll take him to his wife."

"May I come with you?" Rashid asked.

Leine glanced at Derek, who shook his head.

"Of course, Rashid. Meet us here after dark," Leine said, ignoring the look Derek gave her. "Where does Hugh's wife live? We'll need to inform her of her husband's death."

Rashid squared his shoulders. "I will go to Captain Hugh's home and tell his wife."

"Are you sure? Would you like one of us to go with you?" Leine asked.

"No. I will do this thing." He climbed back into the pickup and drove away.

Leine watched him go, anger at Wang rising in her chest.

"Why did you tell him he could come with us?" Derek stood

in front of her, legs spread and his arms crossed. "He'll end up being just one more complication to worry about, you check?"

"And if I didn't tell him he could come along?" Leine crossed her arms to match his. "Did you notice the determined look on his face? Rashid was going back to get Hugh with or without us. I'd prefer we kept the casualties to a minimum, if that's all right with you."

Derek stared past her, his jaw set, reminding Leine of a little boy who didn't get his way.

"Whatever," she said, not waiting for his answer. "Pissed off or not, I refuse to be responsible for another innocent life cut short by Wang's men. *You* check?" With that, she started for the main building. She'd have to give Hattie and Alma the bad news. Derek didn't follow right away.

Good, she thought. It would give them both time to cool off.

As Leine expected, Alma and Hattie didn't take the news well. When she told them they were going back that evening to retrieve Hugh's body, Alma protested.

"One body's enough," she said. "Those men demonstrated that they'd shoot anyone who came close to the camp. What makes you think there won't be someone watching the balloon, or that they haven't already taken the body away?"

"We've got it covered, Alma," Derek said. "We're going to do recon before going in. We'll be fine."

"Maybe you two will be, but what about Rashid?"

Derek gave Leine a look. "I have every confidence that Rashid will do as we say."

"He would have gone in on his own," Leine added. "If he tried that, the chances are high he'd be killed."

"Oh. Well. That's different." Alma shook her head. "Hugh

was such a good man." Tears welled in her eyes and she turned away.

"I'm so sorry, Alma. We didn't realize..." Leine searched for an adequate explanation but found nothing to help.

Alma wiped her cheeks with her sleeve. "It's not your fault, Claire. Hugh knew what kind of man Wang was, knew there'd be risk involved. This *is* Africa."

Leine was beginning to hate that saying.

30

VICTOR WANG STUDIED his cigar, enjoying the sweet, spicy scent of the expensive tobacco. He produced a silver cutter from his pocket and expertly snipped off the end. With the strike of a long wooden match, Wang held the cigar a distance from the flame, allowing the sulfur to burn away before he warmed and eventually lit the end. He extinguished the match and dropped it into the crystal ashtray next to his chair.

Sapphire had poured him a measure of Tasmanian scotch, neat, and Wang held the glass beneath his nose, giving it a delicate sniff. He'd gotten the last bottle of the award-winning single-malt whiskey and had paid more than £1,500 for the opportunity.

Today, however, the whiskey and fine cigar did nothing to dispel Victor's bad mood. He disliked doing business with the men who were coming to meet him today, preferred to conduct meetings in his adopted city of Bangkok. He realized if he wanted to continue to operate without restriction in Tanzania, he would have to strike a deal with the devil, which was how he viewed impending negotiations. Besides, they *had* delivered several fine specimens for his "lion reserve," as well as the girl Zara, whom the men had reported as being a kind of big cat whisperer.

Wang had to admit she worked well with the abandoned cubs and the juvenile males that he'd purchased, although she tended to bond too strongly with them for his taste. He hadn't explained what she was training them for, nor would he. She could easily become a liability if she knew his intention of becoming the biggest canned hunting operator in Tanzania. Let the South Africans have their cheap camps for those who wished to feel the thrill of killing a tame African lion. Victor Wang would give his large cats only enough exposure to humans so that they could easily be moved from camp to camp. The rest of the time he intended to make sure the feline's ferocious reputation as "man-eaters" was honed to a fine edge. Then he could charge a premium, adding the Asian tigers from his last shipment to the menu as another incentive.

Sapphire appeared in the doorway, wearing nothing but one of his expensive Saville Row dress shirts and a lazy smile. The electronic shock collar around her neck gave her a butch appearance that Wang liked. She studied him with her almond-shaped eyes as she touched herself through the fabric, her nipples hardening. Wang sipped his whiskey and glanced at his watch to gauge the time. Doctor Death, as the militant leader liked to call himself, was notoriously late to anything except an execution. Wang deemed he had close to an hour before Death's entourage arrived. Victor opened the top of his oversized pinkie ring to reveal a chamber filled with gray powder, and shook some of it into his drink. He then swirled the glass, giving the golden liquid a cloudy cast.

Sapphire's lazy smile turned into a knowing one as she watched him take a sip of the whiskey. She unbuttoned the shirt, eyes riveted to his, and ran her fingers along her neck and down her chest to circle first one nipple, and then another. Her hand dipped lower, and she began to touch herself, emitting a soft moan as she did.

Wang shifted in his chair, his erection growing. Sapphire closed her eyes as she brought her fingers to her mouth and licked each one. Keeping his eyes on her, he finished his drink and stood, his breath coming faster. He unbuckled his belt, sliding it through the loops until free. Coiling it around his hand, he stepped closer, still watching her, his erection throbbing.

Her eyes opened to slits, she moved backward into the tent until she was next to the bed. He followed, stopping in front of her.

"Turn around," he commanded, his voice hoarse. "And take off my shirt."

Sapphire did as she was told, draping the expensive shirt over the end of the four-poster bed. Wang licked his lips, taking in the curtain of dark hair cascading down her back, hiding the ugly discoloration from their previous session, now yellow with a hint of black. He enjoyed looking at her small, firm buttocks and slender legs. The blood pulsed through his temples, the purported aphrodisiac qualities of the black rhino horn sweeping through his system. He felt invincible, convinced he could read minds, fuck for hours, and rule the world. His mind raced, unwilling to believe the sensations were due only to a placebo effect.

He *had* to figure out a way to acquire more rhinos.

"Fucking endangered list," he muttered.

"What did you say, my king?" Sapphire asked, turning her head at his words.

"Do not speak," he snapped, and dropped one end of his belt so that the heavy buckle dangled freely. Sapphire hunched her shoulders and ducked her head, growing quiet. Victor Wang drew his hand back and swung the buckle through the air so that it landed with a sickening thud against her lower back, clearing the other bruises by several inches.

Without saying a word, she grabbed the bedpost with both hands and squared her shoulders, bracing for more. Wang continued, raising angry red welts the length of her body, filling in where he'd left off the day before.

He reined himself in just shy of a complete beating and dropped the belt to the floor.

AN HOUR LATER, VICTOR WANG LEFT SAPPHIRE ON THE BED, passed out from the pain, and walked onto the front deck. Several men wearing sunglasses and holding AK-47s stood next to a group of late-model four-wheel-drive pickups. A broad-shouldered, powerfully built man wearing a beard and head scarf leaned against the fender of the front vehicle, grinning.

"You are like the animals your guests hunt, eh, Victor?" The man laughed and the rest of the men joined him. "I have never seen such a beast. You take what you want and act out your fantasies with the whore." He shook his head. "If I did not know any better, I would think you had been sampling the dark powder."

Victor Wang smiled, hiding his distaste for the militant and his men. "Welcome. Will you join me for a drink?" He held out his hand, indicating the chair next to his.

Assad Khouri, known to his men as Doctor Death, shrugged off his rifle and handed it to the man next to him before ascending the steps to take Wang's seat. He sniffed the empty glass on the table.

"I will have some of that," he said, waving his hand dismissively as he leaned back in the chair, his legs splayed in what could only be considered an insolent posture.

Wang walked over to a nearby bamboo cabinet to retrieve a lesser bottle of scotch and another glass. He returned to the table and poured a measure of whiskey for each of them.

"Only the finest for you," Wang said, smiling.

Doctor Death picked up the glass and sniffed. As Wang had anticipated, he downed the drink in one gulp.

Wang poured another for him, set the bottle on the table, and picked up his drink. Unwilling to spend more time with his guest than was absolutely necessary, Victor eschewed diplomacy and got down to business.

"Do you have what I requested?"

Assad threw back half of his scotch before replying. "Eighteen hundred kilos."

Wang gave him a sharp look. "I asked for twice that."

He shrugged. "You will get it. The drones are becoming a problem. We were lucky to find what we have."

"Where is it?" Wang asked, scanning the pickups. Transporting that much ivory in open pickup beds would arouse suspicion. The shipment required a larger, enclosed truck.

"The load is on its way to Dar. I don't feel comfortable having so much with me."

Heat rose in Wang's face. "We had a deal," he said, his voice flat.

Assad waved his concerns away. "It is much safer this way. Now, it is only two of my men who are at risk. And, when you call your people at the port, there will be no problem."

Victor Wang swallowed his anger and raised the glass to his lips. He took another sip and set it back on the table.

"That is not what we planned." The words exited his mouth like sparks from a welding torch.

Assad leveled his gaze at his business partner and smiled, reminding Wang of a snarling tiger.

"The plan needed to change. It was not safe." He raised his eyes skyward. "They have drones everywhere now. Even at night they can see you."

"My source tells me they have not yet reached this area." Wang struggled to reassure the paranoid militant. "The organizations who spearheaded the campaign are working on funding, but they haven't yet saturated our section of Africa with their foul machines. Besides," Wang swept his arm in front of him, "we are surrounded by many kilometers of wilderness here. I doubt you need to worry."

Assad slammed his glass on the table. Wang's drink danced, sloshing whiskey over the sides.

"You do NOT argue with me. It is done."

Wang took a deep breath to calm himself. "Then I have no choice but to withhold payment until your portion of the bargain is complete."

Assad's face split into a wicked grin, revealing two pronounced canines, one gold, the other gleaming white. A small diamond, embedded in the gold one, glinted in the sunlight. He lifted his hand and the men near the trucks raised their guns, aiming them at Wang.

"This is unacceptable," Doctor Death said.

Victor Wang assessed his situation, not at all happy with the probable outcome. He thought allowing Assad and his men to train nearby would give him an extra measure of protection, not extra headaches. He pulled a linen handkerchief from his pocket and dabbed at the perspiration on his forehead, giving his guest a placatory smile.

"Of course, we can renegotiate terms," he managed, his earlier belief in his indestructibility having now evaporated.

Assad leaned back and gestured to his men, who stood down.

"Good choice. Renegotiation includes receipt of all monies up front, with final delivery of the merchandise once evidence of drone activity is demonstrated to be nonexistent."

Wang refrained from rolling his eyes. "And how do you think I can manage that? The drones are deployed at several thousand feet. Far higher than I am able to monitor."

"You have friends. Use them."

"I do not have friends in these organizations. My 'friends,' as you refer to them, hold government positions and are not aware of our partnership."

"The drones must be cleared to fly, yes?"

"I suppose." Wang wondered where he was going with his line of questioning.

"Then, it should be easy," Assad said, spreading his hands wide. "Tell your friends that you need the information because you believe the drones are disturbing your precious animals. Demand to receive the information in writing, and then forward the response to me." He poured himself another drink and took a long swallow. "I will view this as evidence that you are right in your assumption there is no drone activity here. Then, and only then, will I fulfill our agreement with the rest of the ivory." He finished off the scotch and poured another.

Wang did the same, resigned to the onerous task of asking his contact in the Tanzanian government to forge a signed missive on letterhead stating the absence of drones over this part of the country. Actually requesting the letter would signal to the ruling party that there was possible poaching in his territory, thereby bringing unwanted attention. Wang tended to keep a low profile, at least with officials, bribing those that could be bought, and seeking favors only when absolutely necessary.

The little boy who had accompanied Sapphire in the shipment from Bangkok walked around the corner of the tent carrying a tray filled with sweets and savory bites. He hesitated at the bottom of the steps, waiting for permission. Victor motioned him forward and the child climbed the stairs, careful not to drop the tray. He set it on top of the table and took a step back, keeping his eyes downcast.

"Well, now, who have we here?" Assad said as he leaned forward and smiled, a calculating look on his face. He turned to Wang. "Where have you been hiding this one, eh?"

"He belongs to the whore," Wang said, nodding toward the tent. Jaidee peeked at Assad, his attention riveted to the gleaming diamond in his gold tooth. Assad laughed and motioned the boy closer.

"Do you want to see my diamond, boy?"

Jaidee nodded and stepped forward, peering into the man's mouth. After he'd gotten a good, long look, he backed away, consternation clear on his face.

"What's the matter, boy? Have you never seen a rich man's teeth before?" Assad's laughter exploded around them. He leaned toward Wang and said in a low voice, "Give me the boy, and I will reconsider my demand for full payment."

The curtain fluttered near the entrance to the tent, and Wang caught a glimpse of Sapphire standing in the shadows, her position concealed from the rest of the men. She shook her head, silently pleading with him to refuse.

"Take him," he said with a shrug. "I have no need of one so young."

Assad nodded and threw back his drink. He stood and walked over to Jaidee, who backed away, his eyes like saucers. Just before the terrorist reached the boy, Sapphire stepped through the curtain toward him. Jaidee cried out as Assad grabbed him and lifted him onto his shoulders.

"Stay where you are," Assad said, his voice dripping menace, "or you will be my men's entertainment for the evening."

Sapphire stilled, her face drained of color. Assad walked down the steps to a pickup and handed Jaidee off to one of his men before climbing into the front seat.

"We will meet again soon, my bruthah." Assad saluted Wang and the group roared off.

Sapphire rushed across the wooden deck and clutched Wang's arm. "You know what they do. He just a boy—" she pleaded, panic filling her voice.

Wang shrugged her off. His closed fist connected to her jaw with a resounding crack. Hand to her face, Sapphire careened backward and stumbled to the floor. She was on her feet in an instant, a grimace of pain on her face as though she expected more. Wang ignored her and picked up one of the sweets.

At least I'm not out the cash.

31

HERE THE HECK is my buddy Victor?" The tall, barrel-chested man with the florid complexion and booming voice scanned the camp in search of Wang.

Ghanima bowed low in front of the camp's new guests, as did the few trusted staff that joined her.

"Mistah Wang is come soon. He has been delayed."

"Well, then. My wife and I are gonna need a li'l somethin' to wet our whistles." The man grinned at the tan, Botoxed blonde with the big hair standing behind him. "Ain't that right, Bobbi Jo?"

"It sure is, Clarence. Come to think of it, I'm mighty parched."

Ghanima turned to the man guarding the couple's seven suitcases.

"You hear what the man say," she demanded.

The porter's eyes grew wide as Ghanima's expression told him she meant to throw him under the bus if he didn't deliver drinks to the couple, pronto.

"And make mine some of that Tasmanian scotch." Clarence drew out the word Tasmanian.

"I'll have an old fashioned," Bobbi Jo added.

"Go on, then. Get the man and his lady a drink." Ghanima rolled her eyes in frustration as the ersatz bellhop scurried to the kitchen to fetch them their drinks.

Kylie watched the little drama play out through a gap between the tent walls as she peeled potatoes and carrots in the kitchen. With the exception of the women Wang kidnapped in Bangkok, most of the other "employees" at the camp had been lured into service by the promise of better jobs in another country. Once they landed in Africa, the amount they owed increased by an insurmountable percentage, essentially enslaving them in a country with no money and no passport where they didn't understand the language. Either way, neither they nor Kylie had any hope of escape. The heavy chain around Kylie's ankles made sure of that.

On rare occasions she'd catch a glimpse of Sapphire, noticing several new bruises on her arms and legs. Obsessed with making contact, Kylie had been caught twice when she tried to slip past Lek in an attempt to see her. Luckily, she'd established a kind of rapport with him by slipping him scraps from the kitchen, and would only receive a warning. Ghanima had been too busy with new arrivals to the camp to be concerned with where Kylie was sleeping, and Lek had conveniently forgotten to chain her to the post.

The man acting as bellhop rushed into the kitchen, panic written on his face. Kylie continued peeling carrots, ignoring his discomfort. When he realized she was the only person in the kitchen other than the guard he let loose, speaking rapid-fire Thai, his hands gesticulating wildly.

She calmly put the carrot and the peeler down and remained silent as he ranted, waiting for him to realize she didn't understand. He ran out of steam soon enough, and Kylie slid off her chair and clanked to the pantry. Lek joined her and produced a key to open the door, revealing a fully stocked liquor cabinet.

The bellhop audibly sighed as Kylie brought out a bottle of the Tasmanian scotch, bourbon, sugar, and a small bottle of bitters. She found two highball glasses and poured the scotch, then mixed the old fashioned, adding a twist of lemon. Then she handed them both to the bellhop. The relief on his face as he took the glasses was palpable, and he gave her a grateful smile. Kylie replaced the bottles and Lek locked the cabinet.

"What you doing?" Ghanima's voice serrated the air. Lek stiffened. Kylie winced and slowly pivoted to face her enemy. Ghanima's eyes blazed with hatred as she advanced on Kylie. Lek stepped forward in an obvious attempt to shield her.

Ghanima looked incredulously from one to the other, hands balled into fists. Her ample chest rose and fell with each labored breath. Kylie tensed for whatever would come next.

"You," she hissed. "Nothing but trouble." She glanced at the half-peeled carrots and potatoes, and flicked her hand as though she was shooing a fly. "This girl don't finish. Look." She jammed her hands on her hips and shook her head, working herself into a state. Her withering glare moved to Lek, who had edged away at her advance.

"And *you*," she said, the words dropping like lead weights between them, "know better. Mistah Wang will *not* be happy." She then seized Kylie by the back of the neck and shoved her forward. Kylie stumbled but remained upright, struggling to take small steps so she wouldn't trip over the chain around her ankles.

"All I did was make drinks for Mister Wang's guests," Kylie protested.

Ghanima cuffed the side of her head. "This girl don't talk.

Ghanima make drinks. *Not* this stupid, clumsy girl." With that, she gave Kylie a vicious shove. Kylie lost her balance and fell to her hands and knees, palms skidding across the sharp rocks.

"Get up!" Ghanima said, the whites of her bulging eyes visible.

Kylie stayed on her knees as she picked out the rocks embedded in her palms before scooting her feet into position to stand.

"You take too long," Ghanima screamed, wiping the spittle from her mouth with the back of her hand.

Kylie turned in time to see the larger woman lunge at her, an eight-inch chef's knife clutched in her hand. Kylie rolled left, lifting her hands to protect her head. Lek sprang forward and grabbed Ghanima by the arms, careful to keep himself from becoming a casualty. Ghanima struggled like an enraged bear against his grip, a stream of what could only be construed as obscenities in Swahili exploding from her mouth. Kylie scrambled to her feet and backed away from the crazy bitch, unsure what to do.

"*Go,*" Lek yelled as he fought to restrain Ghanima.

Kylie spun in place and hobbled from the kitchen.

"WELL NOW, HOW'S MY OLD HUNTING PARTNER?"

Victor Wang, Clarence, and Bobbi Jo had just finished a sumptuous dinner of ostrich and crocodile and had retired to Wang's personal compound for drinks and cigars. They were sitting around a large bonfire in front of the main tent, enjoying the mild evening.

After several glasses of scotch, Clarence's complexion had grown even more florid than when he first arrived. Wang had poured drinks from what appeared to be the prized Tasmanian stock but was actually a lesser brand decanted into the esteemed bottle. He wondered whether his servant had filled the latest one he'd finished. He hoped so. His American friend didn't understand the meaning of the word moderation.

"Business is slow, as you can see." Victor shrugged. It pleased Clarence to think Victor was down to his last shilling and that the American's largesse would help to save his Asian buddy from bankruptcy, so Wang played along.

Which was where his friendship with Clarence and Bobbi Jo Schneider came in. His latest shipment from Bangkok boasted several Asian tigers, one of them a prized white with blue eyes. The Schneiders would pay anything to have a white tiger at their game farm in the States.

Clarence took another long pull on his drink before he leaned forward and slapped his old pal on the back. "Well shit, Victor, then this is your lucky day!"

"And why is that?" Victor asked, a polite smile on his face. Although he could tolerate the Schneider's company when they were sober, when drunk they left much to be desired. Even so, Bobbi Jo boasted that since she came from good Irish stock, she was able to handle even more alcohol than Clarence's pansy-assed German relatives.

Wang shuddered at the memory of Bobbi Jo ambushing him during their annual hunting trip two years before and demanding to know what it was like to ride a "real Oriental." Needless to say, Victor politely refused and found a much younger and more suitable partner for his inebriated guest. The next morning, she was her usual, commanding self and no more was said. He was never sure if she'd forgotten or just ignored what had transpired. Her husband tended to be an easy fix. Just give him anything with long, black hair, almond-shaped eyes, and a pussy, and he was happy.

As long as Bobbi Jo never found out. The woman had a jealous streak a mile wide.

Bobbi Jo uncrossed her legs and leaned forward in her chair, her latest enhancements threatening to pop out of her shirt.

"I'm so *bored,* honey," she said, the faintest of slurs encroaching on her delivery.

Victor looked from Clarence to Bobbi Jo, wondering what the hell her boredom had to do with him, when Bobbi Jo put a hand on Victor's arm and scooted her chair closer.

Oh, no. Perspiration sprang forth from Victor Wang's forehead at the thought of another amorous attempt from the buxom bottle blond. He tried to swallow, his throat suddenly dry.

"But how can you be bored?" he asked, looking to Clarence for assistance. His friend's attention had shifted to one of the more lithesome staff bending over in front of him to stoke the fire, so he was no help whatsoever. "You travel the globe. You live an enviable lifestyle. Whatever you desire is yours."

Bobbi Jo slumped back in her chair, pouting. "That's the problem, Victor, honey. I've already *done* it all, seen it all. There ain't nothin' left."

Victor Wang took a deep breath. He would need to tread carefully. The drinks from his earlier meeting with Doctor Death hadn't completely worn off, and he'd supplemented with several more that evening, so he wasn't exactly sober, either.

"But haven't the hunts I've arranged for you been thrilling? What about the time you took down the black rhino? You insisted on standing your ground as he charged." Wang slowly shook his head. "I must tell you, I thought you would die."

Bobbi Jo rolled her eyes. "Stop being so dramatic, Victor. I'm bored to death hunting game from a helicopter, even if I am on the ground when it's time for the kill." She sighed, a pained look in her blowsy, bloodshot eyes. "Clarence and I have been discussing our annual decision to spend such a large portion of our time and money here, and unless you can come up with something we've never done before, we've decided we're just going to have to take our business elsewhere. I'm sure y'all understand."

At that moment, Victor would've paid good money to see Bobbi Jo Schneider obliterated by the tusks of a raging bull elephant. For years Wang had gone to great lengths to find the perfect hunt for both of the spoiled Americans, always succeeding beyond their expectations. Yes, their lavish spending contributed significantly to the camp's bottom line, and no, he couldn't afford to anger them considering the amount of money they spent on live animals for their farm, but keeping them happy had fast become more trouble than it was worth.

This year, Victor Wang had more on his mind than entertaining a couple of good ol' white folks whose most pressing problem was how much money to contribute to which politician in order to curry the most favors. He doubted either one would last long in the bush with only a rifle and a canteen of water, especially with Assad and his gunmen running loose. An imperceptible smile tugged at the corners of his mouth at the thought of the two out-of-shape Americans scrabbling up a baobab tree to avoid being flattened by a charging rhino, or the look on their faces right before one of the militants took aim.

Clarence put his hand on his wife's arm. "Now, Bobbi Jo, don't y'all think that's a little harsh?" He turned to Victor, an earnest look on his face. "I think what my lovely wife means to say is, although we've appreciated your generosity through the years and will continue to source some of our animals through your company, we've come to the point in our lives that your camp jus' ain't enough. Know what I mean?"

"Of course." Wang nodded his assent. Just then, the front curtain of the tent billowed slightly, offering the glimpse of

Sapphire's outline as she ghosted through the dark interior. Clarence, who was facing the same direction, noticed too, and visibly perked up.

A niggling idea began to form in Wang's mind and grew—an idea that could conceivably eliminate two irritations at once, while keeping intact his business agreement with Clarence. He sipped his drink, wondering why he hadn't thought of it before.

"In light of your need for even more adventure," Wang continued, "I have an idea that might be of interest to you, but will need some time to formulate the execution." He placed his drink on the table and smiled at Bobbi Jo. "I think you'll be pleased."

32

ASHID ARRIVED BACK at Rafiki late that evening after delivering the news of Hugh's murder to his wife. Once he'd found her another place to stay, he contacted the rest of the balloon company's small staff to warn them not to speak to anyone asking questions about either Hugh or the company. He'd then destroyed the few personnel files that existed in case the gunmen came to do some digging to find out who they might have missed. It had been a stroke of luck for all involved that Hugh kept terrible records, preferring to pay his employees under the table.

Derek and Leine were waiting for him outside of the compound. They stored their weapons in the backseat of the pickup and joined Rashid.

"You know this is going to be a long shot, right?" Derek asked, handing him a pair of night vision goggles. "They've probably already moved the balloon and gotten rid of Hugh's body."

Rashid nodded.

"All right then," he said, leaning back in his seat. "When we get within a couple of kilometers, put the NVGs on and turn off the lights so they don't see us coming. At one kilometer, we'll get out and walk."

The dirt road fell away beneath the truck's headlights. Wang wouldn't want evidence of a murder committed near his camp, and he sure as hell wouldn't want to be involved in anything that scared off tourists. Leine wasn't sure why he sent his men to gun down an errant hot air balloon, and had expressed her concerns to Derek, who agreed. They'd both come to the conclusion that the gunmen were probably not on Wang's payroll at all. A sobering thought, considering he was a formidable enough adversary. That, coupled with Zara's disappearance, convinced both Leine and Derek they were dealing with someone other than Wang's thugs.

About three kilometers out, Rashid slowed the truck and slid on the NVGs. He cut the lights and crept along the dirt road, a death grip on the steering wheel. Leine scanned the terrain with binoculars. She spotted several pairs of glowing eyes staring back at her from the bush but confirmed they belonged to a pack of hyenas.

A short while later, Rashid stopped the pickup and turned off the engine. The three of them exited the vehicle.

The African night chorus was in full symphonic resonance as they crept along the dirt road, a robust soundtrack of birds and insects, replete with an elephant trumpeting in the distance and the high-pitched song of a cheetah. As they approached the flat expanse where Hugh had landed the balloon, a low growl brought them up short and the three of them froze. Perspiration slid down the side of Leine's face. The weight of the .45 Alma had given her wasn't reassuring.

The growl came again, this time directly behind them, and Leine reached for her gun.

"Don't move," Derek whispered. Leine stilled.

The breeze rustled the grass, fluttering her hair. They were downwind. Leine wondered if the animal was close. Her breathing shallow, she blinked the sweat from her eyes, hoping this wasn't the end, the big dirt nap, her last hurrah. Too many things she wanted to do. Being ripped to shreds by a lion or leopard didn't seem like the best way to go. No, lying in bed with Santa, arms and legs entwined after some amazing sex and a great meal would be more her style.

How her life had changed.

Several moments passed before Derek slowly turned.

"It's gone," he said, and Leine and Rashid both exhaled.

Leine checked at the weakness in her knees and shook it off.

"Are you sure?" Rashid asked, his voice an octave higher than normal.

"Yeh. That was a close one." Derek shrugged. "Must not have liked the way we smelled."

They resumed walking, the three of them hyper attentive to their surroundings. They approached the area where Hugh had landed the balloon, but both the basket and the balloon were gone, a patch of flattened grass the only evidence anything had been there. Rashid refused to accept that his mentor and friend had been taken and continued to hunt for his body.

A short while later Derek muttered, "He's had enough time. We need to go."

"Let's give him a little longer," Leine said. "If we stop him now, he might not be satisfied and may try to come back."

"All right. But no more than a few minutes, *ja*? I don't want to be here if those gunmen decide to come back."

"Agreed."

They didn't have long to wait. Less than five minutes later Rashid stopped in the middle of the clearing. His shoulders slumped forward as he slipped off the NVGs and hung his head. Leine waited a few beats and then walked over to him.

"Hey," she said gently. "We need to go. I'm sorry he wasn't here."

Tears glistened on Rashid's cheeks. He nodded and wiped his face with the back of his hand. "I will miss him very much."

They turned and walked back to the pickup. Rashid slid on the NVGs and climbed into the driver's seat.

"You remember where you're going to meet us, yeh?" Derek asked.

Rashid nodded. "Yes. I will be there."

"Good," he said, and checked his watch. "See you in a couple of hours."

Leine and Derek set off at a brisk pace toward Wang's camp, slowing when they came to the perimeter. Derek handed Leine a radio, keeping one for himself. She keyed the mic and lowered the volume, then slipped it into her pocket.

"Meet you on the other side," she murmured and set off in the opposite direction.

There wasn't much activity in the central meeting area; the last embers of a campfire glowed red in a metal ring. Leine checked her watch: 02:35. That gave them plenty of time for reconnaissance. She doubted many staff would be up before dawn.

A man wearing fatigues and carrying a rifle walked past, and Leine melted into the shadows. The uniform and weapon didn't match the ones from before, giving her more proof that it hadn't been Wang's people that shot and killed Hugh. Alma had said something about the militants who'd taken Zara being outfitted with new vehicles and weapons, something most armies in the area would be hard pressed to do.

She supposed Wang could be funding them, but being a party to murdering Hugh still didn't feel right, didn't seem like something Wang would risk. Why put his camp and everything he'd worked for in danger by offing a local whose main business was taking tourists for balloon rides?

Leine made her way past the main section of the compound and what appeared to be guest tents, following along the perimeter to the group of brightly colored tents she'd seen from the air.

Her best bet for finding Wang.

33

KYLIE SAT WITH her back against the wooden pillar and picked at the chain, trying to remain calm by whispering song lyrics. She listened for Zara, her spirits lifting every time she thought she heard something. She forgot to be frightened when she was around. Besides, she'd know what to do in case a wild animal got curious.

After the attack in the kitchen, Ghanima had threatened to report Lek if he didn't do exactly as she said, which included her order to stake Kylie outside at night like a dog. He'd acted mean when he secured her to the post and ignored her pleas for help, but she could tell he felt bad. No amount of bribery would change his mind. Lek's fear of Ghanima trumped his desire for anything Kylie could get him from the kitchen.

A deep snort erupted somewhere nearby and Kylie tensed, squinting into the darkness. She wondered if what people said was true—that animals could smell fear. If so, then she was as good as dead.

Unable to see anything, she hugged her legs, attempting to make herself look as small as possible. The scene from one of her mother's favorite movies, *Jurassic Park*, popped into her mind. It was the one with the bleating, sacrificial goat tied to a stake as a tasty snack for the giant *T. rex*. Only this time the sick feeling in her stomach was real, not something conjured up by script-writers in Hollywood.

She didn't like being the goat.

Heavy footsteps echoed in the darkness. She didn't hear the telltale clank of Zara's ankle chains. Who would come to see her at this hour? A bulky form drew closer, materializing at the gate like a specter. Her breath caught in her throat.

Ghanima.

Kylie's heart fluttered in her chest, and she hugged her knees tighter. The older woman unlocked the gate and clomped toward her, wearing a wide grin and carrying a package wrapped in newspaper. She stopped a few feet inside the enclosure and placed the package on the ground.

"Ghanima bring this girl something special," she said. She bent down and unwrapped the mysterious bundle, revealing a glistening, dark mass about the size of a turkey platter. Then she stepped away. "The smell of blood should bring them soon."

"What is it?" Kylie said, panic rising in her throat.

Ghanima laughed and walked back to the gate.

"Ghanima save the insides of the buffalo Mistah Wang butchered for last week's meal. The intestines and heart, and many bones. I think to myself, now, where can Ghanima take this so it not go to waste?" She cocked her head to the side. "You know what I tell myself? Huh?" She waited for Kylie to answer, but when she didn't she continued as though talking about the weather. "I tell myself, why, Ghanima, you should offer the buffalo's insides to Simba. That way, my family stay safe."

Ghanima flashed Kylie a winning smile and walked out of the enclosure. She replaced the padlock and, whistling, headed down the path back to camp.

Kylie climbed to her feet and shuffle-ran to the buffalo

entrails, but the chain stopped her short. She tried yanking on it, hoping it would somehow magically lengthen. It didn't. She dropped to her belly and stretched toward it, but her arms weren't long enough. Her stomach heaved at the rank smell of rotten meat.

She looked around the enclosure for something to throw at the package to push it farther away, but she'd already checked when she'd been there last and found nothing. Tears of frustration coursed down her cheeks as fear clouded her mind. She rolled onto her back and sat up.

"Get as far away from it as you can," she told herself. Hearing her own voice helped, and she continued the one-sided dialogue. "Don't freak out." She got up and shuffled to the other side of the enclosure, muttering to herself and putting as much distance between her and the bloody pile as possible. Without the imaginary safety of the post at her back, Kylie felt even more exposed. The night sounds grew louder, and she clapped her hands over her ears, trying to drown them out. Her teeth chattering, she jumped at every snort, every grunt, every breeze.

"Come on, Kylie. Get a grip. You're going to be fine. Zara says there's plenty of food for the animals this time of year." Kylie kept up the self-talk until she was hoarse and had to stop. The irritating laughter of a hyena serrated the air, the squeaks and yips telling her there was more than one. Did they hunt in packs like dogs? What if the package of organs wasn't enough?

Something moved to her left and she pivoted, saw nothing but dark. Her fingers closed around the knife Zara had given her. She wished it was bigger.

There. Another ghostly shape appeared, and then disappeared, followed by yipping and more hyena laughter. Kylie tried to take a step, but her legs didn't respond. Three more shapes materialized, growing bolder, edging closer to the fence. Glowing eyes stared at her through the wire, the hyena's silhouette visible. It lowered its head and dug at the bottom of the fence, whining.

More joined in, milling around the leader. Several stuck their noses through, looking for a way inside. Kylie watched in dread as first one and then another leapt up and over the fence into the enclosure, easily clearing the barrier. The ones remaining on the outside paced the fence, whining and yipping while the few who'd made it in tore at the bloody package on the ground and growled.

Kylie gripped her knees together to keep from shaking as the hyenas fought over the scraps. She was afraid to move for fear she'd gain their attention. One of the biggest dragged what looked like intestines across the enclosure. Two others followed.

"Kylie."

Startled by the quiet voice, she turned. Zara stood near the back fence, eyes riveted to hers.

"Don't make any sudden movements. I don't think they will attack you since there is food, but you don't want to attract their attention."

Relief flowed through Kylie and her knees grew weak. She took a deep breath and steadied herself.

"Do you have the knife I gave you?"

Kylie nodded.

"Good. You can at least wound them if one attacks."

"I'm scared, Zara," Kylie said, her voice trembling.

"I know you are, Kylie, but you're going to be fine. I'm going to leave for a few minutes. Don't worry, I will come back to help you," Zara said, and disappeared.

A crunching sound, like someone eating popcorn, accompanied the yips and growls of the hyenas as their powerful jaws cracked through the bones. Heart thudding, Kylie searched the darkness for her friend, willing her to reappear. An agony of minutes later, she did.

"Here," she said, and tossed a large rock toward her. "Make a pile."

Kylie caught the stone with both hands and set it near her feet. Zara watched the hyenas feed, waiting until their attention was elsewhere before she lobbed another one to her. It landed nearby with a thud. One of the hyenas lifted its head at the sound and Kylie froze. A few seconds later, it resumed eating and she let out a sigh.

In all, Zara tossed a dozen rocks into the enclosure, which Kylie piled at her feet. Zara gathered several more, keeping them nearby should any of the hyenas decide to attack after their dinner.

The one that had lifted its head at the sound of the rock hitting the ground did so again. This time it slouched toward Kylie with a *whoop*, licking its chops.

"Grab a rock and wait until I tell you. Then throw it as hard as you can," Zara instructed. "I'll do the same from here. It won't know what hit it."

Kylie picked up the biggest rock at her feet and waited. The hyena inched closer, sniffing at the air and vocalizing. Another hyena lifted its head to see what was going on, but ignored them and went back to the feast.

The hyena edged closer to Kylie—now only a few feet away. Its powerful shoulders and sloping back reminded her of a werewolf she'd seen in a movie. Slick with sweat, Kylie's hand shook, and she almost lost her grip on the rock.

"Wait," Zara urged.

Kylie took a deep breath and let it go, her heart thundering in her ears.

Increasingly bold, the hyena inched closer, faking a move to the right, watching her. It sniffed the air and whined.

"Now," Zara yelled, and both women screamed as they hurled their rocks, striking the lone hyena on the skull.

Surprised, the hyena yelped and danced away, shaking its head. Kylie grabbed another rock and heaved it at the stunned animal, this time hitting its flank.

It yipped and ran back to the others who were finishing their meal. The other three scattered and milled around, confused.

"Get out of here!" Kylie shouted, sending another rock sailing at the group. Zara followed up with two more. One fell short, but the others glanced off two of them, hitting one on the nose. It bared its teeth but backed into the enclosure. With nowhere to go but up, it leapt over the fence and disappeared into the bush.

The two women kept yelling and throwing rocks, some hitting, some falling short, but it was effective. With no more food to be had, the other three hyenas followed the last one over the fence and disappeared.

"They're gone, now. It's okay."

Zara's voice washed over Kylie. She dropped the rock still clutched in her hand to the ground.

"Thank you for—" She stopped short, her voice catching in her throat. "I don't know what I would have done if you weren't here."

Zara followed along the fence line until she reached the gate, the chains between her ankles marking her progress by their sound. She stared at the bloody newspaper. "Who left this here?" she demanded, her voice rising.

"Ghanima. Who else?" Kylie answered, crossing the enclosure. "Earlier, she pulled a knife on me when I dared to make drinks for the new guests."

"My god. She's trying to kill you."

"You think?" Kylie shot back. She hated how afraid she felt, how her knees shook with fear every time she saw her. Hated Ghanima's power over her. But what could she do? Kylie wasn't good at revenge. She preferred to let Karma take care of things.

That wasn't working too well.

"We've got to get you out of here." Zara tugged on the padlock and let it fall. "Who has the key?" she asked.

"Lek did, but Ghanima probably took it from him. And what would I do once I got out of here?" Kylie shook her head, despair landing heavy in her chest. "It's not like I have somewhere to go. I can't just call a taxi, you know?"

"You're right." Zara grew quiet. "I almost forgot why I came tonight. I saw your friend, Sapphire. Wang let her visit the cubs, but the little boy—Jaidee, right?—wasn't with her. When I asked where he was, she told me that Wang sold him to a gunman named Assad." She shivered and crossed her arms.

"That can't be good. Jesus. He's just a kid." Kylie's adrenaline surge from fighting off the hyenas plummeted, leaving her drained.

"She couldn't tell me much more. Wang wasn't with her, but she had two guards. She looked pretty beat up."

Kylie winced at the expression on Zara's face. Her stomach churned at the thought of Wang using Sapphire as a punching bag. "So, what, this Assad is going to use Jaidee as a servant? He's six, *maybe* seven, Zara." She paused. "You know something, don't you?"

Zara bit her lower lip. "It's the same man who kidnapped me." She stared into the darkness. "You have heard of boy soldiers?"

Kylie nodded.

"He will teach Jaidee how to be a soldier and convince him to join his cause, whatever it is. Eventually he will learn to kill."

Kylie unclenched her fists and leaned against the post. She slid to the ground, any fight she had now gone.

"That's it, then. We're all going to die."

Wang would probably beat Sapphire to death, and Jaidee would have a short, violent life as a child soldier. Ghanima would eventually succeed in getting rid of Kylie, and, unless Zara was able to breed more lions and tigers for Wang, he'd tire of her, too.

The idea of Jaidee being trained as a murderous soldier depressed Kylie the most. Her brother had died of violence in his own city, near his family. Jaidee would die of violence in a strange country, away from family. How lost and alone he must feel, thousands of miles from his home. At least Brandon had been surrounded by people who loved him when he died.

"Don't think like that, Kylie. There was a reason that we were able to fight off the hyenas tonight. You must have hope."

Kylie smiled at the earnestness in Zara's eyes. Hope. Something that had been in short supply since Brandon was killed.

"I don't believe in hope."

34

Victor Wang approached his tent quietly. Loud, guttural snores emanated from the interior. He mounted the steps and tiptoed across the deck. With a look over his shoulder, he slipped inside.

Naked, with the sheets twisted between his legs, Clarence Schneider lay passed out next to Sapphire, who also appeared to be asleep. The bed was surrounded by gauzy mosquito netting, giving the scene a pseudo-romantic feel. Lamps glowed in the corner of the room, bathing them both in amber light. An empty bottle of scotch lay on its side on the floor.

Perfect.

Victor Wang left them and made his way to the Schneider's tent. A half bottle of bourbon and an empty glass rested on the nightstand next to the king-sized bed. Wang pulled back the netting as Bobbi Jo snorted and turned onto her side. Spittle dribbled from the corner of her open mouth and down her chin, hovering just above the pillowcase. He stilled, listening for the sound of footsteps telling him Clarence was trying to sneak back into bed with his wife.

Hearing only the chirruping of crickets, Victor leaned over

and shook Bobbi Jo. She didn't respond. He tried again and this time was met with a sleepy grunt. Victor scanned the room. His gaze fell on a thick, leather bound book lying on top of the bookcase. He retrieved it and returned to the bed. Raising it high above his head with both hands, he slammed the book on the floor.

Bobbi Jo bolted upright.

"Wha—what's happening?" she croaked, blinking. Wang sat on the edge of the bed.

"You must come with me, Bobbi Jo," he whispered, being sure to put some urgency into his tone. "Your husband—" He stopped and lowered his gaze, waiting for her reaction.

"Clarence?" She glanced at the empty space beside her. "Is he all right?" she asked, alarm creeping into her voice.

"He is, but—" Wang bowed his head, working to appear ashamed. "I thought you would want to know..." He let his words trail off.

Bobbi Jo pressed her lips together, her eyebrows struggling to frown. "Want to know *what*?" The last word exited her like the crack of a whip. She threw the sheets off and clambered to her feet.

Wang jumped up, handing her a robe. She tore it from him, shrugged it on, and knotted the belt. "Where is he?" she asked, her voice dangerously low.

"You do not deserve to be treated this way, Bobbi Jo. You must know the truth. I'm so sorry." Victor Wang lowered his gaze again. "He is in my quarters."

Bobbi Jo pushed him aside as she charged onto the deck and down the steps, headed for Victor's tent. Wang slipped his phone out of his pocket and followed after her. The screen glowed as he recorded.

"Oh, my God—who the hell are *you*?" Bobbi Jo's angry voice exploded inside the structure. "Get away from him, you fucking bitch!" she screamed. There was a loud slap, followed by a string of expletives. Bobbi Jo stormed out of the tent, dragging Sapphire by the hair.

"Let go!" Sapphire yelled, clawing at the older woman's hand. Clarence stumbled from the tent, a sheet bunched around his torso.

"Now, Bobbi Jo, darlin', there just ain't no need for you to treat this li'l girl that way. No need at all." He reached for her hand but stopped short at the look on her face and began to slowly back away. "Now honey buns, don't you look at me like that. I can explain things, see—"

"Oh, I think I've seen all I need to, Clarence, *darlin'*." Bobbi Jo gave Sapphire a vicious shake and let her fall to the deck, then kicked her in the ribs. Sapphire grabbed her side and doubled over, wheezing. She climbed to her knees and scrambled to the corner, drawing her legs up for protection while Bobbi Jo, seething with anger, advanced on Clarence. Wang stopped filming and slipped the camera into his front pocket.

"I guess I ain't enough for you anymore, huh?" The blonde drew herself up to her full height and thrust out her chin, getting in Clarence's face. "And now I suppose my mama's money ain't enough, either."

"No, now sweetness, you know that ain't right," Clarence pleaded. "I had a moment of weakness, that's all. Why, this vixen came to *me*, not the other way around." He pointed an accusing finger at Sapphire huddled in the corner, and shook his head. "If it wasn't for her comin' on to me, slidin' her naked body all over me and makin' me lose my mind, well, I'd a still been yours truly." He cupped her face in his large paw and dipped his head, looking in Bobbi Jo's eyes. "You got to believe me, baby cakes," he finished, his voice a soft caress.

Bobbi Jo glared at Clarence, her chest heaving. He continued to make soothing sounds and touch her gently until her shoulders dropped and she melted against him. He returned the hug and glared over her shoulder at Wang, waving him away. Stifling a smile, Wang nodded and yanked Sapphire to her feet.

"We must leave, now," he said through clenched teeth.

"But what about the collar?" she asked, tears rimming her eyes.

With an impatient sigh, Wang took out his phone and tapped the screen.

"There. Now come." He seized her arm and dragged her down the steps, headed for the main camp. Bobbi Jo and Clarence disappeared into Wang's tent.

Wang would have everything cleaned once they were done. If all went according to plan, the result would be worth far more to him than the price of a new bed.

FROM THE SHADOWS, LEINE WATCHED VICTOR WANG DRAG THE girl toward camp. He wasn't supposed to be there. Hadn't Derek said Wang preferred Bangkok? They'd need to rethink their plan to pose as guests.

She slipped past the larger tent into which the American couple had disappeared, and followed the other two at a safe distance.

"Wang's headed into camp from the north," she said into the radio, her voice low. "Where are you?"

"East of camp, near a group of three huts. Meet me here," Derek answered, his voice terse. Leine keyed the mic.

Wang paused at a small structure, unlocked the door and shoved the young woman inside. He made sure the door was secure, and continued into camp. Keeping to the shadows Leine followed him, noting the hut's location. He disappeared into one of the smaller tents surrounding the main courtyard. Leine waited to see if he reappeared. The light that had been on inside the tent went out. She gave it a few more minutes before she worked her way east, avoiding two guards before finding Derek.

"Wang's here?" Derek whispered. Leine nodded. "Then we can't pose as fucking tourists, can we?"

"On to Plan B," Leine whispered back.

"I think he's keeping the women here," he said, nodding toward the three roughly built structures.

Leine stepped next to the back wall of one and listened. Soft snoring emanated from the interior.

"There's a smaller one just like this back the way I came. Wang locked a young woman inside. It looked like she was wearing a radio collar."

Derek nodded, keeping an eye on the path next to the huts. "Seen enough?"

"Yes. Have you checked the area east of here?"

"Not yet."

"Let's finish up. We can still get to the truck if we head that way," she said.

A dozen yards past the huts, they came to a large enclosed area. Made of wood backed with reinforced metal, the fence stood at least twelve feet high.

"That's robust," Derek commented, scanning the enclosure.

"I wonder what's locked up in there?"

"Can't hurt to look."

They followed the structure until they came to a padlocked gate. Leine peered through the bars.

"Some kind of arena." She moved closer so she could see more of the darkened space. "There are several stalls at the other end."

"Probably where the fucker keeps the animals he says he's going to save."

Leine was about to reply when she caught movement in her periphery. "Wait a second," she murmured. "Someone's there."

A dark silhouette moved across the empty arena. The figure turned for a moment, and Leine caught a glimpse of a face.

"It's a woman." Leine stepped aside so Derek could have a look.

"Christ," he said, his hands gripping the bars. "It's Zara."

"Are you sure?"

Derek nodded and snapped his fingers. The woman turned at the noise and started toward them. Leine scanned the area behind them to make sure none of the guards were nearby.

When Zara was close enough to see who it was, she gasped. "Derek? What are you doing here?" She covered his hands with her own, tears shining in her eyes, and bent to kiss his knuckles. Derek dipped his head and kissed her through the gate. She pulled away.

"You have to leave. It's too dangerous."

"What are you doing here?" Derek asked.

"Assad sold me to Wang, along with the cubs from Rafiki." She glanced behind her, as if expecting to see Victor Wang or one of his gunmen. "He says he wants to rehabilitate the babies, but it's obvious he doesn't care. He's trying to breed them, even though they're too young." For the first time she acknowledged Leine. "Who are you?"

"This is Claire." Derek stepped back, scanning the gate. "We've got to get you out."

"I'm looking for some people—mainly women—who arrived here a few days ago from Bangkok," Leine said. "One of Wang's shipments. Have you seen anyone new?"

Zara nodded. "Yes, there have been several new people in the last few weeks, both men and women. The most recent shipment was a few days ago, as you said. But I think only a few were from Thailand."

"It's possible most of them come from western countries. I'm looking for one in particular."

"We need to get her out of here, Claire. You can talk all you want when we're safely away," Derek insisted. Zara's eyes widened and she shook her head.

"It's too dangerous. Victor's guards patrol the grounds with automatic weapons."

"We can't yet, Derek," Leine said, catching his gaze.

"The hell we can't." Derek reached for his gun, but Leine wrenched it from his hand before he had a chance to aim. He grabbed for it, but she pushed back. A second later he had a knife in his hand, the blade glinting in the moonlight.

"Give me my gun," he said, grinding out the words.

"What are you going to do?" Leine said, aiming the gun at Derek. "Shoot the lock? Then what? Do you even have a plan for when all those guards she was talking about come running?" She shook her head. "And what about the others? What happens when they realize someone broke in and rescued Zara? I guarantee this place will go into lockdown so fast a fucking beetle couldn't get past the front entrance."

"She's right, Derek."

He glared at Leine, who glared right back. After a few moments he nodded, took a deep breath, and put the knife away. "Claire's looking for someone named Kylie—"

"Nelson," Leine said.

"I don't know her last name, but there is a woman named Kylie here," Zara said.

Leine's heart rate picked up. "Where is she?"

Zara leaned closer to the bars. "At night, they stake her out in a pen like a dog. I think they're trying to kill her. One of Wang's kitchen staff left raw meat inside the enclosure. I helped her fight off a pack of hyenas earlier tonight. I don't know if I can be there when it happens again."

"You're allowed to go free?" Leine asked.

"Wang lets me out at night to walk around camp. He thinks the special treatment keeps me happy so that I'll continue to work with the babies. I don't tell him otherwise. Although," she looked down at her feet. "I have to wear leg irons. Kylie has them on all the time."

"Tell me more about Kylie. What does she look like?" Leine asked.

"Shoulder-length brown hair, kind of wavy. I think she's about nineteen. She said she was from Arizona."

Leine retrieved Kylie's photograph from her pocket and held it up. "Is this her?"

Zara glanced at the picture. "Yes."

"Tell me where the enclosure is," Leine said, sliding the picture back into her pocket. "I promise, when we come for Kylie, we'll come for you."

"What time do you usually go for your walk?" Leine asked after Zara described the pen's location.

"I don't have access to a clock, but the guard comes to get me around moonrise."

Leine looked at Derek.

"Eleven o'clock, give or take," he replied.

"Can you keep Kylie company tonight?"

Zara nodded, hope lighting her eyes. "I was planning to, anyway." She touched Leine's arm. "Please, don't wait too long. I don't think Kylie can survive many more nights out there."

"We'll do our best, Zara." Leine turned to leave.

Derek held out his hand.

"My gun."

Leine gave him a look. "Do we have a deal?"

Derek nodded.

She pulled the .45 free and handed it to him, and then walked away, giving them both a moment alone.

"Where'd you learn that move?" Derek asked when he caught up with her.

"You mean when I took your gun away?"

"Yeh."

Leine sighed. "Long story. It comes in handy."

"I'll bet."

Leine led the way to the location Zara described. By the time they reached the enclosure, a guard stood next to Kylie in the pen. Leine and Derek remained hidden and watched. The guard unlocked the chains attached to the center pole and led her out of the fenced area, back toward camp. The chain clanked as she walked. Her clothes were torn and dirty and she looked exhausted, but otherwise appeared in good physical shape. Pieces of torn, bloody paper lay strewn across the pen.

Leine checked her watch and glanced at the sky. The stars had just begun to fade. There wasn't much time before sunrise.

"What's our Plan B?" Derek asked. "Obviously, acting as guests won't work, as long as Wang's here. How do we get both of them out and not alert the guards?"

"I have an idea. But we need to get back to the Rover, asap."

35

VICTOR AND BOBBI Jo set out in Wang's safari vehicle before dawn, towing an enclosed trailer. The sky had turned a deep indigo, signaling the approaching sunrise. He'd woken the American heiress a short time earlier with the lure of a hunting expedition designed especially for her, ostensibly to get back in her good graces. Intrigued, and still livid about her husband's infidelity, she rose without waking Clarence and joined him.

Wang made sure to equip the vehicle with champagne and orange juice as well as a bottle of premixed cocktails in order to help lighten her mood. She sampled two mimosas and enjoyed a Bloody Mary before curtailing herself, citing the need to remain sharp for the hunt. Noticing the trailer, she asked if they were going to hunt on horseback. Victor Wang told her no.

They drove several kilometers down a deeply rutted road, finally stopping near a huge, flat-topped acacia. Bobbi Jo had asked him to stop when they passed a group of giraffes, expressing the desire to "bring one down to watch it fall," but Wang dissuaded her, reminding her that he'd set up the morning's hunt specifically for her.

The two exited the vehicle and gathered together the equipment Bobbi Jo would need.

"May I?" Wang asked, holding his phone up. Bobbi Jo smiled.

"Hell, yes you can video me. This hunt you dreamed up is gonna be a doozy, huh?" She rubbed her hands together in anticipation. "I can't wait. What am I goin' after? It doesn't sound too active." She nodded at the trailer.

Wang smiled. "It's a surprise."

Bobbi Jo giggled as she loaded her rifle. As planned, the drinks Wang supplied on the journey had reinvigorated her buzz from the night before. Of course, the light sedative he'd added probably helped. She closed one eye as she tried to zip her vest, staggering back a step before succeeding.

"Hey, where's my scope?" she asked, checking the backseat.

"I think the reason you are bored is because hunting has become too easy for you," Wang offered. "I did not bring a scope so that your true talents can shine through."

She tilted her head, smiling. "You know, you're right, Victor baby." She tottered toward him, leering suggestively. "How 'bout after this here hunting expedishun, you an' me go an' have ourselves a little ching-chang?" she asked, reaching for his crotch.

A shudder slid through him, and he took a step back. Mustering a smile he wagged his finger. "Your offer is tempting, but if you don't begin soon, the hunt will not go as planned."

Bobbi Jo saluted and wheeled around, gun at the ready. She sank to a crouch and peered into the shadows. "Okay, killjoy. Let 'er rip!"

"Close your eyes. I will tell you when to open them." Wang walked to the back of the trailer and opened the door. He climbed inside and grabbed Sapphire by the arm, leading her out as he would a horse. She didn't make a sound. The tape across her mouth helped, but so did the fear in her eyes.

Wang turned on his phone and checked that the signal from the radio collar was working. He leaned in close, could smell the shampoo she'd used the night before.

"When I tell you to run, you run."

Sapphire's gaze flicked to each side, never settling on one point. Her eyes glistened with tears as she shook her head.

"I will give you a head start, to make things fair." Victor Wang enjoyed the ruse. Giving the whore hope. Even if she did manage to escape, he'd find her using the app on his phone. The range before losing the signal was generous. "You must remain quiet or you will be punished. Do you understand?"

Sapphire closed her eyes and nodded, tears streaming down her cheeks. He turned her and unlocked the handcuffs.

Everything was in order.

"*Run*," Wang growled into her ear, and gave her a shove. Startled, Sapphire sprinted forward and stumbled, but then recovered and ran, her head bobbing as she sprinted away. He waited until she became a dark speck on the horizon before he joined Bobbi Jo.

"Open your eyes," he said.

Bobbi Jo did and looked around. Wang pointed at the rapidly disappearing speck. From where they stood Sapphire resembled some exotic animal darting through the brush.

"Your quarry."

She narrowed her eyes and nodded. "Kinda small, ain't it?"

"Ah, but a worthy opponent. You will see."

"Anything I need to be aware of? Is it dangerous? Teeth? Claws?"

"Get no closer than thirty yards and, to make things interesting, you must make the kill before sunrise."

"Oh, good." Bobbi Jo smiled. "A challenge. And when I succeed? Are there more I can take back to the game farm?"

"I'm sure something can be arranged." He scanned the horizon, searching for Sapphire. The shadows had swallowed her whole. "You'd better hurry."

Bobbi Jo laughed and slung her rifle over her shoulder. "This is gonna be fun," she said, and started after her prey.

Wang smiled as he turned on the recorder and followed her.

TWENTY MINUTES LATER, BOBBI JO STOPPED TO CATCH HER BREATH.

"Where the hell *is* it?"

Victor hadn't figured on Bobbi Jo being as out of shape as she was, and switched to the tracking app on his phone. The screen showed Sapphire two hundred yards to their left. The blinking icon didn't move. He searched the area but saw only grass and shadows. She was probably lying on the ground, hiding. Bobbi Jo raised an eyebrow and cocked her head. He pointed to his left and she nodded.

Wang watched the gap narrow between them and the icon at their approach. The sun had just tipped the horizon, so there was still time, but Bobbi Jo would have to shoot now, or she might realize what she was aiming at. He worried that the drinks she'd had on the drive were wearing off. She seemed more focused and determined than she'd been in the beginning.

As Wang had hoped, their approach flushed their prey. A dark shape rose from the grass. Wang's heart raced in anticipation, filming everything in a wide angle. Bobbi Jo stopped and raised her rifle.

And fired.

The dark form staggered and dropped.

"Yes!" Bobbi Jo lowered her rifle and pumped her fist.

Wang zoomed in on her triumphant smile, and then zoomed back out to capture the action.

She strode to the inert form, slowing as she approached. Wang zoomed in yet again. A look of confusion crossed her face, replaced by horror as she drew close enough to make out Sapphire's body. Her face drained of color, Bobbi Jo's gaze skated to Wang.

"It's...it's..." She stopped and looked down again, unable to voice the words.

The sun had breached the horizon, creating the perfect light. Wang framed Sapphire's face with his phone, peaceful in death, and congratulated himself on the timing.

"Stop filming, you ass," Bobbi Jo hissed. Victor lowered his phone, but didn't turn it off. He glanced down to make sure he'd angled the lens correctly.

She stared in horror at the woman she'd just killed. A moment later, she squatted to get a better look, and brushed away the black hair covering Sapphire's cheek.

"Is this...is that the woman who seduced Clarence?" she asked, tilting her head.

"Yes."

Bobbi Jo glanced at Wang and their gazes locked. He waited, wondering how she would react, his free hand inching toward the gun in his waistband. She blinked, and looked back at the dead woman.

"Oh," she breathed.

Bobbi Jo rose to her feet and slung her rifle over her shoulder. She hesitated a moment before she drew back her foot and kicked the dead woman in the ribs, hard, and then did it again. Grimacing, she continued to kick the body, muttering epithets under her breath, working herself into a frenzy before Wang stepped in, murmuring softly as he took her by the shoulders and led her back toward the truck.

"The whore deserved it," she sputtered, climbing into the passenger seat.

"Of course, Bobbi Jo. Things are back to normal now, aren't they?" Wang nodded and smiled, and opened the console for a bottle. "Here, have a drink," he urged, pouring the contents into a large cup.

Bobbi Jo accepted the Bloody Mary without saying a word, her gaze focused on the horizon. Wang watched her, calculating his next move. Filming the murder took care of the Schneider's ill-fated decision to seek out another hunting camp, and eventually another wildlife supplier, putting Wang in the driver's seat. Unfortunately, with Sapphire's death, he was now in the market for another companion. He ran through the available women at camp, but his interest flagged. There had to be someone who hadn't been tainted by his guests.

His attention wandered to Zara, the lion-whisperer, but he nixed the idea before it took hold. Without her acquiescence, his dream of becoming the go-to hunting camp in Tanzania would be that much harder to achieve. No, there had to be someone else.

36

B ACK AT RAFIKI, Rashid dropped Leine and Derek off and headed home. All three of them were exhausted. When Alma asked them what happened when they tried to retrieve Hugh's body, Derek shook his head and told her what they'd found.

Alma's cheeks grew red, her anger bubbling to the surface. "Someone has to answer for the death of that good man," she declared, fists clenched. By this time, Hattie had joined them and tried to calm the older woman down.

"You can't fight Wang," Hattie said. "You know that, Alma. We can't win against his money or influence."

"I don't think it was his men," Leine said. "The gunmen who shot at us were dressed differently and didn't carry the same kind of weapons."

"Then who?"

"Didn't you mention the men who took Zara looked like they were well-funded?" Leine asked. The two women exchanged knowing looks.

"So you think it was Assad." Alma nodded. "Of course."

"We found Zara," Derek said, leaning against the Rover. "Wang's keeping her locked up in an arena with the cubs."

Alma's eyes widened. "Zara? She's all right? Oh." She whispered the last word, steadying herself on the side of the Rover. Hattie led the older woman to the back of the vehicle and helped her sit on the tailgate.

Leine and Derek joined the two women.

"How is she?" Alma asked. "Why didn't you bring her home?"

"She's fine. And we will. Tonight." Leine described their plan. When she and Derek finished filling them in on the details, Alma shook her head.

"You can't do this. It's much too dangerous. For God's sake, a man was *murdered* because he got too close."

"Yes, but now we know the camp's layout and have a general idea where the guards patrol," Derek added. "We'll be careful."

"Do you know where Assad and his thugs will be when you arrive at the camp?"

Derek sighed. "No. But if we don't go in and at least try, then you'll likely never see Zara again."

"He's right." Hattie took Alma's hand. "Come on. Let's leave them alone so they can put together the things they'll need for tonight."

Alma nodded. "At least we can make breakfast. I'll bet you two are starving."

"I could eat," Derek replied.

"Would it be all right if I used the sat phone again?" Leine asked.

"Of course," Alma replied. "You know where it is."

Alma and Hattie left, while Leine and Derek combed through the Rover, putting together supplies they'd need to prepare for that evening's operation. They inventoried the gear they'd managed to take from Derek's house in Dar. In addition to the semiautomatic pistols, their cache consisted of two MP5s, the sniper rifle—which Derek re-sighted after Leine's mishap on the roof—as well as three pair of NVGs, binoculars, and enough ammunition for the attempted rescue.

"You take the girls. I'll cover you." Leine said as she loaded a magazine.

"Wait a minute. Why don't I cover you? I've got more experience."

"Think so?" Leine picked up one of the 9mm pistols and fired three rounds into a post several yards behind Derek.

He turned to look at the perfectly centered shots and whistled. Then he picked up the .45 lying on the tailgate and carefully aimed at the small branch of a baobab tree about twenty-five yards from him. He pulled the trigger and the branch dropped to the ground.

"Nice." Leine fired three more rounds near Derek's feet, making him jump.

"What the fuck was that?" he sputtered, his face turning crimson. "You could've hit me."

"But I didn't, did I?" Leine set her gun on the tailgate and leveled her gaze at him. "Look, we're both tired. You can shoot. Great. So can I. We'll probably have to play it by ear on this one, so let's not get too attached to our roles, okay?"

"Hey, you were the one making up the rules, not me."

"Okay, Derek. Whatever." Leine finished loading the magazine and placed it in the back of the Rover with the other gear. Tired of his alpha male stupidity she said, "Looks like we're done here. After I call Lou, I'm going to get some breakfast and then I need to sleep." She stood up and headed toward the outdoor kitchen, following the smell of coffee and fried eggs.

KYLIE OPENED THE TOP DRESSER DRAWER AND RUMMAGED through Wang's clothes. She was sure she'd seen him hide something there when he thought she wasn't looking.

Underneath the perfectly folded undershirts, her fingers curled around a small plastic thumb drive. She glanced to the side to make sure her captor wasn't nearby and pocketed the device.

Wang had liberated her from the kitchen earlier that morning without an explanation. Ghanima had been livid but hid her displeasure well; Kylie could feel her eyes boring a hole into her back as they walked out of the camp headed for Wang's tent. She didn't want to think about what would happen if Wang decided to return her. Kylie had no doubt that it would be her death sentence.

She nosed around the well-appointed room, tugging at the weird butch collar Wang insisted she wear around her neck. He'd warned her not to step outside the perimeter of the deck unless he was with her, and suggested she try while he was there. When she did as he instructed a hot, shooting pain arced across her throat and neck. Surprised, she yelped and jumped back, her hands gripping the collar as she tried to tear it loose.

Wang had laughed and patted her head on his way to taking his extra special guests on a hunting expedition. She didn't like the look the bleach-blond woman had given her, even though her husband, a big man with an even bigger belly, hardly gave Kylie a second glance. After they'd gone, Kylie tried to get the collar off, but the band was too strong and wouldn't budge. She'd even gone under the shower to see if she could short it out, but when she'd tested it again, she gave herself another shock.

She spent the afternoon looking through Wang's things and lying on the king-sized bed, alternating between relief that she no longer had to wear leg irons and sleep outside unprotected, and fear of what this new development portended. Where had Sapphire ended up? Had Wang grown tired of her and put her back into rotation for the guests?

Kylie shuddered at the idea of having sex with Wang, but was resigned to the reality. How long would she be able to hold Wang's attention before he grew bored with her, too? Would he beat her like he did Sapphire? Tentacles of depression began to weave their way through her mind, reminding her she had nothing to look forward to, that life would go on after her death as though she didn't matter, just like after her little brother Brandon died.

You have to keep your mind away from such negative thoughts, Kylie. She climbed off the bed and busied herself with cataloging every item in the tent. The few books she found on the shelves were all written in Chinese, and after she'd gone through the photographs and drawings, she was back to thinking.

The thumb drive intrigued her, and she searched the room for a laptop or other device she could use to view the files. She figured the information it contained was probably boring like spreadsheets and business stuff, but with nothing else to occupy her mind, even that could be interesting. Besides, Wang must have had a reason to hide the drive, and Kylie wanted to discover what it was.

Unable to locate a laptop or tablet to read the files, Kylie fished the drive out of her pocket and put it back in the drawer. Knowing Wang, he'd look for it, find it missing, and blame her. He'd be right, but she didn't want to give him a reason to use the shock collar.

Kylie had finally drifted off to sleep when a noise woke her. At first disoriented, she snapped fully awake at the voices outside the tent.

"I don't think Mistah Wang take her," a woman said in a low

voice. Kylie's heart fluttered in her chest at Ghanima's unmistak-able voice.

"Are you sure? He brought the other one with him." The man's voice was louder. It was Ubaya.

"Yes. Now go inside and bring her out."

Kylie rolled off the bed and onto the floor, careful not to make any noise, and slid underneath. The sound of footsteps walking onto the deck told her one of them was coming inside. Both Ghanima and Ubaya would certainly look under the bed if they were searching for her. Kylie cursed her shortsighted impulse to hide in such an obvious place.

She turned onto her back and looked up. The underside of the bed was made of wooden slats running widthwise an equal distance apart. She grabbed hold of the slat directly above her face, testing her grip by lifting her head and torso off the floor. Then she eased the toes of first one foot and then the other between the mattress and the slat near her feet.

The floorboards creaked and Kylie turned her head. A pair of lace-up boots with the pants tucked inside moved across the floor.

The boots stopped, turned. "No one's here," the man said in a loud whisper.

"You look?" Ghanima demanded. Footsteps pounded up the stairs, crossed the deck and stopped. "What about there?"

"The door's open. I looked," he responded.

"Ghanima have to do everything," she sputtered. Heavy foot-falls tracked across the room to the *en suite*, and then came back, pausing at the side of the bed. Breathing heavily, Ghanima's feet shifted as she got down on one knee. At the last second, Kylie pulled herself up tight to the underside of the bed and held her breath.

The older woman's wheezing told Kylie she was still looking. There was a brief pause and Kylie squeezed her eyes shut, trying to make herself smaller. The weight of the mattress above Kylie's right hand grew heavy as Ghanima used the bed to hoist herself to her feet.

"All right, then. She not here. Mistah Wang must have her." Ghanima shuffled across the room toward the other man. Kylie quietly exhaled and lowered herself back to the floor. Both sets of feet turned and walked outside.

"We'll come back another time?" the man asked, the crunch of gravel fading as they walked.

"Oh, yes. Ghanima will come back." The determination in her voice sent chills down Kylie's spine. She'd have to do something to keep the sadistic bitch away from her.

37

LATER THAT EVENING, Kylie watched through a slit in the tent wall as Victor Wang sipped his drink and forced a smile at Clarence's joke about God being a big game hunter. Flames crackled and snapped in the large fire pit, sending sparks into the dark sky above them. Bobbi Jo was watching Wang, a calculating gleam in her eyes. The woman was trouble, Kylie thought. She would need to stay clear of her while the two were Victor's guests.

Wang excused himself from the fireside chat, insisting he needed to oversee the kitchen staff to make sure the buffalo Bobbi Jo brought down that afternoon was seasoned correctly. He refreshed his drink and turned to leave. Bobbi Jo stood up from her chair.

"Would you mind waiting a minute, Victor?" she called. With a sigh Victor turned and waited for her to catch up with him.

Bobbi Jo smiled at her husband and then joined Victor, the smile vanishing.

"What the fuck are you going to do with the video?" she asked, her voice low.

Victor smiled coldly and took a sip of his drink. "Keep it as insurance."

"What do you mean, *insurance*? I demand that you delete every copy you made, or I'll have the law come down on you so fast it'll make your head spin."

Victor Wang laughed, and turned away. Bobbi Jo grabbed his arm. Wang glanced down at her hand and then at her. "I advise you to tread carefully, Bobbi Jo."

She let go, but leaned closer, getting in his face. "No court in the world would convict me of murder. You tricked me into thinking that girl was some kind of animal. I only killed her because of you."

"Then how do you explain what you did afterward?" Victor asked.

Bobbi Jo's cheeks turned several shades darker. "You stopped filming. The phone...you weren't..." She snapped her mouth closed, shock sliding over her features.

"Yes. I was. I watched it this morning. Your actions would be construed by anyone viewing it as quite vicious."

"You fucking asshole," Bobbi Jo fumed.

"Now, then. Are we in agreement? My company will supply all stock required for your ranch, as well as being the one and only safari camp you and your husband will use and recommend, yes?"

Kylie sucked in a breath. Afraid Wang or Bobbi Jo would see her, she took a step backward, intending to cross to the other side of the tent. As she did so, she knocked against a glass vase on the dresser. She lunged to grab it before it toppled over and broke, but missed and the vase hit the floor, shattering into a thousand pieces.

In seconds, Wang was at the door, with Bobbi Jo close behind.

"What are you doing?" Wang demanded. When Kylie didn't

respond, he strode over and slapped her across the face. Kylie put her hand to her stinging cheek.

"She heard everything, you know," Bobbi Jo said. "You'll have to get rid of her, too. Just like you did the other one."

"Shut up," Wang said through gritted teeth.

"I didn't tell you, Victor, but apparently the girl cornered one of your guests yesterday. Told him she'd been kidnapped and was being held against her will. Begged the poor man to help her." Bobbi Jo sneered at Kylie. "I laughed and told him that would never happen here. That she was a disgruntled worker and to ignore her." She shook her head, her eyes gleaming. "You just can't find good help these days, can you?"

"I said *shut up*, Bobbi Jo." A muscle twitched in Victor Wang's jaw. "Clean this up. Now," he said, addressing Kylie. He pivoted and strode from the tent, Bobbi Jo behind him. She paused at the entrance and gave her a look that told her Kylie had made another enemy.

"You best be careful, darlin', or you'll end up like that Asian bitch," she said, and walked out the door.

Knees shaking, Kylie ran to the bathroom and threw up. She cleaned up before she grabbed the broom and dustpan and went back to the shattered glass.

They killed Sapphire? Kylie thought. *Why?* If Wang really did trick Bobbi Jo into killing her, then what would stop him from doing the same with Kylie? Especially now that Bobbi Jo had told him she was trying to escape. What if the USB drive in the drawer had a copy of the video? She went over to the dresser and opened the drawer. It was still there. She picked it up and looked around the room for a good hiding place. No way would she risk being caught with the thumb drive on her.

Nothing looked safe enough, so she slid it into her pocket, intending to find a place later on, after everything died down.

Kylie had just dumped the last piece of glass into the garbage when there was a commotion outside. She raced to the slit in the tent and looked out as three late-model pickups roared into camp, skidding to a stop a few yards from the campfire.

Each truck bed held between three or four men armed with machine guns, wearing fatigues and short-sleeved khaki shirts with epaulets and shiny brass buttons. Some wore dirty T-shirts underneath, while others didn't bother and were bare-chested. Kylie shrank further into the shadows, doom twisting her gut.

The lead vehicle's four doors swung open, disgorging as many men, all wearing sunglasses even though the sun had long since vanished. A man with a beard emerged from the front passenger seat. Wang and the couple watched with wary expressions as he removed his sunglasses and grinned.

"Well, well, well. What is this? A party to which I was not invited?" The man pursed his lips in a mock pout and walked over to Wang's empty chair.

Bobbi Jo and Clarence both eyed the rifles they'd left leaning against a tree. Victor caught Bobbi Jo's gaze and gave a slight shake of his head, an obvious warning to not try anything stupid. She leaned back in her chair and lifted her glass.

"Who's your friend, Victor?" she asked, her smile forced.

The man bowed, sweeping his hand back in an exaggerated gesture and said, "My men call me Doctor Death." He straightened. "But you may call me Assad. And you are?"

"Mrs. Schneider, and this is my husband, Mr. Schneider," she said, with a scowl. "We're Victor's *guests*."

Her emphasis on the word wasn't lost on Assad. Grinning, he dropped into Wang's vacated seat.

Assad? A jolt of fear flared through Kylie. Hadn't Zara told her Wang sold Jaidee to a man with that name?

"It appears we are all the *guests* of our generous host," Assad shot back, his mock-friendly demeanor devolving into an icy stare.

"Appears so." Bobbi Jo's gaze met Wang's with a look that said, *who the hell is this asshole?*

Victor Wang ignored her and snapped his fingers at the tent. "Come," he commanded. Kylie froze, panic blooming in her chest. She attempted a deep breath but only managed a shallow gasp. Wang's face grew red at the delay, his anger obvious.

"Come out. *Now.*"

Knees shaking and her shoulders inching toward her ears, Kylie stepped into the open, pausing near the doorway.

Wang waved his hand impatiently. "Down here."

"But the collar..." she said, her voice quiet.

With an exasperated sigh, Wang slid his phone out of his pocket and tapped the screen.

"Come," he repeated. All eyes were on Kylie.

Worried her legs would buckle and still anticipating a shock, Kylie slowly made her way down the two steps. She exhaled in relief when the shock didn't come.

"But where is the other one? The Thai woman you kept?" Assad asked.

Wang shrugged. "I let her go," he answered, his gaze meeting Bobbi Jo's. Bobbi Jo shifted in her seat and looked away. Kylie kept her face impassive.

"Pity. You should have offered to sell her to me. The child needs more tending than I am prepared to do." He nodded at one of the men standing near his truck. The gunman reached inside and dragged Jaidee into the open. He wore a boy-sized set of fatigues and his hair had been cut in a military style. A pair of sunglasses hung around his neck.

Kylie gasped. Jaidee saw her and started to cry. "Kylie," he wailed. She smiled, trying to calm him.

"You see?" Assad said, obviously irritated. He waved his hand in the air. "That is what he does, all day long."

"It's all right, Jaidee," Kylie soothed. Watching her, Jaidee gulped in a breath and quieted.

Assad's shrewd gaze settled on Kylie. "Perhaps we can work something out, Victor."

Kylie stiffened. Wang wouldn't let him take her. *Why wouldn't he*, a voice inside her argued. He'd done the same with Jaidee, and now she posed a threat to Wang. The implications of her tenuous situation hit her with the force of an oncoming train. Her mouth ran dry as beads of sweat pooled at the small of her back.

"Why not choose a whore who pleases you?" Wang asked.

Assad gave him a sly grin and leaned back in his chair. "But she does please me. I prefer white women."

"Even though she does not follow the Prophet?" Wang countered.

"Conversion is always an option," Assad answered with a shrug.

"Let's not make a decision yet," Wang replied. "I was about to check on our meal for the evening before you arrived. I would be honored if you and your men would join us," he said, bowing.

Assad glanced at the small army of gunmen standing near the trucks. "On behalf of my men, I accept."

"Good. Now, if you'll excuse me." Wang grasped Kylie by the arm. The Schneiders' worried expressions mirrored Kylie's own tremulous emotions. Wang's firm grip on her arm told her he wasn't about to turn her loose. In any case, she didn't dare try to run—not while Wang still had the controls for the collar.

Wang marched her toward camp before Assad could protest. Relieved that Victor Wang wasn't going to give her away, Kylie went willingly. Wang muttered to himself in Chinese the entire time. The only words Kylie recognized were Assad and fuck head.

Mouthwatering smells of roasting meat wafted toward her,

telling her they were close to the cooking area. Instead of continuing on, they stopped in front of a wooden hut used as a storeroom. Wang dragged a key ring from his pocket, selected a key, and unlocked the door. Then he shoved her inside.

"I thought you wanted me to help you with the food?" Kylie asked, wondering what he wanted her to do in the dark space filled with jars of spices and bags of flour.

"Your services will no longer be needed this evening," Wang muttered, and slammed the door closed.

LEINE AND DEREK SKIRTED THE CAMP'S PERIMETER, HEADING FOR the fenced enclosure where Zara said she would meet them. Both carried a side arm and extra ammunition, a knife, and an MP5 slung across their backs. In addition, Derek wore a rucksack with extra gear, water, and ammo. They reached the pen with the pole in the center at 23:30. No one was there.

"Shit. Now what?" Derek paced, glancing at his watch.

"We wait," Leine answered. Earlier, when she informed Lou she'd found Kylie at Wang's camp, he'd told her to stand down, wait for reinforcements. Knowing that support would take several hours to mobilize, Leine had explained that leaving Kylie alone in the enclosure would be too dangerous but that the other victims would still need assistance and to send help regardless. Especially when Wang learned of the two women's escape. The possibility of removing his staff and vacating to another location was high. She'd also asked about April, calling Lou on his evasive tactics.

Lou had sighed—a long, drawn-out, world-weary sigh.

"Brigit and Andrew tracked her to Riyadh, to a pseudo modeling agency there. But," Lou paused.

Leine gripped the phone. "But what, Lou?" she ground out through gritted teeth.

"They lost them, Leine."

"Lost them—" Leine repeated. "How the *hell* did they lose them?" She paced the woodchip path, anger and concern combining in a slurry of emotion she found hard to control.

Lou had assured her they were doing everything they could to find April and the other women, and not to worry. Brigit and Andrew were some of their best operatives. Leine had lost her temper and ended the call, seething with impotent rage, knowing there was nothing she could do. Not from a remote area in Tanzania.

Snapping back to the present, Leine noticed movement in her periphery. She dropped, pivoting, her gun aimed in front of her. Derek mirrored her actions. Zara emerged from behind a gnarled thorn tree, accompanied by the clank of leg irons.

"Don't shoot. It's me," she whispered, her hands up. Leine eased her finger from the trigger and exhaled.

"Jesus Christ, Zara. You could have been shot," Derek said, reaching her before she could take another step. Opening the ruck, he pulled out a pair of bolt cutters and crouched at her feet. The tool bit through the links next to both ankle cuffs. Mindful of the noise, Derek placed the chain on the ground and then stood.

"Thank you, Derek." Zara threw her arms around him. Clearly embarrassed, Derek peeled her arms from around his neck.

"Where's Kylie?" Leine asked, scanning the pen and surrounding area.

Zara shook her head. "She wasn't here. I checked the kitchen where she usually works, but she wasn't there, either."

"How long until you're missed?" Derek asked.

"It depends on the guard. Tonight it's Ubaya. He lets me walk by myself most of the time, so I think we're all right for now."

"Do you know where he is?" Leine asked.

"He usually sits by himself under a big baobab tree just outside of camp and drinks beer. That way, no one can find him to make him work."

"Derek, you take Zara back to the Rover and wait for me there," Leine said. "I'll find Ubaya. Key the mic if you see anyone. If it's Wang or Kylie, let me know asap."

"But what about the others?" Zara asked. "They're being treated like slaves, too."

"We've got that handled. Derek will fill you in when you get back to the Rover."

Derek handed Leine a canteen filled with water. She took a quick drink, replaced the cap, and left, melting into the shadows.

K YLIE PUSHED THE bags of flour and rice onto their
sides and lay across them, trying to get comfortable.
She heard snatches of conversation and the sound of
footsteps hurrying by. Probably staff getting the big dinner
ready. The distant laughter of the main camp's guests filled the
air. Her chest squeezed tight at the ache of revived memories—
of family dinners and celebrations, and happier days when
Brandon was still alive.

The rich scent of exotic spices filled the small hut, and Kylie
wondered if Wang would leave her there all night. She hoped so,
since it would delay the inevitable. She refused to think about
what would happen to her if she ended up with either Wang or
Doctor Death. Or his gunmen, for that matter. Even though she
didn't have much experience with sex, she wasn't stupid.

Whatever it was wouldn't be pleasant. The one time she did
think things through, she'd broken down and sobbed, fear blos-
soming inside of her like a drop of blood spreading on an oily
surface. Now that Wang knew Kylie had overheard his and
Bobbi Jo's conversation about Sapphire, she didn't know how
long she had before he'd try to do the same to her.

Seeing Jaidee brought another ache to her heart. He was alone, afraid, and at Assad's mercy. Her fear of the militant and his men trumped her maternal feelings for Jaidee, although if she ended up with the gunmen, she'd try to make the best of things. Either way, she didn't see much of a future, for her or Jaidee.

Her fingers curled around the knife she kept hidden in her bra. Good thing Wang wasn't very thorough. He never patted her down.

Kylie turned onto her back and stared at the ceiling. The image of her mother and father appeared in her mind and tears welled in her eyes. Where were they? Why hadn't they found her yet? Didn't her mother's friend, Leine, look for people like her? She'd been so excited when she thought she'd seen her on the ship. Did she travel this far? The army certainly did. She liked to imagine an elite Special Forces team ghosting their way through camp, immobilizing the guards as they searched for her. She'd like to get one to immobilize Ghanima.

As soon as the thought crossed her mind, her good angel chastised her. On the other hand, her bad angel heartily congratulated her on her awesome imagination. Soon, she drifted off, dreaming of handsome men in camouflage carrying guns and coming to take her home.

Kylie snapped back to reality at the sound of gravel crunching outside the hut. Disoriented, she climbed to her feet. Had Wang decided to come for her anyway? She wasn't sure how long she'd been asleep, but no one was talking or laughing outside.

A key scraped the lock and the door opened. Ghanima's familiar silhouette filled the doorway.

Kylie backed up until she hit the far wall. Holding something behind her, Ghanima advanced into the hut and closed the door. A filtered glow from the walk lights outside leaked through the gaps in the wall, illuminating the woman's face and eyes and giving Kylie the impression she was an extra in some B-rated horror flick.

Except this wasn't a movie. And she wasn't an extra.

"What do you want?" Kylie asked, trying to see around her. Ghanima moved, too fast for an overweight spawn of the devil, swinging what looked like some kind of a bat. Kylie ducked at the last minute, feeling the swish of air past her head as the weapon came close.

Kylie cried out and feinted to the left. Ghanima lunged for her, missing her again by mere inches. Kylie wouldn't be able to get away with the same ploy again, and she waited for the other woman to make the next move.

The sound of Ghanima's breathing echoed against the walls of the small space. She raised the bat. Kylie frantically searched for something to use as a weapon. Then she remembered the knife.

She reached for the hilt the same time the bat sliced through the air toward her. Kylie tried to get out of the way, but was a split-second too late. The wood connected with her head, knocking her off balance. Stunned, Kylie stumbled against the wall. Ghanima came at her again, swinging the bat for all she was worth. Kylie dropped to a crouch and slid the knife free as the bat whooshed above her.

Expecting resistance, Ghanima staggered forward. Kylie sprang to her feet and lunged, burying the knife in her throat. The larger woman's eyes bulged in shock and a sound like a strangled cat wheezed from her mouth. The blade still in her throat, blood poured from the wound, the stain burgeoning on the front of her shirt.

Kylie stared in horror at the woman, at what she'd just done. The bat clattered to the ground. Ghanima slumped to her knees, a horrific gurgling coming from her throat. She hesitated a moment, and then collapsed face down in the dirt. A dark stain spread beneath her.

Panic clouded Kylie's mind, and she stood rooted to the spot. *Oh my God. Oh my God. What have I done?* The words played a loop in her stunned brain, words she was unable to shake free.

Time passed before she came back to herself. She shook her head to clear it and stepped over Ghanima's inert body, shuddering as she did. She turned away and headed for the door. Blood roaring in her ears, she inched open the door to check if anyone was nearby. She saw no one.

Her brain frozen, Kylie blanked on what to do next. She couldn't stay in camp. How much range did the collar have? She had to get as far away as possible. Then she could figure out the rest.

She slipped out the door, closed it behind her, and started running.

———

LEINE CREPT UP BEHIND THE MAN SITTING ON THE GROUND NEAR the huge baobab tree. Three beer bottles lay scattered next to him, a fourth in his hand. His gun was propped against the tree, a few feet from him. She waited until he brought the bottle to his lips and tipped his head back before she eased the gun out of his reach.

"Nice night, huh?" she said, stepping around the tree, her gun aimed at him. Startled, the gunman put the beer down and scrambled to his knees before his gaze cut to where his weapon should have been.

"Looking for this?" She held his gun up with her free hand. A wary expression crossed his face. She removed the magazine, jacked the cartridge out of the chamber, and set the weapon on the ground. He glared at her.

"Lesson one, never allow your weapon out of range." Leine shook her head, studying him for a moment. The moonlight picked up a sheen of sweat on his forehead. "You're Ubaya, right?"

He hesitated before he nodded.

"Good. I'm looking for Kylie, and I've been told you know where she is."

"No," he answered, swiveling his head, searching for help. "I do not know this person."

Leine smiled. "Of course you do. I would never have known you were here if someone didn't tell me where to find you. They said you would help me find her."

"I cannot." Panic filled his eyes. "I will lose my job if I tell you."

"You'll lose more than that if you *don't* tell me." Leine aimed her gun higher, in line with his sweaty forehead. He fell silent, the sheen spreading. "What's it going to be, Ubaya? Stay mute and you can die, or tell me what I need to know and finish that beer." She nodded toward the bottle on the ground next to him.

The beer won.

"Mister Wang took her. She stays in his tent on the other side of camp." His gaze flicked to the bottle.

"Was that so hard?" Leine picked up the cartridge she'd ejected from the chamber of his gun and slipped it into her pocket. The magazine went into a side compartment of her pants. Then she walked over to Ubaya. "Hands behind your back."

"But they will look for me. When they find me they will know you are here."

"I don't intend to stick around that long. Hands," she ordered.

"What about the animals? I will not be able to defend myself if they come."

"You probably should have thought about that when you chained Kylie to the metal pole and left her there all night."

Ubaya swallowed. "But she did not die."

"Hands."

Ubaya bowed his head and did as she instructed. Leine pulled out a length of rope and tied his wrists. Then she had him lie prone while she used the same rope to tie his feet, trussing him like a Christmas turkey.

As she started to walk away, he rolled onto his side.

"What about the beer?" he lamented. "You promised."

Leine shrugged. "I lied."

39

W ANG WALKED THROUGH the remains of the evening's festivities, picking up glasses and half-empty bottles of wine and booze, while one of his staff cleaned the rest in silence. Wang had instructed him to not disturb the militants or the Schneiders.

Bobbi Jo and Clarence had disappeared into their tent as soon as dinner was over. Wang wished he'd been able to do the same.

The evening had progressed into a bacchanalia as Assad and his men grew increasingly drunk, to the point that several began singing at the top of their voices and firing their weapons into the air. Wang had pleaded with Assad to get a handle on his men for the sake of the paying customers in the other section of the camp, but Assad just shrugged and said, "Let them have a taste of the real Africa." They continued well into the evening, stopping only after Wang doctored a bottle of whiskey with sedatives and poured liberal drinks for them all.

Assad had passed out on the bed in the remaining guest tent, sprawled drunkenly across the 1000-thread-count sheets, his muddy boots leaving dark streaks on the pristine fabric. The child had curled up on the floor next to him. A few of Assad's men slept in their pickups, while others rolled out blankets nearby.

Victor Wang considered having Assad and his men killed as they slept, but discarded the idea. Because of the crackdown on poachers by so many African agencies, massive quantities of elephant ivory and rhino horn were getting harder to come by. And, most poachers were small operators, unable to supply the amount Wang needed. If Assad were to cease operations, Wang would be forced to deal with less acceptable groups who might or might not believe in keeping their part of the deal.

Or, he'd have to decentralize and use several individuals, which brought its own set of headaches. Either way, the logistics were a shitstorm waiting to happen. Once the supply line was interrupted, his business partners would leave him in droves.

The thought of working with individual poachers reminded Wang of his orders to hunt down Derek and the woman. He hadn't received word of their capture, had only heard second-hand reports of the debacle at the poacher's home in Mikocheni. It would be the last time he used contract assassins instead of his own men.

Victor was in the process of combining two bottles of scotch to make a fifth, along with figuring out his next step to find the runaway Afrikaner, when his phone vibrated. Caller ID told him it was his driver, Tai. Irritated by the intrusion, he set the bottle down and walked to the edge of camp before answering.

"Ghanima is dead," Tai advised. "The girl is gone."

Wang swore. "Did anyone see where she went?"

"No. What do you want me to do?"

"Have you removed the body?"

"Of course."

"How did she die?"

"A knife to the throat. It was still in her neck."

How did the girl obtain a knife? Wang clenched his jaw, his irritation rising. He'd have to concoct a story to tell Ghanima's family. They'd want the body.

"Bring the truck. We'll track her from there. The helicopter will wake too many people." Wang ended the call. Alone with no weapon the girl would have little chance in the bush. They'd have to find her soon, or he'd be out what he paid for her. She'd be an easy mark for a lion or leopard.

Wang hated losing an acquisition.

"Is there a problem?"

Assad's deep voice startled him.

"Nothing you need to be concerned about." Wang turned and smiled. "A small administrative glitch."

The gunman grinned, the diamond in his tooth sparkling in the dim camp lights. "Why do I not believe you?" He scratched his balls and yawned, looking toward Wang's tent. "Where is the girl? I could use some company."

"I'm afraid she's not here."

Assad's sharp gaze snapped to Wang's. "Where has she gone?"

Wang maintained eye contact. "She's not here," he repeated. His fingers itched to activate the app on his phone. The shock collar had a range of two miles. If she was hiding within that distance, they'd find her. But he had to leave, now.

Just then, Tai pulled up next to the main tent in the all-terrain truck. He cut the lights and idled, waiting for his boss. Assad studied the truck and then Wang. Wang gave him an apologetic smile.

"I'm afraid there are some pressing matters I must attend to." He straightened, his face a mask of calm. "If you'll excuse me." Wang turned to go, but Assad grabbed his arm. Wang checked the impulse to deliver a blow to the man's windpipe.

"I think this 'pressing matter' must have to do with the girl," he said. He released Wang's arm, his eyes narrowing. "She has run away, yes?" When Wang didn't reply, he continued. "My men and I will help you." He brought his fingers to his lips and whistled, the sharp sound piercing the night.

"Get up, all of you. Now," he shouted. Groggy from being sedated, his men were slow to respond. Assad strode to one of the men still in his sleeping bag and, before he could rise, slammed his foot into his stomach. The man doubled over, wheezing.

"Get up. We are leaving," he commanded. Most now awake, his men snapped to and climbed to their feet. Assad walked to the lead vehicle and slid into the passenger seat. His driver was there in seconds.

"Fucking terrorist," Wang muttered as he walked to the truck. He brought out his phone, activating the shock collar, and dialed up the intensity. The amount of electricity delivered would be enough to slow the young woman down but not inflict lasting damage. He glanced at the power level. She'd been wearing it for twenty-three hours. There was perhaps an hour left on the battery, although the monitor on his screen showed even less. He edged the limit higher. He'd have to make the first charge count.

Wang climbed into the truck and nodded at Tai. His driver shifted into gear and roared out of camp, leaving Assad and his men in the dust.

40

L EINE WAITED UNTIL Wang and the gunmen had left before she emerged from the shadows. The guy cleaning up the party debris had gone, dragging a sack filled with garbage behind him, headed for the main camp. She checked the tents for Kylie—except for the American couple asleep in the far one, none of the others were occupied. She walked out of hearing range and radioed Derek.

"Where are you?" she asked.

"Zara and I are...we're at the Rover," Derek answered.

"Great. I found Ubaya and I'm at Wang's compound. Wang just took off in a hurry. A group of men with guns in late model pickups followed him. I'm pretty sure they had on the same uniforms as the guys who shot Hugh. One of them said something to Wang about Kylie escaping. Wang didn't disagree and she's not here, so I think we can safely assume she's on the run."

"Shit. How do we find her? It's a big fucking world out there."

"Good question. We need to track them, see where they're headed. Meet me where Rashid parked the last time."

"Uh, sure. Yeh. We can do that."

"What's going on, Derek? We don't have a lot of time here."

"I...it's nothing. We'll be there in a couple of minutes."

Leine slid the radio into her pocket. Something about Derek's tone put her on edge. Had they been compromised?

She arrived at the rendezvous point a short time later. Derek and Zara were already there. Leine studied the area through the NVGs, searching for signs of company. There didn't appear to be anyone else nearby except him and Zara. She keyed the mic. Derek brought the radio to his ear.

"Almost there," she said.

"Roger that." Derek put the radio back on the Rover's dash and said something to Zara. He glanced behind him several times, giving Leine the impression there was someone hiding behind the seat.

Sliding her gun free, she crept up next to the Rover. She listened for a moment, trying to determine if there might be more than one person in the back, but the only thing she heard was the sound of paper crumpling.

Leine eased her fingers around the handle and took a deep breath. Then she flung the door open, stepped back with both hands on the gun, and shouted "Hands up!"

Derek and Zara spun in their seats. Derek drew his weapon but Leine's position blocked a clear shot.

"Claire?" he asked, peering around the headrest. "What are you doing?"

Several sets of eyes stared up at Leine from the newspaper-covered floor. It took her a second before she realized what she was looking at and lowered her gun.

A half-dozen curious, mewling cubs tumbled over each other in an attempt to get to their new visitor. Recovering, Leine glared at Derek.

"What the—?" she said. Her initial surprise morphed into anger at the possibility of getting her head blown off for nothing.

Derek's sheepish expression told her everything. She looked down at the cubs and shook her head.

"You couldn't leave them," Leine said. It was more a statement of fact than a question.

"Look, Zara said she wasn't leaving without them and I didn't want to leave Zara." Derek shrugged. "What could I do?"

Leine bit back a comment, but realized it wasn't worth it. And, she had to admit the goddam things were cute.

You're getting soft, Basso.

Leine slid her gun into her holster before carefully closing the door and crossing to the passenger side.

"Slide over, Zara."

———

Leine pointed Derek in the direction Wang and his driver had gone. A short time later, they picked up fresh tire tracks heading east.

"They're headed toward my old stomping grounds," Derek said.

"What's the terrain like?" Leine asked.

"Low mountains, lots of trees and scrub. Good cover. And, this time of year there's running water."

Leine checked her watch. Half past two. Sunrise wouldn't be for several hours.

"How are they tracking her?" Derek muttered. "I mean, it's bloody dark out here. Even with NVGs, they'd have to have an idea where she was headed."

"Wang likes to keep track of his property," Leine said.

"Meaning," Derek prompted.

Zara answered. "Meaning he put a collar on the women he kept. Sapphire told me that the one she wore would shock her if she tried to go outside of a prescribed area."

"Wouldn't be difficult to have one that also tracked the wearer," Leine added.

"Like a dog training device," Derek said. "So we're talking about maybe a half-mile to a mile range, depending on the charge."

"There are some that will work as far as two miles, but the majority of them are in the shorter range." Leine leaned back in her seat and listened to the grass and brush hit the underside of the Rover. They needed to get to Kylie before Wang and the rebels did, but how?

Half an hour later, Derek cut the Rover's running lights and slipped on the NVGs. Wang's vehicle left an obvious trail through the grass, as did the pickups belonging to the other gunmen.

"I think I know where they're going," Derek said, and peeled away from the tracks, heading north. "We'll loop around and come at them from another direction."

"How can you be sure?" Zara voiced what Leine was thinking.

"The way they're headed they'll be on foot before too long. If your girl's smart," he said, glancing at Leine, "she's working her way into the rocks so her position will interfere with the radio collar."

"What happens when he shocks her?" Zara asked. "Wouldn't that make it difficult for her to keep going?"

Derek shrugged. "Maybe not. Depends on the collar. Whenever you use the shock capability it drains the batteries. Especially when it's operating at a distance."

They continued along a path only Derek could see, following a narrow valley. The evening smelled of ozone and verdant vegetation, and Leine sensed a charge in the air. As they crested a rise, the sky lit up like a rocket, creating a stark relief of their surroundings. Seconds later, the deep roll of thunder signaling an impending storm rocked the ground beneath them. Anxious, the cubs whined in unison.

"Shit," Derek said, glancing at the sky. "Looks like a good one coming."

The way ahead narrowed to the point that they couldn't go any further. Derek pulled over and parked next to a stand of trees. He slid the .45 from its holster and handed it to Zara.

"You know how to use this?" Derek asked. Zara nodded. "Good." He gave her the extra magazine. "There's food and water in the back." He peered at the gauges in front of him. "Plenty of fuel to make it back to Rafiki."

"Wait. You're coming back, right?" Zara glanced at Derek and then at Leine.

"I think what Derek is implying is that if by any chance we *don't* make it back, you'll be able to get home."

"Yeh. Exactly."

Zara placed the gun on the dash before she leaned over and kissed Derek.

"That's to remind you," she said in a soft voice. He smiled.

Lightning flashed again, followed almost immediately by a clap of thunder.

"That was close," Derek said. "Let's go before things get hairy."

Derek gave Zara some last minute instructions along with the directions for home before exiting the vehicle. Leine was already in back, gearing up when he joined her.

Fifteen minutes later, the two set off in search of Kylie.

41

KYLIE WINCED AND shrank back at the great thundering boom, waiting until the sound rolled off into the distance. She grabbed on to the next hand-hold in the ancient granite and pulled herself up and over, sliding across the rough surface and dropping down to the other side. Her grandmother used to assure her that thunder was the sound God made when he was bowling a perfect game, because, hey, God always bowled a perfect game, right? She smiled at the memory, comforted for a moment.

But then the next shock came. Though less intense this time, she stopped and clutched the collar.

Either they're moving further away and the signal is getting weaker, or the batteries are dying. Both scenarios gave her hope, and she continued to work her way forward, moving deeper into the valley.

Each time the collar went off, her resolve to escape grew. She couldn't stop, not now. Not after what she'd done. Her punishment would likely be worse than what Wang did to Sapphire. Fear coursed through her at the thought of the bruises she'd seen on her friend.

What if he became so angry he beat her to death?

Kylie picked her way along the bank of a stream. She followed it like a road, not sure where it would end. She had to keep going until the batteries died or Wang gave up the search.

The night sounds were more ominous this far from camp. A lion's roar echoed nearby, accompanied by an animal she couldn't identify screeching in the distance. She tensed at a far-off hyena's *whoop*, remembering in vivid detail the night in the enclosure when Zara helped drive them off. She wouldn't last long without some kind of weapon, but the fear of what Wang would do if he caught her spurred her on. She'd figure out her next steps when daylight came.

If she survived.

Kylie had run to the nearby valley because she didn't know where else to go. Whenever she worked outside the kitchen tent peeling vegetables, she'd gaze at the distant valley with the scenic outcropping. Surrounded by trees, the gray and white rock formation shimmered in the sun, eliciting thoughts of one of her favorite movies, *The Lion King*. That was before Ghanima had banished her inside with nothing to look at except pots and pans and the stainless steel sink.

She pushed the thought of what she had done to Ghanima to the back of her mind. Thinking about it now did her no good, not when she was running for her life.

She'd been fortunate to find her way in the darkness, her luck holding with a bright moon illuminating the way. Lucky, at least, until the winds kicked up and blew the clouds in.

Tired and hungry and weak from the sporadic shocks, Kylie yearned to lie down and rest, even if just for a moment. But her mind wouldn't let her, whispering to her that if she stopped now, she'd be dead.

Partially due to fear and partly from exhaustion, her knees shook as she continued to follow the stream. Soon, the path began to rise. Heart hammering in her chest, she scrambled over the loose gravel, gouging her hands on the jagged rocks. She didn't want to climb too far—she knew that cell phone service worked better without obstruction and assumed the same was true of the collar she wore. That, and she'd read somewhere to get to lower ground if caught outside in a thunderstorm.

Raindrops splatted her face, and she veered away from the small stream, further into the dense bushes. Storms came and went quickly here, dumping loads of water in a short amount of time. The small stream could easily swell to a raging flood, and she didn't want to take any chances.

The prickly shrubs scratched her arms, but she was beyond caring. The wind whipped at her clothing, indicating rain would soon follow. She needed to find shelter.

She broke through the brush and found herself in a small clearing surrounded by trees.

What was it she'd read about taking cover outside in a thunderstorm? Find a group of trees but don't stand under the tallest one. She thought about retracing her steps to lower ground but decided against it, worried that it might bring her closer to Wang.

Lightning flashed again, illuminating the clearing. Kylie glanced up to see which of the trees were taller. She picked the shortest one and squatted beneath it as the thunder crashed around her.

Did radio collars conduct electricity? She had no idea. The sporadic drops became a wall of rain, drenching Kylie and everything around her. Crouched in a ball, she squeezed her eyes shut and covered her ears against the storm, waiting for the next shock.

LEINE PUSHED THE HAIR OFF HER FACE AS SHE FOLLOWED DEREK UP and over a boulder. Assuming Kylie would opt for the path of least resistance, they'd been tracking the main artery of a stream, which was now overflowing its banks. The intensity of the storm pushed them further into the bush, making the already difficult hike a hard, soggy marathon.

"Not much further, now," Derek shouted over the wind. "I don't think Wang and the gunmen will get very far with the storm raging on like this. And, I doubt Kylie will, either. I say we take shelter until this lets up."

Leine nodded and followed Derek through the bush. He led them to a shallow overhang where they propped their weapons against a rock. Leine wrung the water from her clothes while Derek leaned back against the rock wall behind them and stared at the rain.

"It's going to be hard to track her in this," he commented. He opened the top on his canteen and offered it to Leine. She took a drink and handed it back.

"Hopefully it'll stop soon."

Lightning flashed, followed by a deep rumble, punctuating her words.

"Hopefully."

"So tell me about Zara." Leine squeezed rainwater from her hair and shook the excess from her hands.

"Not much to tell, really."

"You two obviously care for each other."

Derek dipped his head in acknowledgement. "We do. But caring and actually being together can be...difficult."

"You mean because of working on opposite sides?"

"Yeh," he said with a wry smile. "Let's just say my profession causes a lot of arguments."

"Then stop poaching. Start working with her instead of against her. You heard Alma."

"It's not that easy, though, you see?" Derek shook his head, staring off into space. "How do I earn a living? They live hand to mouth at Rafiki, relying on donations. A man's supposed to take care of his woman."

Leine rolled her eyes. "That's chivalrous of you, Derek, but most single women I know don't require that a man take care of them." She ran her fingers through her hair, shaking the last of the rain off. "Most want someone who can take care of themselves, who don't expect them to cook every night or clean up after them." Memories of Santa came out to play and Leine indulged for a moment before snapping back to real time. "Honestly. I think your girl Zara fits the bill."

He grimaced. "What kind of world do you live in? Most women I meet are interested in one thing: how much did I earn last year, and will I exceed expectations in this one?"

Leine shook her head. "Then you're meeting the wrong women."

Derek grew silent, watching the downpour. Eventually, the rain eased and then stopped.

She checked her watch and glanced at the sky. The stars were fading. The sun would soon rise and take the safety of the darkness.

They continued along the still-swollen stream, working down the steep slope. Derek stopped when he spotted a blade of grass bent a certain way, or a broken branch, things Leine would easily miss in the dark. At one point, he pushed through the brush, coming upon a clearing surrounded by trees.

Stooping beneath a stunted tree, he shoved his NVGs up as he took out his flashlight and shined the beam on the ground.

"She sheltered here," he said, conviction in his tone. He followed the tracks leading through the small stand of trees. Pivoting in place, he scanned the area. "She's climbing."

"How did we miss her?"

Derek shrugged. "She isn't following the stream. She must have passed by when we stopped to wait out the storm."

Following the prints, they scrambled over loose rocks and climbed, leaving the swiftly moving stream behind them. The sky grew lighter as they progressed, and the sun peeked over the horizon, throwing long, dark shadows across the landscape. Half an hour later, they reached the top of the outcropping.

Leine checked the way they'd come, making certain no one was behind them. She turned back to Derek.

"Look for signs that someone's been here," Derek said, eyes on the ground as he walked, studying the terrain. Leine scanned the rocky promontory, pausing at a shadowy opening near the base of a large rock.

"Over there," she said. Derek followed her gaze. "Looks like a good place to hide."

They split up, each coming at the area from opposite directions. They were within a few feet of the opening when Kylie broke cover.

"Kylie! Wait." Leine started after her. "Your mother sent us."

Kylie disappeared behind a mound of rock.

A few moments later, she called out, "How do I know I can trust you?"

"Your mother is Mindy Nelson and your father is Paul," Leine said. "You live in Phoenix, Arizona, and last year your little brother was murdered."

Kylie didn't respond. Leine continued. "My name is Leine Basso and I work for an anti-trafficking organization called SHEN. We help the victims," she said, ignoring the look she got from Derek. "We met once, briefly, after your brother died. Your mother and I used to work together. I also know you were backpacking in Southeast Asia and ended up here. We want to help get you back home."

The top of her head appeared as she peeked over the rock. "Who's he?" she asked, giving Derek a wary look.

"His name's Derek. He's the muscle."

"Leine Basso, huh?" he muttered.

Ignoring him, Leine waited as Kylie emerged and walked toward them, her distrust of Derek obvious in the way she held herself, as though coiled to run at the slightest provocation. She stopped several feet from them. Leine opened her arms. Kylie hesitated a second, her face twisting in an effort not to cry. She took a tentative step forward before she crossed the distance between them and fell into her arms, sobbing.

"It *was* you on the ship, wasn't it?"

"Yes, it was me," Leine murmured as she stroked her back. "It's okay, Kylie. You're going home." Her hand brushed the radio collar. A thick, plastic-coated wire band encircled her neck. The built-in transmitter was sheathed in a hard plastic casing and lay against her throat. The band itself would take a metal cutter to remove.

"Let's do something about this thing." Leine pulled out the multi-tool she'd purchased in Dar and, using the pliers, slid the jaws around the transponder and squeezed, fracturing the screen. She repeated the process until the unit had been damaged sufficiently enough to render the device inactive. Derek offered his canteen to Kylie. Wiping her eyes she took it and drank.

When she was finished, Kylie handed the water back to Derek. "We have to go. Victor Wang is close."

"Have you seen him?" Leine asked.

"No," she said, indicating the collar. "The shocks. The last time was right before the storm quit. The jolt wasn't as strong as before, so I think the batteries are getting low."

"Come on, then," Derek said. "Let's go before we find out for sure." He started for the edge of the outcropping, but Kylie didn't move.

"Wait," she said. "They've got Jaidee."

"Jaidee?" Derek stopped.

"He's a little boy from Bangkok. He was taken the same time as me. Wang sold him to some scary-looking guys with guns, but they brought him back, saying he was too much trouble." She looked at Leine. "We have to help him," she pleaded.

Leine glanced at Derek.

"Oh, no. No." He shook his head. "I didn't sign on for that." Before Kylie could protest, he turned around and headed toward the ledge.

"Listen," Leine said. "I'll report Jaidee's abduction to SHEN. We'll look for him, I promise. Okay? But we have to go. Now."

Kylie nodded. "There are others," she said quietly.

"I know," Leine answered. "We're taking care of that."

42

THEY MADE IT back to the Rover with no sign of Wang or Assad. Even though the sun had climbed above the horizon, the temperature still ranged between pleasant and bearable. Although, after the heavy deluge of rain the night before, the cloudless, sunny sky promised a soggy, humid day ahead.

Zara ran from the Rover to meet them.

"Thank God, you found her." The two women hugged each other. Zara stepped back and held out a canteen of water. Kylie smiled in thanks and took a drink.

Derek walked to the Rover and was about to open the door when the sound of revving engines shattered the silence. Three vehicles—two pickups with a Land Cruiser in the lead—roared up the hill toward them. Leine counted five men with machine guns in the pickup beds, and at least two occupants in each cab.

"Get to the truck—now!" Leine yelled. Kylie dropped the canteen, and she and Zara took off at a dead run, with Leine close behind. Derek dove behind the back wheel well and aimed at the approaching vehicles with the MP5, shouting at Zara and Kylie to stay down.

Leine reached the Rover and set the M21 on the hood, flipping up the dust covers. She sighted on the lead truck, her finger on the trigger. She waited until she knew she had the shot, and fired.

A hole appeared in the windshield on the driver's side and the Land Cruiser veered right. Leine sighted on the passenger and squeezed the trigger, but he lunged for the steering wheel at the same time and she missed.

She swiveled at the rapid thud of automatic gunfire strafing the ground near the Rover. Two men fired at them from the bed of the lead pickup. Kylie and Zara screamed and covered their heads. Leine shifted her stance, aimed at the two men, and fired. The one on the left snapped backward and tumbled out of the pickup. At the same time Derek returned fire, smashing through the windshield. The passenger dropped from view, but Leine couldn't tell if he'd been hit. The driver leaned out of the window, shooting with one hand. Derek fired again, this time hitting the driver. The pickup bounced over a rock and sent the second gunman flying from the bed. He landed hard and rolled. Leine watched him for a moment, but he didn't move.

The remaining pickup went wide, heading around them. Leine changed her position to accommodate. Derek flung the back door open and motioned to Kylie and Zara.

"Get in and stay down," he yelled. The two women climbed inside the Rover, and Derek slammed the door shut. He fired on the other pickup while Leine turned back to the Land Cruiser.

A young boy sat on the hood. The man behind him held a gun to his head, the barrel resting on the child's temple.

She was certain the man holding the boy was Victor Wang, as he wore the same clothes he'd been wearing at the camp. Leine searched for a shot but couldn't find it. Standing behind the front wheel well of the Cruiser eliminated the possibility of shooting his legs out from under him.

Gunfire erupted behind her as Derek attempted to hold off the second pickup.

"Fuck—" Derek gasped, clutching his arm. He'd been hit.

Leine pivoted and dove for the MP5. At the same time, a searing pain bit into her calf. Gripping the gun, she rolled onto her back and fired.

The second pickup swerved and pulled to the left, headed for the other side of the Rover. Leine tossed the MP5 back to Derek and grabbed the M21, which she'd left when she went for the machine gun. Ignoring the pain in her leg, Leine rolled onto her stomach and slid underneath the Rover. The pickup was coming around for a second pass. She shot the front tire, but it didn't blow like she'd planned.

The assholes have run-flat tires, she thought. "Coming your way," Leine yelled to Derek.

"Got 'em." Derek sat with his back against the wheel, holding the MP5 in his good hand, the stock braced against his chest.

Blood pounding in her ears, Leine keyed in on the Land Cruiser. Wang had stepped from behind the vehicle, still holding his gun to the boy's temple while he watched the action.

The weight of the child must have been too much, or maybe Wang assumed Leine and Derek were out for the count, because she had a clear shot. Wang was smiling, clearly thinking he'd won. Leine sighted on him, took a deep breath, exhaled.

And squeezed the trigger.

Wang's head jerked back and his knees buckled as he collapsed to the ground, still holding the boy. The boy struggled out of Wang's grasp and climbed to his feet.

Leine swore. "Stay there, stay there, stay there," she muttered under her breath. He stared at Wang lying on the ground until another round of gunfire split the air. Startled, he broke into a run, heading for a clump of dirt nearby. Relieved he was out of the line of fire, Leine craned her neck to see whether Derek needed help.

He wasn't there.

"Come out, come out, wherever you are." It was a man's voice. Leine's stomach twisted at his cheerful tone.

"I have your friend, so if you refuse I will have to kill him. Although," he paused. "He's already been shot and looks weak. He might bleed out soon." The man's laugh echoed against the surrounding hills. "And don't forget—your gun comes first."

Fighting to quell the anger burning in her chest, Leine shoved the rifle out from under the Rover. A pair of military-style boots appeared and someone picked up the weapon. She unbuckled the shoulder holster and slipped it off, hiding the PPK in the waistband of her pants.

"You are taking much too long," the man scolded.

"I've been wounded. It's going to take time."

The same pair of boots walked to the Rover and crouched down. He reached underneath, seized her ankles, and dragged her out. A stabbing sensation shot through her calf, arcing up the back of her leg. Leine gritted her teeth against the pain.

She sat up to the barrel of an AK-47. Two men in military uniforms, one on each side of her, aimed machine guns at her head. The bearded man Leine had seen at Wang's camp stood to her right, grinning. A gold tooth with a diamond embedded in it glittered in the early morning sun. Next to him was another thug holding Derek at gunpoint. His complexion gray, Derek looked like he was going into shock.

"He needs a doctor," Leine said, gripping her own leg to stop the bleeding.

"That won't be necessary," the man with the beard said. "I am a doctor."

"What?" Incredulous, Leine stared at him.

"My men refer to me as Doctor Death. Although, my women

call me the Amazing Assad." His smile vanished. "Open it," he snapped at one of the gunmen, gesturing toward the Rover.

The man stepped past Leine and reached for the door. A distant crack split the air, followed by a thud. The gunman lurched forward and collapsed to the ground.

Assad's eyes widened, and he threw his head back, searching the sky. "Drones," he breathed.

Leine yanked the gun from her waistband and fired, catching the two remaining gunmen off guard. With what must have been his last ounce of strength, Derek knocked his captor's weapon to the side and head-butted him.

Dazed, the gunman staggered back. Derek stepped away and Leine finished him off with two rounds to the chest. She scanned for Assad but didn't see him.

"Where'd that come from?" Leine asked, gripping the door handle and pulling herself to her feet. She searched the surrounding hills, looking for Assad and the mysterious gunman as a wave of dizziness spiraled through her. She put a hand out to steady herself. Derek slumped against the Rover.

Leine got to him before he fell and threw his arm over her shoulder. Whoever had killed the other gunman weren't interested in shooting them, or they'd be dead by now.

"Come on," she said, and limped with him to the back of the vehicle. Opening the door, she eased him onto the floor of the cargo area, laid him on his back, and elevated his feet. Kylie and Zara peered over the backseat, their faces drained of color.

"Are they gone?" Kylie asked, her voice shaking.

"Heads down," Leine ordered. Both of them ducked out of sight. "I don't know, but we've got a lull. Derek's not doing too well."

"I have first aid training," Kylie said softly.

"So do I," Zara added.

Leine sighed. "Okay, you—" She stopped short at the sound

of a vehicle approaching. Remaining behind the Rover, she stepped away from the cargo area and raised her weapon.

An open, military-style jeep with two men came toward her but slowed to a stop several yards away. A larger pickup followed behind.

"Drop your weapon." The man riding shotgun spoke into a PA system.

Leine squinted, trying to make out who it was. He seemed familiar.

"Drop your weapon," he repeated.

Leine glanced at Derek. He looked bad. "I've got wounded here," she yelled. She tossed her gun to the ground and stepped away from the Rover, hands up.

"Identify yourself," the man continued.

"Leine Basso," she yelled back. "I'm American."

The jeep pulled forward and stopped in front of the Rover. The second vehicle followed. The man who was using the PA climbed out.

"You. What—" Leine said when she recognized the uniform. It was the man from the lion encounter. "Where did you come from? Naasir, right?"

"Good memory. I thought your name was Claire?" Naasir glanced at Derek and motioned to his driver. "We'll need the first aid kit. He looks like hell."

"What are you doing here?" she asked.

"A mutual friend told me you needed help." He eyed the dead bodies surrounding them. "I'm not so sure he was right."

"By any chance, are you talking about Lou?" Leine asked.

Naasir nodded. "Lou Stokes and I go way back. Went through covert ops training together. We keep in touch— Christmas cards, that kind of thing. When you notified him of your need for support he thought of me right away. Sorry we didn't arrive sooner." He glanced at the carnage surrounding them and whistled. "Lou mentioned you knew how to handle yourself."

"Yeah, well, I had help."

She glanced at Derek. His skin didn't look as pasty, and he was talking to the medic. Leine limped to the passenger side and opened the door. "You can come out now."

Kylie and Zara emerged from the backseat. Kylie's knees buckled and Naasir grabbed her before she collapsed. Zara looked shaken up but otherwise appeared to be in good condition. The cubs were all strangely quiet. A couple of them gazed up at Leine with inquisitive blue eyes. She was glad to see none of them had been hurt. The loud gunfire must have scared them silent.

Then Leine remembered the boy. She started for the rock where she'd last seen him.

"Wait. What's the hurry? You've been hurt." Naasir followed her. When she didn't respond he looked up, following her gaze.

Jaidee hovered near the rocks, his eyes round.

"Jesus," Naasir breathed. "Where'd he come from?"

"It's all right, Jaidee," Leine called to him. "You're safe." She reached toward him, smiling. Brows drawn together, he grimaced, making a valiant effort not to cry. "Come on," she urged.

Naasir stepped back in a clear attempt to lessen the perceived threat. Jaidee took a tentative step forward and looked around, his expression wary.

"It's okay, I won't hurt you—I promise," Leine coaxed.

"Jaidee!" Kylie shouted from behind Leine. The boy shifted his attention to his friend and after a moment's hesitation, ran to her.

Leine limped to the passenger side of the Rover and parked herself in the seat. Lifting her knee, she pulled her pant leg out of her sock to assess the damage to her calf. The skin was chewed up and a painful, bloody mess, but it didn't look like the round had penetrated. She tore a paper towel from the roll on the floor and pressed it to the wound, wincing as she did.

"Daniel," Naasir called to the medic. "When you've got him stabilized, bring the kit over here. The lady has a flesh wound."

"How did you find us?" Leine asked, leaning her head back.

Naasir glanced skyward. "Unmanned aerial vehicle." He returned his attention to the dead bodies. "Is that Victor Wang?"

"You know him?"

"A man named Assad Khoury's been linked to several terrorist organizations. We've been monitoring him for quite a while, hoped he'd lead us to his backers. Thought it might be Wang." He shook his head. "It wasn't, although Wang used Khoury to move massive amounts of ivory. We could never prove it."

"Assad was here," Leine said. "He muttered something about drones before he disappeared."

"I saw him run." Naasir's gaze was intense. "We had to let him go. We still need to track the money."

"What happens to Wang's people now? Most of his staff are victims."

"All of them are being taken care of. My unit is there now, making sure everyone has a chance to contact their families and friends, let them know where they are."

"You wouldn't happen to have a phone on you?" Leine asked. "I'd like to call Lou, let him know what's happening."

"Of course." Naasir whistled and raised his hand. "Phone." One of his men ran over with an iridium satellite phone and handed it to Leine.

She entered Lou's number and waited.

"Lou, it's Leine," she said when he answered. "We found Kylie. She's fine. I'm sitting here with your old buddy, Naasir."

"It's good to hear your voice, Leine," Lou said. "I can book you both on a flight home tomorrow, if you're ready."

"Book a flight for Kylie back to LA," Leine said, her tone sharper than she intended. *Fuck it. He knows I'm pissed.* "I'm going to Riyadh."

"Leine, calm down. Everything's okay. We found April."

"You—what?" Leine shoulders dropped in relief as she let out a sigh. April was safe. She allowed the exhaustion she'd been keeping at bay to sweep through her now that she didn't have to hold on, didn't have to keep going for her daughter. Tears pricked her eyelids, but she kept her emotions in check. No sense breaking down now. If she waited long enough, her feelings wouldn't be as strong, wouldn't sideline her, like they did when April was being held by that lunatic, Azazel.

"I said, April's—"

"—she's fine, I know. I got that." Leine took a deep breath. "Thank you, Lou."

"She's on her way back from Riyadh. Should be home this time tomorrow." Lou paused for a moment. "I'm sorry things went sideways, Leine. Somehow, someone tipped off Wang. I don't know who."

Leine closed her eyes. "I do."

"Need any help?"

"Nope. I've got it handled." She'd postpone *that* call until she found a burner phone, something she could pitch afterward.

"Okay then. When you get back, I'm giving you some time off. Maybe paint the living room like you've been threatening to do."

"Yeah. I just may take you up on that."

43

One week later

K AVI STOOD ACROSS from the shop where his contact said to meet him. Traffic sped past, agile motor bikes and smoke-belching *tuk tuks* by far the most prevalent. No one had gone into or out of the rare goods store in several minutes, which told him Abraham had closed for the meeting. With one last glance to each side, Kavi crossed the street and tried the door, surprised when it swung open. The bell jingled as he entered the cool, dark interior, expecting to see his old friend behind the counter.

At first glance, there didn't appear to be anyone in the store —only shelf after shelf of ivory Buddhas and trinkets. Most, Kavi knew, were made of illegal ivory with falsified papers. The people who came to this store didn't care.

Curious that Abraham didn't come out to greet him, Kavi skirted the glass shelves, headed for the back room. His eyes took their time adjusting to the dim light, and he stumbled over something next to the counter. He turned to see what his friend had left lying in the middle of the floor and froze. Abraham lay face-down, the back of his head a bloody, tangled mess. His prized lion-tooth necklace had broken, the teeth scattered around him.

His heart racing, Kavi stared in horror at his dead friend. He backed up until his hand hit the counter and then turned and started for the door. A man dressed in black holding a gun fitted with a suppressor stood not ten feet away. His head was shaved except for a long ponytail that fell below his shoulders. On his neck was the triad's familiar tattoo.

"Where did you come from?" Kavi asked, his heart racing. Perspiration beaded on his neck and slid between his shoulder blades. He hadn't heard the man enter the store.

"My boss is not happy, Kavi. You used his resources for your own personal vendetta." He advanced toward him. "Not only that, but now we will have to find another pipeline. Victor Wang was much more valuable than you could ever hope to be." The man's expression remained implacable.

"I can explain..." Eyes riveted to the gun in the other man's hand, Kavi inched toward the back room and the rest of his life.

"I'm waiting," the man said, tracking his progress.

"She would have disrupted Wang's supply chain if I hadn't warned him."

The man in black smiled. "And yet, instead of killing her, which would have been the prudent course of action, you told Victor to sell her at auction—that there were many who would pay to exact their revenge." He raised the gun. "You preyed on Wang's greed only to satisfy your need for vengeance."

Kavi's mouth ran dry as his mind raced for a way to bargain for his life. But then he stopped. Phan was going to be very upset when he didn't bring home the vegetables she'd asked for.

"How did you know?" Kavi asked, the air escaping his lungs as though the man had stuck a needle through his chest.

"It appears you underestimated your enemy," the man replied. He fired two rounds, one to the chest, one to the head.

The gunman picked up the two spent casings on the floor before he unscrewed the suppressor. Then he walked over to the body, leaned down, and pressed his fingers against Kavi's carotid to search for a pulse.

He didn't find one.

———

LEINE PUT THE LAST STROKE OF PAINT ON THE WALL AND STEPPED back, admiring her work. The calming shade of green was exactly what the apartment needed, what Leine needed. Especially after Africa.

Her phone rang, and she dropped the roller into the paint tray. She wiped her hands on her jeans before she answered.

"Hi, Mom," April sang out cheerily.

Leine smiled. Ever since her daughter had helped bring down the traffickers in Riyadh, she'd acquired a new self-confidence, something Leine both appreciated and dreaded. Relieved that April's first undercover assignment for SHEN had turned out so well—her actions helped save seventeen women and children from a brutal life—Leine was also leery of that same confidence and hoped that her daughter would temper her newfound ability with prudence.

"Hi, sweetie. What's up?"

"I just sent you a link to a video. You have to see this."

Leine walked into the kitchen for her tablet, opened her daughter's text message and clicked on the link. The video began with a screen giving the date, location, and three names. Leine leaned forward in her chair at the first name: Victor Wang.

The other two, Bobbi Jo Schneider and Sapphire, meant little to her.

The picture quality was good but jumpy, zooming in and out, and picked up the sound of the videographer's footsteps as well as his breathing. The woman captured in the video looked like one of the guests who had been staying at Wang's camp. Leine enlarged the picture for a better view.

The video showed the woman carrying a hunting rifle and creeping through the dark, giving the impression she was tracking prey. She stopped and the picture zoomed out, showing a dark silhouette in the distance. She raised her rifle and fired. The dark shape dropped, the bullet obviously finding its mark. The next scene panned in for a closeup, the woman staring down at her kill, clearly shocked. A second later the video zoomed out to capture not only the hunter, but also the prey—a pretty young Asian woman, obviously dead. Leine stopped the video.

"It's all over the Internet," April said. "Isn't Victor Wang the guy you went after in Tanzania?"

"Yes. Do you know who uploaded the file?"

"Someone calling themselves Justice K19. Heard of them?"

"No, but I have an idea." It had to be Kylie. She'd told Naasir to check Wang's computer for a video file showing the murder of a woman who'd been trafficked the same time as she was. Leine hadn't heard anything about the video after that and assumed someone had wiped Wang's hard drive before it could be searched. But if Kylie had a copy, why hadn't she given it to Naasir?

"It says in the article that the woman with the gun was brought in for questioning. She claims it was all faked. That it was a bad marketing ploy to get people to go to their company's website," Kylie said. "She and her husband own one of those wildlife ranches where you can pay to hunt exotic animals."

"Has anyone reported the other woman in the video missing?"

"The article doesn't say, but the way the video's taking off, I wouldn't be surprised if either she steps forward to prove she isn't dead, or a family member does."

Leine made a mental note to check in with Kylie, ask her some questions. After making plans to see April for dinner, Leine ended the call and read the article. She'd gotten through to the last paragraph when Santa walked in the door, carrying a large bouquet of flowers and a shipping envelope.

"You shouldn't have," Leine said, smiling. She kissed him and took the flowers into the kitchen to find a vase.

"Beautiful flowers for a beautiful lady." Santa set the over-sized envelope on the counter. "That's for you, too. Looks like Derek sent you something."

Leine finished arranging the flowers in the vase and wiped her hands before opening the package from Kenya. She turned it over and shook out the contents: a handwritten letter folded into thirds, and a shallow box. She opened the letter and read:

Dear Claire/Leine,

Please accept this gift in the nature intended. Our adventure in Tanzania and the resulting conversations we shared had a profound effect on me and I now find myself working part time with the Rafiki Conservation Center. It's helped me to put my past behind me as did something you said while on the ship. "It's not what you did, it's what you do." I've changed my ways and am on the path to a new and better life. You check?

I've decided to take your advice to heart and have decided to rectify the damage I've done to this mysterious continent I call home. Your work with SHEN has inspired me to take action. The nature of my specific skillset has made it a bit tough to decide on the right path, but I now believe I've found exactly what I am meant to do. The neck-

lace is my gift to you as well as to Tanzania. I hope my efforts will help in some small way.

Take care of yourself, and if you ever need anything, please don't hesitate to ask.

Yours Sincerely,

Derek van der Haar

Leine put the letter down and picked up the box. Inside was a beautifully beaded necklace, evoking the fine work of the Maasai. She lifted it out and only then realized its significance. The focus of the piece glinted in the sunlight.

Nestled in a cluster of gleaming sapphires was a diamond embedded in a gold tooth.

Ready for more Leine? Start reading The Last Deception, the next book in the action-packed Leine Basso thriller series!

ACKNOWLEDGMENTS

I'd like to thank the following people for their help and support in writing *Cargo*: first reader and confidence man, Mark Lindstrom; my stupendous editor, Laurie Boris; intrepid adventurer and chief hot air balloon pilot Mike Carnevale for fact-checking my Tanzanian/Maasai references and providing the framework to write about life in East Africa; Kathryn McNeil for initial input regarding Bangkok; my writing group: Ali Mosa, Jenni Conner, Darlene Panzera, and Sharon Kleve; Mistress of Mayhem and Prodigious Plugger of Plot Holes, Ruth M. Ross-Saucier; and early readers Michelle and Brian Yelland, and Bev and Larry Van Berkom. Special thanks to TSODA134 (a.k.a. Special Forces Dude)—your detailed input and PowerPoints on weapons, recon, sniper protocol, comms, SE Asia, et al, add an element of realism to my novels that I wouldn't be able to achieve without your help.

Writing is never a solitary endeavor.

ABOUT THE AUTHOR

DV Berkom is the USA Today bestselling author of riveting action-adventure and crime thrillers. Known for creating resilient, kick-ass female characters and page-turning plots, her love of the genre stems from a lifelong addiction to reading spy novels, thrillers, and action/adventure stories.

A restless soul and adventurer at heart, she spent years moving around the US and traveling to exotic locations before she wrote her first novel and was hooked. More than twenty books later, she now makes her home in the Pacific Northwest with her husband, Mark, and several imaginary characters who like to tell her what to do.

Her most recent books include Claire Whitcomb Westerns *Legend, Gunslinger,* and *Retribution,* and the Leine Basso thrillers *Terminal Threat, Fatal Objective, A Plague of Traitors,* and *Shadow of the Jaguar.* DV's currently hard at work on her next book.

For more information, visit her website at www.dvberkom.com. To be the first to hear about new releases and subscriber-only offers, go to: bit.ly/DVB_RL

ALSO BY D.V. BERKOM

Gunslinger

Legend

Printed in Great Britain
by Amazon